ORION'S SOULMATES

ORION'S SOULMATES

JOHN CECCA JR.

Giuliana and Robert
Love Pa.

ORION'S SOULMATES

1

Beneath the Jungle

**"Day six went awry.
Perfect is what perfect does
Beings' imperfect."**

The dry jungle underbrush offered little resistance for the intense archaeology graduate student. Knowledgeable well beyond the novice stage, the scientist with machete in hand forged ahead as the searing heat of the Belizean summer moistened her clothes and skin as though she had just been caught in that early morning downpour. It's been hours since petrichor's taste and sweet smell evaporated into a salty, dry-lipped trek. The spirited sounds of a jungle humming with life, Howler monkeys playing atop the thick canopy, and the buzzing of insects played like a joyous symphony. Hedging towards the fabled ruins of Xunantunich, mapping various locations, hoping to find a discovery, or adding new information to old theories.

The autonomous Harvard University doctoral candidate had separated from the group, hoping to add a possible topic on the Mayan civilization's extinction theories or everyday life for her nearly completed thesis.

Halting at a fork in the path, she rubbed her sweated ancient Mayan medallion and checked her GPS, locating her associates. They were nearby, heading in the same direction. The diverging paths exit and merge at the end of the jungle, a little under a quarter of a mile away, where they will meet. Sending her location and continuing to explore her surroundings, peering through a bush, she noticed a small cluster of ruins, not uncommon in this well-explored and documented jungle. Still, something seemed different. Piquing her curiosity, she created a path that opened to the area of a small cluster of ruins. Climbing onto a structure, she noticed a stone with markings, approached it to take photos, then slipped, slid, and tumbled out of control on the opposite side. Down the smooth, slippery, hard surface, falling much further than the distance she had climbed. Landing with a thud, scraping her face, banging her hands, arms, and legs, she roughly rolled into a cave. Light shone down; she located her dropped phone. The fall was about 15-20 feet. She collected herself, a little stunned, but was well equipped for emergencies: flashlights, water, bandages. She slowly rose to her feet, shaken but not frightened.

Standing momentarily, ignoring her injuries and any plan for an immediate exit, she succumbed to her intense archaeological curiosity, now examining the surroundings. Dimly lit, using a flashlight, she observed, and then she entered a small chamber showcasing a small stone altar. It was a simple structure with a tabernacle in its center and a thin stone slab covering the opening. She removed the slab and brushed off the dust and dirt without trepidation. Briefly examining it for markings, she saw there were none. Flashing her light, she could see a square object within the tabernacle. It looked like a wooden frame. Removing it and then raising it to eye level, she noticed that there was not a speck of dirt or dust on it. Looking more closely, she discovered that a metal disk appeared to be wedged inside its center; the metal object was inscribed with writings, symbols, and runes, not just Mayan, but many cultures, increasing her breathing and professional interest. Her thoughts and imagination were going berserk. Investigating further, she determined that nothing else was of interest, and then trying to take photographs proved useless; she placed the relatively light 8x8-inch object into her backpack.

A dampening effect was blocking her communications. The hour was getting late, but she had no means to prove it. Genny Giuliana Cantalupo, scientist, Harvard doctoral candidate, alone and hurt in the jungle. Apprehension suddenly took control of Genny. She rubbed her necklace…hard. The tomb smelled suffocating, like graveyard dirt. She could taste blood from her fall. Her injuries and their pain made their presence. Slowly retracing her steps to where she fell. Genny realized she couldn't make the climb; smooth, steep, and slippery, the effort outweighed her increasing pain. Flashing her light for an exit, she noticed a passageway. Heavy breathing continued, and fear had arrived as she entered the narrow, claustrophobic way. She traveled a short way into it and was surrounded by dense forest greenery; sunlight filtered through the canopy. It was getting brighter. The passage abruptly ended; she was out. Genny's heart thumped, exhaling a sigh of relief, and she managed a victor's aura with a beaming smile. Her phone was nearly dead, but she could inform the group of her situation.

Attending to her injuries, the archaeologist team listened to her story, but she never revealed her discovery. Genny was confused, losing time. The daylight was fleeting, and they would meet with another group to share a return ride to the hotel. The expedition had little time, but though they tried, they could not verify Genny's story. She sat quietly, thinking about her discovery during the ride back.

***

The university's physician addressed Genny's injuries, smiling, informed her she couldn't continue on the dig and would have to return home. Rubbing and pulling at her medallion, she took the news surprisingly well.

Spending hours examining the artifact, she came to the disappointing conclusion that it was a hoax. The frame looked like cheap material, and the cuts were modern. The disc was just a bit larger than a compact disc and looked like it was recently manufactured. She recognized most inscriptions, such as Egyptian, Mayan, and others. She guffawed, noticing that they were laser cuts. Laughing out loud at her ignorance, filled with frustration, she sighed, "Fuck, I thought I had something!" Her injuries hurt. She tossed the disc with her personal effects as a mere souvenir.

Arrangements were made for her trip home; she would leave early in the morning. The University and Belizean law required a manifest for her archaeological finds collected over the past three weeks of the month-long excursion. The artifacts were subject to the approval of the Belizean government before they could be exported. They were packed according to the law.

Genny then arranged her possessions into suitcases; they also required a manifest to include all souvenirs. She included the disc. Her luggage would make her flight unless there were unforeseen problems. The archaeological items were subject to delay. A luggage service would come by in the morning to pick up the trunk and luggage. A carry-on bag was all she needed for the flight. The school would pick up her luggage at Logan International Airport in Boston, MA.

The trunk and luggage were labeled:
Harvard University
School of Archaeology/Receiving
21 Divinity Ave.

Cambridge, MA. 02138
c/o Genny Giuliana Cantalupo

An exhilarating chill consumed her, as did the thought of Autumn in New England and finalizing her dissertation.

***

"Before you leave today," the professor said, eyes twinkling. "I want to tell you a short story and leave you with a thought. You can ponder until the next meeting," the handsome archaeology professor addressed his students. "Not on any test. You can find it in my book." He winked, catching smiles, "and could win my favor very easily." Jokingly.

The class quieted, some smiling, already familiar with his strange tales.

"On a trip to the Yucatan Peninsula, not the most recent, years ago, I was with my mentor, a professor who taught history here at the University. He has sadly passed on. It was only a day or two before we would leave Mexico and head back to Boston. He put his arm around me, whispered that he had something special to show me, and invited me to accompany him. We visited a Mayan shaman, sometimes called J'men." He wrote that on an overhead projector. "I went along, and I was introduced and warmly greeted by the shaman. The shaman told me I had a good soul; protect it." Laughing. "He was very, very old. His home was plain and traditional, with some statues and artifacts indigenous to his people. He sat comfortably in a soft fabric recliner, asking us to sit on the sofa. He offered us a glass of balche." The professor put the word on his overhead projector. "It's an alcoholic beverage. His granddaughter served us, and then she left. It was tasty, and man, it was strong." The class laughed. "The three of us were alone, and then, collecting his thoughts, he started speaking softly about his life. Talking about his gods and how his time on earth had come to an end, saying his reflection had eyes that never changed and that his daily collapsing body, supported by this accompanying, undying, eternal traveler, always made him feel that he was not old at all. He then whispered, *'You are not your body. You are what never changes.'* His hand touched my heart, and I got goosebumps as he sat back in his seat, smiling. I observed him as he continuously rubbed an ancient Mayan medallion that hung around his neck, and then he took it off and handed it to my associate with words, sort of a prayer. The shaman died the following day." He paused.

"Spooky stuff, no?"

"Ooh!" The class teased and mocked.

"Think along with the thoughts of the shaman. Even at your young age, I'm certain some of you have experienced the sensation of your body changing, but something inside you never gets older." Pausing, "We just accept this as part of life. And it is."

"Yes, you may have experienced that; look into the mirror, timekeeper. Here's the point, when does that unaging thing begin its Journey? At birth? Conception? Before either? It gives you a mortal feeling and makes you wonder about our existence. The mystery of life, and no one has the answer. Does anybody here have it?" He lightened the mood as they chuckled. "Our lives are filled with so many distractions and misdirection. We don't have time to ponder our existence, as they say. Meditation is an exceptional way to calm and focus your thoughts on life and this course." They laughed.

"What is this presence called, or known as?"

"Your soul," the class said in unison.

"Maybe it is our soul or something else, something older. Something placed here?"

They listened. "I don't think anyone has the answers to this question."

"Do you know what this is called?"

"Ensoulment," the young student replied.

"You read my book!" with a big smile.

"Yes, I did, and I especially enjoyed your thinking on how difficult it is to change mainstream thinking."

"I appreciate this and will cover that at a later date."

Someone shouted out, "What were the shaman's last words?"

"Another time. Thank You."

"Think about what we were discussing. That's your assignment."

The class ended, and the professor was satisfied with his lecture and even more so with the first puff of his Gitane cigarette.

2

The Disc and the Doctorate

Soft, classical music quietly filled the room. The perfumed scent of freshly cut flowers surfed the air, and the early morning May breeze, open windows, raised curtains, and soft sunbeams illuminated the worldly and ancient room's charm.

Claire gazed into the eight-foot antique oval mirror, admiring the beauty it reflected, a chamber that could have only been furnished by a disciple of Cleopatra. The greatest beauty was her wife of the past eight years, Prisha, helping her prepare for today's Ph.D. ceremony. Prisha, Indian, beautiful, with dark black pearl eyes, long, sensual jet-black hair, and a red bindi that framed her brown, delicate, alluring face atop a goddess' five-foot-five-inch frame. Her good looks are matched only by her intelligence and dedication; she is an MIT Ph.D. graduate in Earth, Atmosphere, and Planetary Science; she now works for the US government. Sharing the magnificent brownstone in Boston's South End with her wife.

Caressing Claire's shoulders, a kiss on the neck, with a slight accent, she said, "You seem more excited than usual today?"

Claire Marie Randolph-Mishari, born into Yankee wealth, was afforded the best classical education in the world, several master's degrees, two PhDs, and her most cherished one, four years at Cambridge University in Cambridge, England. She was now a long-time faculty member and the Academic Director of the School of Archaeology at Harvard University, Cambridge. Massachusetts. Today was a memorable and joyful day. Her student and blossoming friend, whom she had mentored for years, was receiving her doctorate today. The tall, almost five feet ten inches, elegantly fit woman gazed into her hazel brown eyes, checking her short, brushed-back, dark, dirty blonde hair, smacked her beautifully red-lined, thin lips, a color that complemented her light complexion, lifted her eyes that so well fitted her perfectly angular face.

Reaching for Prisha's hand, "Prisha Harshita Mishara-Randolph, I love you so much that I get a tingling sensation gazing into your eyes. I'm happiest when we are together." Sighing, "Although our work has been keeping us apart. To answer your question." She put her index finger across her upper lip and started rubbing a little, a habit she would do forever while thinking. "Today is special because Genny is receiving her doctorate. I'm presenting it to her. I've known her since I interviewed her when she applied to Harvard as an undergraduate. I advised her on her master's at Cambridge. We've been on archaeological digs. She has helped me with papers and research." Claire lit up the room with her smile.

Prisha was taken aback, seemingly a bit jealous. "We have been apart!" with a sense of coolness. "Why haven't you ever mentioned her?"

"Oh, Pri, I have. I understand how busy you are at work; conversations or words sometimes seem hollow. She's special, and I feel I'm sharing her accomplishment."

Prisha returned a suspicious look.

"Oh no, Pri! Nothing like that." She got up and affectionately hugged Prisha. "When you teach, you build a relationship with your students. Most come and go. Some stay in touch. And a rare few become friends and colleagues. They look up to you, and you respect them. You are their mentee. They are your protégées. In my field, it is exciting to watch young minds learn and grow. Please, Pri, do not upset yourself by raising suspicions. You will know! When you meet her tonight."

"Oh! That's where we are going." Prisha smiled and apologized for her foolish thought. Claire said she would text her to arrange a time to meet at Artu's Italian restaurant in Boston's North End.

"I think the reservation is at six o'clock." Claire got a text that her limousine had arrived. They hugged and kissed.

"You better not have smudged my lipstick!" Claire laughed as she entered the limousine.

Prisha flashed her beautiful smile, "Love ya."

***

Rolling up her yoga mat and lowering the stereo's volume, the sweating but relaxed soon-to-be doctoral graduate sipped her water as she toweled herself dry. With a satisfactory grin, "I did it!" She thought, like Elle Woods in *Legally Blonde,* a well-deserved tribute.

She had been on a mission since grade school, five feet eight inches with not-too-long dark brown hair, matching eyes, a small nose, and an athletic but not muscular frame. Her smooth olive skin sported several small tattoos, acquired as mementos on her archaeological digs.

Born and raised in East Boston, Massachusetts, she was a Catholic student through the sixth grade and then spent six years at the world-renowned Boston Latin School. She was an outstanding student and athlete, receiving a full scholarship to Harvard University and then successfully enrolling in a double major, archaeology and anthropology, leading to a BA-MA degree. In Genny's senior year at Harvard, she was the team's "Most Valuable Player" in lacrosse for a near-championship season and a star swimmer on the intramural swim team. In her spare time, she became a certified yoga instructor. Upon graduation, with her advisor's help, she enrolled in a Master's of Archaeology program at Cambridge University, Cambridge, England, where, upon completion, she was offered entrance into their prestigious Ph.D. program. She declined, instead going to Harvard University, wanting to be closer to home. The summer before entering the Harvard program, she took a certificate course in Archaeological Art at Cornell University in Ithaca, New York.

Genny Giuliana Cantalupo, GG, to her friends, lived in her late grandparents' home in a historic section of East Boston, MA. It was the generational home of her great grandparents, situated at the hill's peak on Webster Street with unparalleled views of Boston Harbor and the Boston Skyline. The quarter-acre lot, boasting forty-five hundred square feet of living space, a finished basement, a multi-car driveway, and a garage, constantly attracted land developers.

Her mother teaches language skills in the Boston School System, and her father runs his family's variety store, a small grocery market called Tavio's on Sumner Street in East Boston. Her brother Robert is a FedEx pilot living in Memphis, Tennessee.

Genny's dad's parents had run the grocery store for decades until age forced their retirement. They have since passed. Her mother's mom had died of cancer, leaving Genny with few memories. The most influential and guiding force in her life was her grandfather, Enrico, her mom's dad. He was a tenured history professor at the University of Massachusetts, Boston, passionate about archaeology and travel. Enrico inherited land in Italy and sold it for a sizeable amount. He created comfortable trust funds for his two grandchildren, taking care of all his family somewhat equally. Enrico and Genny had a special relationship and spent hours discussing archaeology, history, and science. They fermented their wine, and at times, it was a disaster. They traveled together and shared archaeological digs and findings. He left her the home that she loved! His sudden departure broke her heart.

Today was her day. She rubbed her Mayan medallion, "Thanks, Pa!" She checked around the room to see that everything was in its place, full of items that Enrico and she had collected over the years. She turned on the infuser, the fresh lemon scent and soft Nuevo Flamenco guitar music filling the air, and headed to the shower.

Dressed and ready to go, she heard a car pull into the driveway. The doorbell rang, and there stood Dr. Randolph-Mishari, Claire. They greeted one another with a warm embrace. They had chemistry and had become trusted friends.

"Doctor, you look glorious!" Genny smiled excitedly at her mentor.

"Please, GG, it's Claire. You look stunning!"

"Come in and check out my place?" She said excitedly, gave her a quick history of the house, and poured her a glass of homemade wine.

"Cheers and congratulations!" Their glasses clanging resonated with success.

"Genny, I must be upfront with you. We have been student and teacher, advisor, counselor, and now associates over the past decade." She paused, putting her index finger to her upper lip, and began rubbing. "I have known you as long as I've known Prisha. I have cared and worried about you. I watched you grow and mature. I see you now as a colleague, but most importantly, you have become like family, a daughter to me." A little embarrassed, she took a sip of wine.

"You don't have to be shy about this," Genny said, walking over to her with a hug. "You have been my closest friend and confidante along the way. I put my trust and, sometimes, my life into your wisdom and hands. When Enrico passed, you were there. I loved you for that." They sipped their wine. "By the way, does that put me into the will?" They laughed.

"Your place is magnificent. The views are stunning! All that I thought it would be." Claire started looking around at some of the artifacts. She recognized many of them.

"What is this?" She asked excitedly, picking up the disc from Belize.

Genny rubbed her medallion, explaining that the disc was a souvenir and how she had found it, and concluded it was a hoax.

"My dear GG! You have found something magnificent. I recognize this material—it hasn't existed on Earth for tens of thousands of years, it's extinct!" She was amazed and puzzled. Genny continued to rub her medallion.

"If you have no plans, I want you to start work tomorrow. We can carbon-date this artifact and examine the metal closely. GG, this is extraordinary! We can discuss this in the car; we should leave now."

Genny locked up, and they headed for the ceremony.

***

Soft classical music and lavender fragrance wafted through the comfortable, climate-controlled stretch limousine. The ladies carrying their refilled glasses of wine sat apart, each at the window in the rear seat. Claire gave the driver a nod, and they were off.

They were still early, but the traffic through the Sumner Tunnel in East Boston would add considerable driving time.

"You must send me a bottle of that wine," as Claire sipped.

"I will bring you a couple. This was Pa's favorite and his last batch," Genny said sadly, rubbing her amulet.

"GG," Claire rubbed her upper lip, "You may have made a significant find. Review your protocols with me. It does look like a modern souvenir."

"Dr. Randolph-Mishari," Genny said. Claire smiled, feeling Genny's professional, passionate burst. "I thought for certain that it was an artifact, the circumstances, lost time, unable to use communication devices or cameras."

Still rubbing her amulet, starting to think, she said, "It all seemed so strange, but this area of the jungle has been so thoroughly searched and documented. This couldn't be possible!" Appearing exasperated, she sipped her wine and continued, "I was happy I was sent home early. I was pretty sore from the fall." She laughed.

"If this is an artifact… We must inform the Belizean administration. We have a working relationship and agreements on archaeological findings. With a misunderstanding, we cannot get involved where the school is asked to leave!" Stated in her administrative tone, sipping her wine. "Hmm! This is good. Breakfast was too light." She smiled.

"I took all the proper procedures. I listed it as a souvenir, explaining how I found it. I even talked to one of their agents, and she stated that this is common; there are pranksters and practical jokers always trying to screw you over. I listed it on my manifest. It was examined and had a government seal."

"Oh, you did well!" Claire said, finishing her wine. "GG, is tomorrow ok with you?"

"Yeah, if I'm not too hungover, lol!" They both giggled like schoolgirls, enjoying one another's company.

"I want to start immediately; this may be more than an artifact!"

Genny was anxious and excited, rubbing her hands together.

"We are here, glorious Harvard Yard! We will meet later and drive together to the restaurant," said Claire.

Genny nodded. The chauffeur opened the door. Genny exited to the back of the car and got a hug from Claire, who said, "Congratulations, Genny Giuliana Cantalupo. You have earned this!" They went their separate ways.

***

The ceremony was being held at the Tercentenary Theater, an expansive grassy area smack in the middle of Harvard Yard. The place was packed; tens of thousands of graduates and their families also live on cable TV. Somewhere in the crowd were Genny's mom and dad. Her brother Robert was in Memphis and could not fly because of bad weather.

Doctor Claire Marie Randolph-Mishari presented Genny with her Kenneth C. Griffin Graduate School of Arts and Sciences degree.

She met her parents after the ceremony, but could not find Claire in the crowd. They hugged, beaming with love and pride. Genny was the family's first female doctor. They walked around the yard, but not for the first time, and inhaled history. They departed, looking forward to this evening. Genny gave hugs and kisses and thanked them for being such supportive parents. They left; Genny met Claire back at the limousine.

"Well, Doctor!" Claire giggled.

"Yes, Doctor!" Genny laughing.

"Can't wait to introduce you to Prisha." Claire beamed.

"Looking forward to it." Genny released a vast sigh, a relieved smile, a load off her shoulders. She had her Ph.D.

***

Artu's is an exquisite Italian restaurant at 6 Prince Street in Boston's North End, steps from Paul Revere's house. The Cantalupos had made a reservation for 12-14 guests. The owner was friends with the Cantalupo family, both growing up in East Boston, and they also had a business relationship with the store and the restaurant. Tavio's imported specialty items from Italy for the restaurant. Artu's is not a large venue. The owner reserved an area for the party steps up from the bar. There was plenty of room to enjoy the evening.

Michael and Ginerva Cantalupo were warmly greeted and then taken to their seats. An aunt, uncle, and two Cantalupo cousins found their way up the stairs. Two of Genny's college friends were greeted and seated with their significant others. Claire and Genny arrived, and as they entered, the bartenders, old friends, toasted Genny, a gesture that prompted many customers to stand and applaud. A server handed her and Claire a glass of champagne. A very emotional Genny lifted her glass. "Cheers and thank you," she said to the bartenders. Smiling, they nodded. Genny had been coming here for years and knew the staff and many customers.

They joined the rest of the party. Her aunt, uncle, and cousins immediately greeted and hugged Genny. Her friends came over and did the same. Then, she introduced Claire to her family. Michael and Ginerva got up and affectionately greeted Claire.

"I can't thank you enough for watching over my baby all these years." Ginerva smiled with tears.

"I remember you from ten years ago or so. My GG has talked about and looked up to you with so much admiration and trust. I also can't thank you enough. GG has been special ever since she was a baby…" Genny interrupted Michael.

"OK, Dad. We are doctors." The sound of doctor sounded so good. "Please!"

"OK, GG, but Claire, thanks."

Claire was unaccustomed to this type of family emotion. She got chills. She was enjoying herself. She politely checked her phone, waiting for Prisha, whom she had texted earlier.

Prisha stood at the entrance at the end of the bar. The place got quiet. The patrons, bartenders, and servers tried to be as unobtrusive as possible, but could not ignore her beauty. It was as though a celebrity had entered. The host led her to the party. Claire greeted her at the top of the stairs with a hug and kiss. She introduced Genny to her. They hugged.

"Prisha!" said Genny excitedly, "Thank you for coming. I'm so happy to finally meet you. Claire has told me so much about you. I feel like I know you." Taking the shy Prisha by the hand, Genny introduced her to her family and friends as Claire's wife.

Then Genny proclaimed, "Let's drink, eat, and be merry! Yahoo!" And they did.

It was a festive time. The food was sumptuous. The owner provided a singer with a guitar, who serenaded the party and the rest of the restaurant. Prisha danced with Claire. Genny danced with Claire and Prisha; they all danced, drank, ate, and had a great night.

Claire's giggling, "GG, not too early tomorrow."

"You got it, boss, doc, ah, Claire!" A smiling and somewhat inebriated Genny saluted Claire. "Bye, Prisha!" They all laughed.

Hand-in-hand, Claire and Prisha thanked the Cantalupos and slipped into the night.

3

Parked Chevrolet

A pre-football game day din could be heard down the corridor. Professor Lucas Johnny Chevrolet shook his head as he approached the lecture hall. The unruly first-year students chirped and chattered like farm animals upon his arrival. General Science 101 was offered as one of the soft sciences required for the liberal arts program at the university. "What the fuck am I doing here?" Lucas whispered, shaking his head, as he entered the lecture hall. On his arrival, the room settled a bit; nearly all the 100 or so students were surfing their phones, laptops, or tablets as though the apocalypse were upon them.

Lucas had just finished an archaeological, photographic expedition of the Yucatan Peninsula and Belize, doing research for his second novel. The little over six-foot, bronze-skinned, bluish-eyed, and sandy-haired Californian was drawn to this temporary position for a second year for some needed money and the proximity to the educational and cultural benefits that the city of Boston and the surrounding area offered. Boston, aka the Hub of the Universe. He taught three sections of GS 101 and an elective, "Mesoamerica Gateway of the Alien Gods," a visual presentation of architecture and culture. The class was based on his first novel, *Mesoamerica—Stones of the Gods,* and his upcoming novel.

Lucas, the son of a Swedish/African mother and a French-born father, grew up on sunny Californian beaches, allowing him to excel in water sports and short drives to the mountains for winter activities. He did his undergraduate work in astrophysics at the University of California at Los Angeles with a minor in visual arts. He then received his doctorate in Cosmology from the California Institute of Technology. To this day, he does not know why or how he did it. His passions have always been research, writing, photography, history, archaeology, and travel.

He stepped into the classroom and put his coffee cup on the podium. Frustrated by the students' lack of interest, this part of his job, "What the hell am I doing here?" the thought echoed, taking a sip of coffee. "Ah! Now that's truly a gift of the gods." He grinned.

"Class, I would like your attention today." His three teaching assistants, overhearing his comments, gave him a quizzical look. His usual routine was to put something on the board and ask if everybody had done the reading. He would work straight from the university's syllabus and then ask prepared questions. The same few would answer. Then, he'd ask each teaching assistant to lecture for five minutes. It would end with "follow your syllabus, expect a quiz, visit your TAs, and "You know my office hours."

The students continued with their blasé attitude that the world owes them. He knew that they would. He then took the quite voluminous, heavy textbook and, with all the irritation he was feeling, slammed it to the floor with all his force. It sounded like a car backfire. The room got still, very still.

"Hang in with me a few moments. Please!" Lucas was relieved.

"That was somewhat of Newton's Third Law. Every action has an equal and opposite reaction. With this slamming sound, I got your attention." He chuckled. "I'm feeling a little bit like you today. Unsure about the future! It is real. It isn't easy. Sometimes, it can be frightening."

"So, kindly listen to my lecture, have some fun, and walk out of here this morning with a smile and a thought." He had their attention. There was an almost unrecognizable silence.

"One of the great disappointments in life is staying stuck in time. If you ever get a chance, read Kurt Vonnegut's *Slaughterhouse-Five* about Billy Pilgrim getting unstuck in time." He sipped his coffee with an air of confidence.

"Part 2 of today's lecture is not for you to get stuck in time. To be clearer, we are all stuck in time. The key is to make that time yours. This is not a lecture, lecture." Lucas chuckled. "A good friend wrote a song called ah, *Pieces of the Puzzle*, and one line goes." He sings, "Living on autopilot at someone else's pace." The class begins to hum and laugh.

"The next American Idol!" A student cracked, and more laughter.

"What I'm trying to say and probably saying to myself is try not to let circumstances lead you into situations that trap or block your true paths in life. Do not be reluctant to move on or add new chapters to your life; slow down. It's ok to revise your plans. In the end, only you live with the results. You may not realize it, but we only have so much time." Lucas paused, thinking of a cigarette, and continued in a poetic presentation, "We are hourglasses that flow at different rates. So, I'm saying, do what you really want to do with your life if it's legal!" The class laughed. "It is yours and only yours!" Lucas felt good.

"My life story? Well, not today!" He had their attention.

"I'm going way off syllabus today, but just listen and give it a chance." He paused, lit a cigarette, took a significant drag, and put it out. The class got very quiet. "My point is that no matter what you think or believe, you never know what will happen next." He laughed.

"Science and religion are interwoven! I believe that religion may be a misinterpretation of science. I won't be able to cover this in the next twenty to twenty-five minutes, but here is a start."

"How many of you believe in God or a life force that is greater than ours? Don't raise your hands. It's a philosophical question." Sipping his now-cold coffee.

"Do you all believe that history is told and taught to you about how it happened? Let me ask you this? Do you remember what you did yesterday?" He laughed. "I don't, let alone last week, month, or year. You watch news reports covering the same event. You surf or switch channels and get a different perspective: they all differ. For example, view our political parties viewing the same event with opposite perspectives. " His coffee was now gone.

"We must question historical facts! Before social media, news traveled slowly, inaccurately, opinionated, and accepted; how about a hundred, five hundred, or a thousand years ago? There is an adage, 'To the victors go the spoils,' and they write history. And believe me, the Status quo holds hard against change."

"So, I want to touch upon the Science of Ancient Astronaut Theory for the next few minutes. If you wish to leave now, my eyes are closed, no problem. Do it now."

A few students left. He continued with general theories and their timelines for the remaining fascinated students. Then the class ended. "You are welcome to come to my lecture tonight. It deals with ancient alien theorists and their ideas, and my book," pulling a copy from his bag, "*Mesoamerica—The Stones of the Gods*." He held it up. "You will enjoy both. Stay in the back of the auditorium, and I will cue you when to find a seat. I appreciate your attention today, and hopefully, I'll see you tonight." Lucas was pleased.

The TAs said it was the best science class they had ever attended. The students mostly agreed.

Lucas kicked himself, mumbling. "What do I do for an encore? When's the pink slip coming?" He stepped outside and finished his Gitane cigarette. He blew a smoke ring, watching it lazily drift and slowly vaporize.

4

Black Flags and White Coats

It **was a beautiful early spring morning in Boston's Government Center.** The JFK Federal Building, twenty-six stories tall with modern offset towers, stood like a pillar of contemporary society, its steel-and-glass frame catching the Boston sun. Inside, the 26th floor hummed like a machine—cameras, scanners, whisper-quiet drones, and firewalled servers monitoring everything from the Atlantic coast to foreign consulates. Situated across from City Hall, with its controversial design. Its grounds are landscaped with tables, benches, and modern abstract sculptures. The penthouse offices of the JFK Building were recently redesigned to accommodate one of the government's newest agencies, the United Aerial Phenomena Task Force (UAPTF). It analyzes and organizes data that could threaten U.S. national security. The department promoted transparency, no longer keeping the public uninformed, with press releases and a yearly unclassified report. Until recently, the department's internal structure and philosophy changed.

The UAPTF is controlled by a private group of top-level Security Deputies from all parts of the U.S. national defense world. The organization does not answer to the FBI, CIA, or Congress. Information to the public is limited for national security interests.

The agency has become an opaque enigma. The head of UAPTF is someone about whom extraordinarily little is known. Morgan Strassa, whether a real name or a pseudonym, is unclear. What is evident is that Morgan Strassa is feared and respected. He continuously monitors anything alien-related, especially archaeological finds, having placed operatives worldwide.

At its center: Stanley Birk, Director of the UAPTF, six-foot-five-inch, ex-Marine, part bruiser, part politician. A relic of another era—ideally suited to guard the secrets of this one.

Entering the building, a short walk from his Longfellow Place Condominium, to a chorus of "Good morning, sir." Not smiling, swept by security, headed for his private elevator, and up to his plush office. Granted with total authority and unbridled power that exceeds that of local government and most federal agencies.

His graying reddish, slightly balding hair was professionally coiffed, and his fingernails were manicured weekly. He owned a closetful of suits that gave him the stature of a "Man in Black." He had a stare that could make a weak bladder fail.

Born and raised in the D Street Projects in South Boston, a staunch Irish Catholic, he enlisted in the Marines upon graduating from South Boston High School. He served and saw active duty. He was a member of the USMC boxing team and did quite well. Taking shrapnel in the legs in Pakistan ended his military career. He went to night school for Political Science at Suffolk University, located on Boston's Beacon Hill, next to the State House, where he worked as a court officer and developed many friendships and contacts. Upon graduation, he secured a job in Washington, D.C., where he met his wife.

The elevator approached his office, and he thought about his recent divorce, his ex-wife, and their three children, who had moved back to Falls Church, Virginia. He softly punched the door with a closed fist.

His job had become all-consuming, leading to his family's departure. Stanley Birk was angry! He was furious and hateful, but he was addicted to his work and the power and respect it gave him.

The office suite was an advanced electronic, technically enhanced bunker. An American Flag and the Marine Flag flanked his large desk. Behind his desk was a giant poster depicting the crucifixion titled "The Truth is Out There!" He always got a kick out of people's reactions to it. His response was, "Mulder got nothing on me. Oh, maybe Scully." He would chuckle. People would laugh but fear him.

An overturned family photo lay on his desk. Viewing it brought on a momentary rage. He hated his wife for taking his kids. He could have easily prevented her, but he loved his children and tried to do what was best for them.

Checking his agenda, and his first meeting, as he put it, was with that "pain in the balls, Prisha." He reached for a cigar, started puffing, filling the room with smoke, then went to the bar and poured a tall glass of whiskey. "I'm all set." He boasted, "This should piss her off." Kicking back and reading memos, he waited.

***

Prisha arrived in an Uber, filled with doubt and distress concerning her job. She was hired as an Assistant Director of the Environmental Protection Agency (EPA) while working closely with the National Aeronautics and Space Administration (NASA) on a joint interdepartmental project to examine the current climate instability. Her office was in Boston, and she reported only to the project director, Beebe Schwartz, headquartered in Houston.

Prisha had a small but highly committed and productive staff that examined New England and Eastern Canada's climate while working closely with international and domestic agencies. It all changed six months ago, at the beginning of the New Year. Her office had been consolidated, and it would be run out of NASA in Houston, Texas. Beebe informed Prisha in person that she was not offered a position in the realignment. Prisha was hurt. Beebe explained that she was her only choice to run the team, but was overruled. She asked Prisha to compose herself and that the government would never let her go. Continuing, she explained that a new and restructured agency (UAPTF) based in Boston demanded that she be an integral part of the program. Prisha was relieved. Her latest position was as an Assistant Director, studying weather and climate associated with aerial phenomena. It would deal with planetary alignment and all astronomical features at the time of the phenomenon's appearance. Her staff, offices, labs, and everything connected with the project encompassed the entire 25th floor of the JFK building, except for her office, which was situated down the corridor on the 26th floor of her boss, Stanley Birk.

Stanley, a political appointee, was Prisha's Director. She viewed him as a stupid, misogynist pig, yet very adept at communication and socialization. He was an effective bully. She had met him when he had worked for Homeland Security, unimpressed then, overwhelmed now. Her new position did come with a more than substantial pay increase, a car still waiting for approval, and an absurd expense account, highly profiled within the organization yet secretive to the public. The operation was now classified. Talking to your spouses, mates, or family about the research was forbidden, even unlawful.

Her first meeting today was with that "dolt," Birk.

Entering the building, she was afforded all the courtesy of a dignitary. Her beauty and fragrance lifted the spirits of the security and the public as they waited in line to enter the building. She carried herself with an air of importance. She did not have access to a personal elevator, but there was an express elevator for floors 24-26, frequented by staff, U.S. senators, and Congressmen. There was security here, as well as at Birk's private elevator. You needed a passcode to ride. Her presence, along with their morning coffee, lifted the well-being of the few riders. Arriving, she greeted her assistant and then entered her office.

The office was not the size of the Director's Birk but exquisitely decorated. With Claire's guidance, she draped the walls with original ancient art, and statues with an Indian flavor accented the room. The scent of freshly cut flowers was always present. On her desk was her wedding photo. The views of the Charles River and Cambridge, primarily the MIT campus, were breathtaking.

After checking the time and her notes, she grabbed her folder and headed down the long corridor to Stanley Birk's office. She was mentally aloft, not fully present, feeling like she was walking in a bad dream. She loved her work but despised this man.

***

The cigar stench festered upon her approach, stifling any enthusiasm she may have had. Tina, the receptionist, greeted her with a friendly hello. "Doctor Mishari-Randolph, are you here to see the Director?" she smiled.

"Yes." Humbly.

She checked his schedule and informed him that his appointment was here.

"Let her in!" He growled.

The door lock clicked, and Prisha entered.

The battle had started upon her entrance. A cancerous cell by the Montecristo No. 2 cigar devoured her Clive Christian No. 1 scent. She could feel the smoke settle on her soft skin like punishing evil insects; her hair and clothing were being dipped into a pig smoker. The stink of whiskey made for a cheap bar atmosphere.

He smiled, knowing he had saturated the room perfectly.

"Good morning, Assistant Director. Hopefully, you had a pleasant weekend?" Grinning.

Forcing a smile, "Good morning, Sir." He preferred "sir" when dealing with Prisha.

She was seated directly across from him in a strategically placed chair. She refrained from gazing at his ridiculous poster.

Prisha had made public comments about his lack of scientific knowledge and background, a mistake that had gotten back to him. He did not care. It was true, shared knowledge, and it incredibly pleased him that he had something on her. However, his superiors admired and respected her.

"Prisha, we have a call coming in from Morgan Strassa."

Preventing herself from gagging as he puffed away, she nodded.

Tina, a voluptuous, well-educated, knowledgeable, redheaded receptionist, answered the call. Morgan Strassa, a la Dr. Stephen Hawking, communicates through a computer simulation. Was he a male, a female, or a robot? Nobody knew. It was a mystery.

"Director Birk, is Assistant Director with you?" The simulation squealed.

"Yes," he said, not knowing how to address Morgan Strassa.

Morgan Strassa continued. "We have a situation that needs further documentation and examination. It's in Utah at a place well known through a television series on the History Channel, Skinwalker Ranch, or something like that. We have received permission from the owners, who will share information on their recent findings and allow us to do some testing with them. This is an extremely sensitive situation! I want Doctor Mishari-Randolph to prepare and lead a team immediately. Any testing will be a top priority in this department, and the results must be available immediately. This should take two to three weeks, so plan with your families. Any questions will be sent to Director Birk, who will forward them to me." He stopped.

"Yes!" Birk replied. Prisha nodded and couldn't wait to get out of there.

The meeting abruptly ended. Birk knew she was sick to her stomach. Prisha raced down the corridor and waved her hand to her assistant, who understood her distress. She entered, locked the door to her office, and then headed for the bathroom and vomited. Cleaning her mess, she jumped into the shower, scrubbing and washing her hair. Having a change of clothes available, she started her day afresh. She put her clothes into a plastic bag and sent them to the dry cleaners. She tried to remove Birk's entire stench from her and the office, wanting to cry but pleased to get away from him for a few weeks. She spent the day making arrangements for her team. They would leave immediately upon confirmation from her department in Washington, D.C.

She went home.

5

The Thing That Never Changes

Good evening, class. This is Archaeology 411; I've invited some science students to join us today," said Dr. Lucas Johnny Chevrolet. He nodded to the students. "You may find your way to a seat; thank you." His approach and demeanor were a world apart from earlier today.

"I'm hoping you did the reading or at least some of it. It may not fit well with what you are learning as a traditional archaeology student. I want you to be exposed to these ideas because they contradict your learning. Are these findings facts? Yes, they are, but the conclusions you draw from them are up to you. Try to think, as it is said, outside of the box. Don't close your mind, even if you don't understand or believe in something." He paused and looked at his students.

"If time permits, or if you want to stay a bit later, we will have a question-and-answer session," Lucas spoke confidently.

"There was a time, and not that long ago, when we thought the moon was the moon, a celestial body moving in harmony with the earth, tracking time and tides. We did not question ancient cultures' abilities as great builders, contractors of civilizations, the monuments, and the structures they left behind. They were theoretically explained as a step in man's advancement. The explanations at times were argued, slightly different, but were all accepted, that the cultures managed their projects." Pausing, "I remember on grade school field trips to the California Science Center in Los Angeles, that they have this display, a diorama of sorts, of ancient Egyptians building a pyramid: hundreds of enslaved people, pulleys, ropes, levers, and ramps. This is how the pyramids were built. Yes, the California Science Center, you accept this as a fact, live with it, and never question it. You would look at and read about the size and number of blocks and how they traveled and wonder how, but still believe, and if your teacher quizzed you, your answer would be what was told to you. That's how all of history and science is taught and accepted." Pausing.

"Oh, and not too long ago, God was God, accepted, worshipped, loved, and feared. Parents would make their children worship, respect, and never question their beliefs. In turn, they would pass it on to their children, even though they thought it was all bullshit. Fear and rationalization perpetuated these faiths. I still have childhood friends, to this day, who adhere publicly to these teachings, with the thinking that they are mystically protected with prayers and absolved at planned confessions, or whatever their faith allows, will save them. Not believing in what they say but using it as an insurance policy. LOL." Pausing.

"Then along comes Erich von Daniken's *Chariots of the Gods*, and begins questioning all that was taught, not accepting faith, without further examination. He reexamined and reinterpreted ancient texts and the structures they left behind, creating alternate theories on the history of civilization and its timeline. His theories were then supported by a growing number of modern-day Alien Theorists, led by von Daniken and Giorgio A. Tsoukalos, with whom I had the pleasure of attending a lecture series of theirs at Ithaca College a few years ago. They and their associates, a growing number of prominent scientists and journalists, are researching and searching for facts that could lead to a more exact beginning of man, at least a new history. They are convincing us to look up at the sky, the stars, the oceans, and our everyday images with a new set of eyes and an open mind. Their theories present astounding earth timelines, theories of earth crust displacement, Antarctica, and Atlantis; questioning the ancient religious text and giving them new meaning are just some of their interpretations of Earth's and man's history. They have stepped out of that box and are looking around." Pausing.

Lucas went on to give a thrilling lecture with a slide presentation. During his lecture, you could not hear a whisper or a cell phone. He had time for questions.

"Doctor Chevrolet, may I recap a few things? Some theories, let me get this straight. That, I call them aliens, but we may be the aliens, traveled ten, maybe a thousand light years, eradicating dinosaurs, terraforming the planet, seeding it for the growth of new life, which would be similar to theirs?"

"It's just an alternate theory, which may or may not be proved, but it's out there," the professor replied.

"Yeah, way out there!" A student shouted, followed by chuckles.

"Doctor Chevrolet, are you saying they altered the species' DNA over time?"

"You understand that this is just theory. The planet may have evolved according to Darwin's theory. The dinosaurs may have been accidentally eradicated, but the planet and its species, man, appear in theory to have been altered, evolving physically and mentally at a more rapid rate than they should have," he replied.

"Doctor Chevrolet, some of your ideas deal with ancient floods, wiping out most of the world's population, and sinking Atlantis. You even claim Earth's crust was deliberately displaced—putting Antarctica at the South Pole, hiding an ancient civilization, possibly alien, thriving beneath the surface, and has tunneled under the oceans so they can enter and exit their world undetected. Professor, please, this is not an Asimov, Bradbury, or even a Jules Verne class, whereby I could enjoy this poppycock. No offense intended."

Lucas shrugged. "None taken." He smiled, pleased that she got the facts at least. "I live outside of what has been taught to us and do not refute these radically different possibilities. You understand that governments know about these things; none of this will be revealed or proven in our lifetime."

"Doctor Chevrolet, you briefly touched upon the Knights Templar, the Catholic Church, and the papacy in the 14th century. Can you give us more details?"

"Thank you. You can find it in my book *Mesoamerica—The Stones of the Gods*. I will touch upon this in a later lecture. Thank you. It's time for one more."

"Yes," Pointing to a student who looked like a Catholic priest. He stood up.

"You speak of the soul, this…this entity as an alien host, and it begins at conception, or earlier." Then, raising the inflection of his voice, "Is that not God?" The class got very still, waiting for the next word. "This host travels with you until death, then leaves." Once again, raising his voice, "That's why we protect life! God is within you, within all of us. We have free will, good or bad. Gifts!" He blessed Lucas and the class and then apologized for raising his voice.

Lucas, unfazed, thanked the student and told the class they would discuss these ideas later in the course. "Read the book. There is a lot of archaeology and intriguing theories. You'll enjoy it." However, the priest's words resonated in him, A question as old as the rocks he studied.

"Any questions on the architecture, levitation, or anything?"

There was not, and the lecture ended. Several students thanked him. One of his science students shared a cigarette with him, and they talked while walking to their vehicles. Lucas had a good day.

6

Peabody Museum of Archaeology and Ethnology

The **Peabody Museum is affiliated with Harvard University** and was established in 1866 as a gift from a wealthy philanthropist, George Peabody. The large, old museum, which is focused on the archaeology of the Americas, is located on Divinity Street on the Harvard University campus.

***

The campus was tranquil, transitioning into summer break. The Peabody Museum sat quietly on Harvard's campus, its windows reflecting the pale spring sun. Inside, the air was rich with the scent of stone, history, and dust. Claire arrived, pulling into her parking space, marked Dr. Randolph-Mishari, at the rear of the museum. She was greeted by security and continued up to her office suite on the top floor. Her assistant had the day off. Claire stepped into her office, placing fresh-cut flowers into a vase, a daily ritual. She turned on soft classical music, sipped her smoothie, and reflected on yesterday's joy--and the enigmatic disc Genny had brought home. She smiled with a bit of euphoria, sipping her smoothie, listening to Beethoven's Moonlight Sonata, thinking of Prisha and Genny.

Prisha was extremely tense this morning. In a most political, sensitive, loving way, she told her that she did not have to do that job, that they had plenty, and that she could find work for her at any university in her area. Prisha replied jokingly, "You ain't my sugar mommy!" They both laughed and affectionately hugged.

The thought of Genny now played. "I like that girl," Claire said, " I'm incredibly pleased that we will work together. "That disc!"

***

Behind the Museum was a smaller building. It was a testing laboratory. Harvard University, competing for the best students in the world in the archaeological field, acquired the best equipment. All new and old scientific finds could immediately be evaluated on campus. The Museum greatly benefited because all their archaeological digs could be tested using Radiocarbon-14 dating, cutting-edge X-ray fluorescence (XRF) equipment, and the ability to do X-ray diffraction analysis (XRD). Doctor Ditmer Winkler, a German immigrant, managed the facility with a doctorate in mechanical engineering from MIT. A serious, demanding, big-framed, six-foot-something, a little overweight, and a dedicated, diligent colleague, Ditmer was a funny guy, but his humor sometimes gets lost in translation.

Ditmer answered his cell with his deep accent. "My good doctor, something must be amiss to hear from you today. How are you?" he smiled. He and Claire have been associates and friends for two decades.

"Ditmer, it is so nice hearing your voice. Now, can I get a translation?" Laughing.

"Ditmer, are you there for the day?"

"Always for you! Claire." He was sincere.

"I have an item. I'm not certain if it is an artifact. It contains both organic and inorganic matter. This could be of great interest. The fewer people aware of it, the better for this project."

"Yes, I am Claire." The joke blew by her with no response. "Doctor, I understand completely."

"Doctor," she continued. "I need carbon dating and XRF scans. High resolution imaging. Quietly."

"You have it. I'll bring the portable gear to your office. We can get immediate results. I can also get a sample for the carbon dating and start that process, which may take a day or so. You know it will get top priority, nowhere faster on the planet." He was proud.

"Also," She continued. "I need some super high-imaging photography. I want to scan; you will see what I mean when you have it in front of you, all surfaces. I want to scan these photos into the University's supercomputer and get immediate results."

"That can be done. I have an associate here today who can manage the photos without problem. Referencing the mainframe, Dr. Jeffery Drayton is in charge. I had coffee with him this morning. The computer will shut down next week for a few days. If we move quickly enough, we can get this done ASAP. I have an excellent relationship with his department."

Claire was pleased with all that Dr. Winkler was telling her. "OK, great. I'll call you when the item arrives. This will be a long day, and I will send it out for lunch or dinner."

"That sounds great."

"Thanks, I'll text you later." The call ended.
Footsteps echoed outside her door. She didn't need to look--she knew and was excited.

7

The Disc Arrives

Genny awoke to a foul taste and an angry stomach. She made a cup of coffee and sipped a bottle of water. A bit foggy, recapping the events of yesterday. Taking out her yoga mat, she did a quick twenty-minute stretching routine and a short brisk workout on her spin bike. Meditating for a few minutes. She felt better. Her thoughts collected, she raised herself, looked into the mirror, and said, "Good morning, Doctor." She was happy and off to the shower. While drying, she made a protein smoothie. She was quickly dressing, as casually as possible. She was not clear on what her role was. She was hired as an Assistant Professor to teach and do research. She was under Claire's administration. The original plan was to start in late August. Here it is, late May.

Her precious medallion was always the last item to grace her body. She kissed it with a secret prayer, then put it on. Not knowing the parking situation, she decided to take an Uber. She gathered what she thought she would need for the day and two bottles of wine, then placed the disc with them into her backpack, stepping outside and tracking her ride.

She was dropped off in Harvard Square, picking up coffees and healthy pastries, and started the short walk to the Museum. Her cobwebs were fading, and the fresh spring air and the late-morning bustle made her feel alive.

The Museum would not open for another hour, so she approached the staff entrance in the rear. There, she was greeted by the security guard; according to her nametag, Sheila, Genny introduced herself and told her the situation. Sheila, a petite brunette with a ponytail, looked down at a note she was holding. "You must be Genny. You'll need security clearance after today." Smiling, she said. Then, she wished Genny good luck.

Her footfalls echoed throughout the museum as she climbed the stairs, even with running shoes.

The office doors were open, and as she entered, Claire was beaming.

"Morning, Doctor," Genny said, stepping in with coffees and a warm smile."

"Good morning, Doctor. It's day one, and you're my favorite employee!" They laughed.

"Doctor, you understand that we must act more professionally in our day-to-day routine at the University," Claire explained.

"Really!" Silly Genny responded.

"Did you bring the disc?" Anxiously, Claire asked.

She pulled the disc and the two bottles of wine from her backpack. Claire was torn about which one to grab. Taking the wine, she placed it on her desk and said, "These are going home with me!" She then took the disc as though it were the Holy Grail and just stared at it, rubbing her finger across her upper lip in deep thought, placing it on a magnificent medieval table in the room.

"GG, let's sit and have our brunch, and I'll fill you in on today's activities."

"Before I forget, I need clearance to get in here and the parking situation." Genny inquired.

"Already in the process, dear. Just need a photo of you and voila."

Genny was relaxed. Claire continued, "It's like this …" telling her about her talk with Dr. Winkler and today's plan. They sipped their coffees. Genny rubbed her necklace. The day had begun.

They sat together at the medieval table where the disc now lay under a soft beam of light, in joyous, comfortable silence, sipping their coffee.

Genny spoke very softly, almost in a trance, as she continued to rub the medallion, like a habit. "This feels like something bigger than me. Bigger than us."
"Good," Claire said, "Because it probably is. Let's call Doctor Winkler and get started."

"Dr. Winkler, is everything ready?" Claire demanded.

"Yes, just a few minutes to finish packing and off to your office. My photographic engineer, Charlie Zaspa, will accompany me."

"This is all on the quiet. Did you fill Zaspa in?"

"Yes, she is a real professional and the absolute best in her field," Ditmer explained in his heavy German accent.

"Let's say in about an hour. I have a few administrative duties to clear up. Say 1:15. Does that work for you?"

"Yes, doctor, it does. I also contacted Doctor Drayton. He said if we get the images to him late today or early tomorrow morning, he could get us results in less than 8 hours."

"Ditmer, you are a miracle worker. Thank You. See you in a bit." The call was disconnected, and she made another call. Genny was sitting and listening to Dr. Randolph-Mishari, who was taking total charge of the project. Genny admired this.

"Cynthia, how are you? This is doctor…"

"Yes, I know," she interrupted. "I'm all set over here. Your preliminary information enabled me to get a big jump on this. Send her over. It shouldn't take more than 20 minutes. I'll have the credentials and passes ready before you leave today."

Claire rubbed that upper lip, slowly growing into a big smile, "Thanks, Cynthia. I owe you one, and do not be shy to ask!" The call ended.

"Genny, head over to the Administration Building. Ask the receptionist to page Cynthia Robeo. She will handle all your documentation, parking passes, and identification tags. It should take less than half an hour, so be quick. We have Dr. Winkler and his associate coming by in an hour."

***

Genny was out the door, heading for the Administration Building.

"Cynthia Robeo, please?" She politely inquired.

The receptionist picked up the phone and paged Cynthia Robeo. A moment later, the corridor doors swung open, and Cynthia emerged.

She extended her hand to Genny. "You must be Doctor Genny Giuliana Cantalupo?" in a heavy British Colonial accent. Cynthia, a six-foot-two-inch Nigerian, greeted Genny with her beautiful smile.

"I'm the one." Genny chirped.

"Quickly, Genny, I have everything set up. You need to sign a few documents, then I can take your picture, and you will be on your way. I will send a package over to you later today."

They chatted along the way. Cynthia was from Lagos, Nigeria, a place that Genny had visited. They hit it off.

She was out of there in less than 20 minutes. Genny thanked her and said, "When things are settled, they should have lunch."

"I would like that," Cynthia replied, then shook Genny's hand.

***

Genny got back with time to spare. Claire had made room on the large table for the examination. Turning to Genny, Claire said, "Come this way. I want to show you your temporary office." They walked by the assistant's desk and down a hall overlooking the Museum's main exhibit. They entered a small but luxurious office.

"Genny, this may or will be your office. I'll catch flak and jealousy for this. Everything is going fast. You can set up here." There was a beautiful antique desk, Mesoamerican artifacts, and wall hangings. Genny was amazed!

Claire hit a panel in the back of the room, and a door slid open. It was a partially equipped lab. "You can do your dirty work in here," she chuckled.

"Best of all, in the back of the lab is a door." Claire opened the door, and a well-lit passageway led to a door. Inside was another magnificent, fully equipped lab with a library of books and charts.

"This place is freaking awesome!" Genny squealed. Claire smiled, loving the girlish enthusiasm.

"Yeah, but that's not the best part." She opened another door, and there they entered Claire's office. Dr. Winkler and Charlie Zaspa were setting up their equipment.

8

Images and Alloys

Claire, I have looked at the object, and it is fascinating. It looks modern, and I would think nothing of it if you did not bring it to my attention." Ditmer continued, "I think Charlie should set up first. She plans to take macro-photography and overall digital images and go to her lab immediately. She will quickly review the images, send them to Dr. Drayton at the supercomputer, and then forward copies to you. We have looked, and we can see letters, hieroglyphs, or whatever on both sides, and we will be able to magnify them as much as possible."

"Ok, that sounds good. Let's get started." Claire was in control.

Charlie Zaspa, aka Pham Ngyuen, is the daughter of Vietnamese refugees and immigrants. She graduated from the Rhode Island School of Design with a BA-MA in Photography. A diminutive but forceful woman, she took her nickname from a Vietnamese comic strip.

She began her work by setting up her portable studio with lights, a vertical rise-macro photography platform, and a Leica Camera. She was thorough, and her onlookers watched her for nearly an hour, moving with precision and perfection. She finished and was off to her lab. Claire, Genny, and Ditmer thanked her.

Ditmer picked up the object and was weighing it in his hand. Flashing a light on it, it glistened. "This is something he said to Genny and Claire. Tell me how it came about?" He was organizing his equipment as Genny told the story.

"I'm going to cut a piece of this organic material and send it to our lab." He started cutting. "It's almost like braided, coarse hair." He placed it in a plastic bag. He made a phone call, and in less than a moment, a person was waiting for his package. He labeled it and then sent it off to the lab.

Genny and Claire were impressed with Ditmer's steady, well-prepared procedures.

Claire had sent out for coffee and sandwiches. No one was hungry, but everyone enjoyed the coffee.

"I've been excitedly thinking about this since this morning." Ditmer breathed heavily, and then, turning on his portable XRF, he zapped the disc.

Astounded, Dr. Winkler read the results on the machine.

Claire reacted to his astonished look.. "Do you mind sharing?" Claire became impatient.

"I'm going to take a second reading on the reverse side to compare them." He did, and the result was the same.

Breathing heavily with an anxious look, Claire said, "Well!"

"Ok!" Confused. Sighs. "The readings show the following: aluminum, copper, iron with traces of titanium, nickel, chromium, molybdenum, and some other minor trace elements."

"Translation!" Claire excitedly.

"Very odd elements. I do not know how to say this. These elements are used for spacecraft and then some. Aluminum, copper, and iron comprise the greater part of the disc and are known as quasi-crystal alloys. Scientists in Florence, Princeton, and Cal-Tech have been analyzing items found on Earth that contain this pattern. It is a 60-point symmetrical rotation." Ditmer started to shake.

"Claire, this may be alien technology!"

Claire and Genny got goosebumps and chills! They hugged, and Claire, unable to contain her excitement, looked Genny in the eye. "God! I am so proud of you! You did it!"

"We did it!" Genny, with an uncontrollable smile, made it clear.

Dr. Winkler asked them to calm down. "This is what I think, but we must do further analyses."

"That disc is not leaving my possession!" Claire was adamant.

Do you have a file tool? I could remove the disc, file the edges, get a sample, and do a deeper study. We must do this!"

Claire stepped back, entered her lab, and returned with a file and a small jar. Asking, "Can you reinsert the disc?"

"Yes." Ditmer carefully filed only the edges with great care, most of the shavings going into the jar, some on the desk. He took the jar and labeled it. Genny wiped the edges of the disc, collected the loose shavings, put them into a plastic bag, and unconsciously put them into her backpack.

"Dr. Winkler, you know I want this right away!" Demanded as his boss.

"Oh, Claire, I will not sleep until I know for sure!" Claire was happy.

"Genny, Ditmer, this is remarkable! We are a team. As we go forward, we are a team. I do not know where this is going, but we should sleep on it."

"Dr. Winkler, please start on this. I anxiously await the carbon and scanned image results."

"Ok," Breathing heavily.

"We will meet here tomorrow at 9 o'clock," Claire said.

"Good day, and thank you, Dr. Winkler." Claire took a deep sigh, and Dr. Winkler left.

9

Safeguards and Departure

Claire and Genny were alone, pondering what was next. A courier walked in and handed Genny a package. Cynthia had come through.

Claire then texted Cynthia a thank you emoji.

"Dr. Cantalupo." In her most serious voice of the day, Claire, rubbing her finger over her upper lip, said, "This is your find. However, I cannot allow you to take it with you. I know this seems harsh, but believe me, I'm doing this to keep the disc away from harm. I know you kept it, and it was safe; it may have profound importance."

Genny looked relieved, rubbing her medallion. "By all means. Where can we keep it?"

"I think the Museum would be the safest. I have a personal safe, but I cannot give you the access information. Sorry!"

"That's okay. If possible, could you forward me all the scanning information and the carbon results?" Genny asked.

"Of course, Doctor, already in the process. Let's have a drink and call it a day."
Genny's grin said it all.

Claire brought out two bourbon glasses. "Neat or rocks?"

"Neat." She smiled at Claire; they toasted and then sipped their drink with accomplishment and satisfaction, and they departed for their homes.

***

When Claire arrived, Prisha was quiet, packing for her trip to Utah. Claire got nervous that she might have offended her this morning. Prisha turned to Claire, smiling. "It's not what you think." Continued, telling her of her horrific encounter with Birk and her assignment to Utah.

"My poor Prisha." Hugging her. "You still smell of cigar smoke."

"Do you want to go to dinner and talk about this?" Claire asked.

Prisha shook her head no. "I have to coordinate this trip. There is a lot to do and with urgency. I cannot tell you any more than that, or they'll shoot me!" They laughed, lightening the mood.

Prisha continued packing while Claire put on some music. "We'll do takeout later if that's ok." Prisha was okay with that. "Genny sent over some of her grandfather's wine; I think you'll enjoy it."

She continued packing and texting her team and looked up with a smile. "That sounds great with some Thai food."

"Ok, about an hour or so," Claire replied.

Claire did not mention her glorious day.

During dinner, Prisha commented on the fine wine, then, with selfish guilt, blurted out. "Oh goodness, how was your day?"

"A day on which a Nobel Prize was born!" She was excited and told her story. Prisha enjoyed the pleasant distraction.

10

Symmetry

Lucas flicked his cigarette, held his coffee, and entered the building. As he approached the auditorium, he could hear the din of the students. He was feeling bad about yesterday's thoughts. Thinking, "What am I, a jerk? Those students, me, that's who they were. They are just kids finding their way."

The University had offered the job to Lucas, who was highly recommended by their staff members. The arrangement was to teach this entry-level class, for which he was overqualified, and they would give him a class in which he could design a curriculum relating to Mesoamerican archaeology. The University was developing a new department, but only had an opening for a science teacher. They knew his book and thought he might be the professor who would organize their first archaeological dig in the Yucatan.

Lucas had momentarily forgotten the gift bestowed upon him, lost in the research of his developing novel.

He entered the lecture hall with a cheerful outlook, greeting his students with humor and tidbits of related information. The TAs were excited with this newfound positive energy, and so went the following two semesters.

The school contacted him to teach his newly designed Mesoamerica Photo/Art course this summer. Initially, he was reluctant but acquiesced when the school offered him an additional section in the fall and two fewer science classes. He agreed. The first two drafts of his book were completed.

11

The Pattern

Claire and Genny got to the office early. Sitting at the medieval table with their coffee, staring at the disc, Genny rubbed her medallion.

"We should think about getting a paper out as soon as possible, but we should be very cautious," Claire said.

"I'm with you, professor. Let's see the results." Genny stated.

"This could shake history. We could be met with formidable opposition. So, we must be exacting in what we say." Claire whispered, rubbing her face. "You do understand that findings, the discovery of this nature, could bring you a Nobel Prize."

"Yeah, I was wondering when that was going to happen. My doctorate was getting a little stale after two days." They guffawed. This is why Claire needed Genny as part of her life.

Genny, in an honest, frank tone, "Us! We are a team. You brought me to this precipice, and we will share the view."

"It's going to be such a pleasure collaborating with you. I think I will give you a raise." Laughing.

"That's fine with me!" Genny jumped on it.

Claire was getting a call. It was Ditmer.

"I am delayed for a few minutes. We worked all night; I promised that my staff would get a paid day off. I have the analysis for the disc. The carbon testing will be completed in fifteen to twenty minutes. Charlie was able to get the images over to Drayton early last evening. She will send them to you shortly, and the analysis will be within the hour."

"Thanks, Ditmer. The images are coming over now. No problem with the days off. When you arrive, we will examine the images in my lab."

"Great, see you in a few." Pausing, "Not to alarm you, but this is astounding!" In a deep, heavy-breathing accented voice.

Claire got chills. "OK, see you then. Ditmer, one last thing: furnish me with a list of everyone working and working on this. Keep it small and quiet. Thanks!"

"Will do. No problem, all our associates think that this is day-to-day research for the museum."

"That's great, keep it like that!"

"Genny, this is going well. Let's go into the lab and check the images on my desktop. Ditmer will be here in about an hour or less."

"Sure." Genny grabbed the disc and left the beautifully scented room, entering a musty lab.

Claire turned on her desktop with a 48-inch monitor, freshened the room, and turned down the air conditioning thermostat.

"We will work in here today. Sally, my assistant, will be in later this morning. She doesn't need to know what's going on for now. She is dependable and remarkable. I think you may have met her."

Claire was taking precautions to make this as secret as possible until they could figure out what they had.

Claire and Genny examined the images. They were fascinating—sharp, detailed laser cuts over a shiny, bluish metal surface.

"There is a pattern here." Claire pointed them out to Genny, "Maybe twenty or so."

"I recognize many of these ancient glyphs. The different glyphs are grouped." Genny examined.

Genny pointed out, "Egyptian, Mayan, Sumerian, Olmec, looks like Hittite cuneiform, even Chinese ideographic." Pointing, "This looks like Gosford Glyphs."

"Yes, and many more. They appear different than what I'm familiar with." Claire rubbed her lip with her finger. She had intense concentration; her eyes were focused like lasers through her glasses.

"The reverse side is a longer message in one script. I don't recognize any of this." Claire was in deep thought.

"We'll get the computer report, then we'll do our analysis." Claire looked up to Ditmer. He was sweaty and breathing heavily. His yellow buttoned, short-sleeved shirt was wet. It hung over his waist, which had a thin belt overrun by fat, keeping his khaki slacks up.

He apologized for his appearance but said he arrived as soon as possible.

"Thanks." They both replied.

"What do you have?" Claire started right in.

12

The Age of the Disc

Opening a briefcase as old as him, the type with a top handle, **you** open it while it's set up right, like Mary Poppins or a doctor's bag. It had a little latch with a flap locked into the side; he flicked it open and pulled out two files.

This is the report on the disc. He handed each a copy.

"As we observed yesterday, the materials are what they were yesterday. I can now positively state that there is symmetrical rotation, and the aluminum, copper, and iron certainly show patterns of a Quasi-Crystal Alloy. I have found no match for this combination of elements in our data banks. I could argue that this was not made on Earth!" Taking a deep breath.

Genny handed him a bottle of water.

"Well, this is fascinating. But let us try to put all the pieces together first before coming to any preliminary conclusions." Claire was being cautious.

Ditmer handed them a second folder.

"This is the carbon testing, so be prepared to get blown away."

They read the report before he could state it, and their faces lit up with amazement. Claire said, "I knew this material was old when I saw it at Genny's."

"We did this test three times to make sure what we found was correct. The carbon dating process breaks down after 50,000 years or so. This item was assessed beyond that range. It is at least 60,000 years old and could be up to 300,000 years old."

"Get this, my favorite: coarse 'guard hair' from a Mammuthus primigenius, a woolly mammoth that was extinct over 10,000 years ago."

Ditmer could not contain his excitement, glowing with his results; the ladies were taking it all in.

"What's next?" Ditmer asked.

"We are still awaiting the results from the mainframe. Doctor Cantalupo and I will start piecing it together when we get it. I said before, we are a team. For now, we will examine everything from an archaeology perspective. Seek all possibilities until we can produce something. We will research and read if any work has been done in this area. I cannot say exactly. Ditmer, why don't you take the rest of the day off? Doctor Cantalupo and I will go over the report when it shows up. We will be here in the morning and fill you in."

"Good plan. I am pooped!" They laughed.

"You did a herculean job in twenty-four hours. I cannot believe where we are in just forty-eight hours." Claire patted him lightly on his sweating back.

"Genny, isn't being a professor fun?" Claire smiled.

"Yeah, let's get something to eat. All this thinking makes me hungry." Genny's stomach growled.

Ditmer left.

Claire was at the computer. "GG, I sent you a copy of everything. Let's lock the disc up, grab lunch, and discuss this. Hopefully, the report will arrive. It's so nice outside; let's walk over to Dunster Street."

13

The Message

Walking back from lunch, the report came through. Claire forwarded a copy to Genny.

"We'll print this out as soon as we're back," Claire said as she read the short analysis.

When they returned, Claire printed two copies. It was short, four pages.

"Genny, take your report and examine it in your office. Introduce yourself to Sally and return in about 45 minutes. I want to think independently about this and then compare our thoughts. Top secret!" Genny saluted her and smiled.

***

The Report.

Disc Side A

- 22 different sets of markings or glyphs were determined.
- 14 positively identified.
- six partially identified.
- two unknowns
- The 14 identified sets of markings have similar, if not the same, messages.
- The six partially identified markings have similarities to the other messages.

- The messages, though not translatable, contain elements as follows:

-Recognize the Gods.

-Help build civilizations.

- Teach not to harm- never take a life.

- Life begins (not translatable)

- Free will?

- Superior being.

- Create lineage- lesser beings made to understand.

- Rules- impermanent civilization.

Disc Side B.

-Side B Non-identifiable writing—narrative contains some glyphs similar to side A's.

It cannot be determined which side A or B is, and they have been chosen arbitrarily.

***

Genny headed back to Claire's but checked with Sally, who had arrived while she was examining the printout. Middle-aged Sally was a positive stereotype of a professional woman working in a museum as a receptionist or assistant to a director. She was efficient and did everything by the book. Genny reintroduced herself. They had a brief student-administrator relationship.

She was let into Claire's office.

"Genny, in cases like today, just text and use the lab entrance." It was close to three o'clock. Sally had made coffee and sent them in.

"I will; I wanted to meet Sally."

"Ok, let's move on."

"So, what was your first impression?" Claire asked Genny.

"Sally is very nice." They laughed.

Rubbing her necklace. "My first thought is, why? Why am I finding this disc?"

"That's good." Claire, just focusing on Genny's words and thoughts while in her classic pose, asked her to continue.

"The organic material is so obviously placed that someone wanted this disc to be found and dated. The timeline is overwhelming."

"I agree with you. The glyphs" pausing "with the same message sounds like a mission statement, depending on a further translation."

Genny: "Yes, some sales pitch. To a group, I'm assuming."

"This is a lot of science fiction to process. Feels like weeks, not hours; we've been working on this." Claire was saying as she got a text message. It was Prisha. Claire texted back that she was in a meeting and would call her immediately after the meeting. Prisha replied, "Okay," and a heart emoji.

"Yes, doctor, I agree. My thinking on this is treating it as though it were science fiction or an elaborate hoax." Genny said.

Claire smiled. "Yes, and my inner X File raises the principle of Occam's razor. Science fiction will give us fewer assumptions. Let's apply simple fictional thoughts and then tie them into facts."

"Ok." Genny went first. "Simple versus complex, then this seems to be an alien pitch to intervene with human civilization, or a hoax leading us to believe so. But why so intricate and deceptive?"

"Also reminds me of a sales manager giving instructions to their managers. I have no clue, so why a hoax?" Claire said.

"Or generals giving orders to their troops. A hoax is more believable," Genny said.

"It looks like they are coming with rules. Putting them into place, leaving, and letting humans or someone continue. Am I reading into this too deeply? "Claire asked.

Genny: "The rules that can be translated are so specific. Do not kill."

Claire: "Do not take life for any reason. Not specific on when life begins."

Genny: "Create a lineage?"

"Impermanent civilization, meaning their civilization could end." Claire grimaced.

"Free will?" Genny declared.

"Help them build their civilization." This is too much, seemingly science fiction. But why has this disc been found and dated?" Claire continued, "This is only the computer's translation. We must dig deeper!"

They discussed it for hours and agreed to sleep on it, meet in the morning, and devise a plan. Then, they departed.

Claire called Prisha, but there was no answer. She then texted with the same result.

***

Claire returned home and found a note on the table. Prisha explained that her job is shrouded in secrecy, and she cannot communicate for a bit. She is heading to Utah with her team and will get in touch as soon as possible. Claire read this with deep sadness, concern, anger, and regret for not immediately calling her.

14

Astral Projections

Genny made a quick stop, picking up a small pizza and eating a slice on her short ride home from there. "Hmmm!" Munching on another slice as she entered her home. She put her backpack in its corner, then placed the pizza on the kitchen table. She freshened up. Pouring a tall glass of wine from an opened bottle, she took a big gulp, set her glass on the kitchen table, and crushed one more slice of pie before putting the pizza into the refrigerator. Another gulp of wine produced a relaxing tingle. Reaching into a kitchen counter drawer, pulling out a little sewing kit tin, opening it, and removing a half-smoked reefer. She took her contraband to the back porch.

An awakening warm spring evening massaged Genny's tired frame and mentally drained psyche, sinking into the canvas wooden chair. Settling like a bag of sand, the descent was only halted by the end of the stretching seat. Lighting the roach, taking a deep hit, followed by a sip of wine. A stuttering harbor sea breeze was acting as an intermittent stimulus. Lilacs abound, in full bloom, fragrance the area like fairy dust, as caterpillars nested, waiting for their next journey.

Another sip of wine and a last drag settled Genny as she reviewed the day's events. The sun was setting over Charlestown and Cambridge like a giant cherry, shooting off rays, illuminating Boston's skyline and harbor with a candy land sugar coating.

In a meditative state, Genny rubbed her medallion and nodded off to a deep sleep.

She was falling, falling, and falling deeper, deeper, and deeper into the center of her medallion and now floating up, up, up into the evening sky like a super unbound kite, looking down at the city and seeing her sleeping, smiling self on the deck, whereby her body appeared larger than the objects around her, like a giant doll in Barbie's playhouse. She was now riding her medallion like Santa's Sleigh across the sky. Looking down, the harbor looks like a bathtub filled with toys. The city resembles pieces of a model train display. Zooming across the sky, her mind and body were vibrant, feeling more alive than ever, and watching the setting sun was traversed by slowly drifting, passing clouds resembling a herd of happy elephants.

She was traveling over the city, looking down at the State House's golden dome, Boston Common, and the Public Garden. Arriving above Claire's home, seeing through the walls, Claire was reading a note with tears trickling down her cheeks. Zoom... Floating up and away, thinking about Peter Pan and the wind's back, a joyous rapture, and smiling down at the TD Garden. She was on the ceiling of the entry of the Four's Restaurant on Canal Street, rubbing her medallion. The owner greeted her.

"Hey, old friend, sitting at the bar?" He asked.

"I don't know." She was amazed that she was talking from the ceiling.

She looked around and saw all the familiars, staff, and regulars. They all acknowledged her presence.

"Hello!" She giggled.

She was drawn to a man with papers scattered on the bar, working in the corner of the bar, hovering above him. She tried to see what he was writing. It looked like the glyphs on the disc.

The handsome man, with a big smile, introduced himself. "Hello, I'm Lucas Johnny Chevrolet."

"Lucas Johnny Chevrolet! Lucas Johnny Chevrolet! Lucas Johnny Chevrolet..." Echoing at least twenty times.

"I'm Genny." Laughing from the echoes

"I know!" Shouting as though she were far away.

"What?" Genny replied.

"Rico's granddaughter?" He was shouting with a bullhorn.

"What?" Genny cupped her ears.

"The Angel Enrico!" Talking into an electric microphone.

"What? Talk louder!" She grimaced.

"Lucas Johnny Chevrolet!" Shouting into a DJ's microphone at a wedding with the volume jacked up!

"What?" She sighed and cupped her ears, but still couldn't hear him.

"The Yucatan!" Played on the PA system at a Red Sox Game at Fenway Park.

"What?" Shaking her head. Frustrated.

"The Medallion!" In a whisper that was louder than thunder.

"Oh!" She spoke.

She drifted back into space, floating towards the moon. History and knowledge reeled through her thoughts as though all history was downloading into her brain. She passed the planets and then out of the solar system. Mathematical formulas inside cartoon bubbles came in all directions, popping as they touched her. Stars passed like lights in a tunnel of a passing, speeding Bullet Train.

She was on a planet that was not Tralfamadore but was like Earth. Back in college, Harvard Yard, she was doing yoga with a Mayan Shaman and traveling back to grammar school at the Our Lady of Assumption, her communion rosary beads tightening and burning her hands. She picked herself up after falling when she took her first steps and said, "Gravity! Hmmm! Ain't so bad!" Seeing her joyful parents' faces from her crib. She was doing the backstroke in amniotic fluid.

Genny suddenly awakened, damp from an engulfing fog. Her heart was racing, and she was breathing heavily. "What the fuck!" A silent but forceful whisper landed her on her feet. It was early evening. Rubbing her medallion, she whispers, "Lucas Johnny Chevrolet." She collected her things, took them inside, and locked the screen door.

Lucas Johnny Chevrolet plays across her lips in a continuous, endless loop. With her iPad, she does the research. Amazingly, he exists here and now at the University of Massachusetts in Boston. Not thinking she could be freaked out further, she heads towards her library. There was a file cabinet labeled "PA." It was impeccably chronologically organized. His passing was coming up to two years; she had never opened or disturbed any of his papers. Checking on his dates and digs, there it was—a photo of Pa and this man, Lucas Johnny Chevrolet, on a dig in the Yucatan. Enrico was wearing the medallion. Exhausted, she stood motionless and took the photo and some documents. She flopped on her bed and started to read. She paused, and her dream became completely focused as she fell asleep.

15

Black Helicopters

Prisha and her eight associates disembarked from their military transport, a Boeing C-17 Globemaster III, arriving at the Dugway Proving Ground, aka Area 52, and were greeted by a Colonel. They were informed of the guest processing procedure, which would be expedited by scanning and confirming their identity. The Colonel explained that with the cooperation of the owner of Skinwalker Ranch, they quickly built a functional facility that would house them, along with installing state-of-the-art scientific equipment. Then, upon completion of the project, the government will donate any permanent fixtures and electronic devices to the ranch.

Two military guards, male and female, had been assigned to Prisha's team and were at their disposal. They would also stay at the ranch. The Colonel informed them they could not leave the ranch until the project was completed unless extenuating circumstances existed. Their cell phones will be held by security and monitored in case of an emergency. They will communicate with government-issued devices only; measures are taken for security reasons. He continued, saying he was unsure how well they were briefed on this mission. Still, the gist was to do a scientific analysis concerning astronomical alignment along with weather and climate conditions based on information that the Skinwalker team had gathered. The distinct possibility of a wormhole or similar phenomenon may exist. Their time frame was twenty-two to twenty-five days. He thanked them, said the government appreciated their time and service, and ordered his officer to begin the checking-in procedure.

The crew was enthusiastic and excited. This team of scientists was recruited to be the best in their fields and unattached from their family or marriage. They were excited about this unparalleled career opportunity. Prisha was hand-picked as the assistant director because she was the best and only person for the job, selected by a team that worked well inside the government. Her brilliance would overshadow Birk's bungling lack of science.

Prisha's heart sank. She wished she wasn't so proud and took Claire up on her offer. Looking at the team's excitement amplified her loneliness and longing for Claire. She knew she was the best person for this assignment and pulled herself together with a deep sigh.

As they were leaving, the Colonel told them their personal belongings and equipment were being trucked as we speak. It's about a three to four-hour trip. You will fly in a Sikorsky CH-53K King Stallion helicopter, which will get you there in less than an hour. One last note is that you only answer to Stanley Birk per Morgan Strassa's orders. He again thanked them for their time and wished them good luck.

16

The Wait of Silence

Her thoughts of Prisha overshadowed Claire's excitement. She worried about her when she traveled, and now, incommunicado, made her anxious, placing her at the forefront of her mind.

Arriving at work with fresh flowers, she could smell freshly brewed coffee wafting through the foyer. Sally had arrived and, as always, took care of the morning routine.

"Good morning, Sally." An unenthusiastic Claire robotically addressed her.

"Good morning, Doctor. You, okay?"

"Yes, just a lot on my mind." She tried with more enthusiasm, walking over to a small, out-of-view area used as a small kitchen and pouring a cup of coffee. She then picked up the day's schedule from her inbox. She took a deep breath.

"Sally, we may have to alter this today." She looked at her schedule and said, "I'll let you know." As she entered her office, she asked Sally, "Is Doctor Cantalupo in?"

"Yes, before me!" Smiling.

Claire went to her desk and found a coffee and breakfast treat. Genny was not familiar with the morning procedure. She sent Genny a text to come to her office via the lab.

***

Genny awoke early, still dressed in yesterday's clothes. She rose slowly from the bed, walked into the kitchen, made a quick cup of coffee, and went to the shower. Thinking about her dream, rubbing her medallion, and wanting to share it, she quickly got ready, gathered her things, and left for the Museum.

She stopped to pick up breakfast, drove a short distance, and found a staff parking spot. She greeted Sheila, the security guard, and gave her a piece of pastry. Sharing pleasantries, she was off to her office. She was the only person in the building; a janitor was hiding, but it was quiet. Hearing whispers, secret stories of the museum's artifacts, as she passed them. Rubbing her medallion, she climbed the stairs and strolled to her office.

When she arrived, she took Claire's breakfast and placed it on her desk like a good little Catholic schoolgirl. She returned to her office, rolled out the yoga mat she grabbed on her way out of the house, did a twenty-minute routine, then sat for twenty minutes or so in meditation, focusing on last night's dream, until she heard someone come up the stairs. It was Sally Pedroia, Claire's assistant. She put the mat away and sat at her desk, organizing it. She started listing things she needed to make her office and lab feel like home. She could hear Sally setting up. She stepped out of her office and over to a startled Sally.

"My goodness! Early bird catching worms?" Sally joked.

"No, Sally, just anxious today. This will not be my routine." She laughed.

"I'm making coffee; there is tea, cocoa, milk, and juices if you like." She highlighted assorted items in the little area that she was showing Genny, pointing out a microwave, air fryer, toaster oven, and a good-sized refrigerator."

"Wow, thanks for the information and tour. Is there anything else I should know?"

"You can bring whatever you want or need. I know you may be working late some nights. Please give me a list so I can pick it up. We have an expense account. If we go over, I'll ask for the money." She was all business but all smiles.

Genny liked her. "Ok, I will. Thank you very much."

"It is good to have you aboard, and when the thing gets settled, don't hesitate to ask for my help. The Doctor would only give up that space to someone important to her. We try to be a happy work family." Sally was pleased.

Returning to her office, reviewing the glyphs, and then starting to do research for any connection, she got a text. It was Claire asking her to come over to her office.

***

"Good morning." Genny greeted her mentor.

"Good morning, Genny."

Genny could feel Claire's lack of energy, and the void of classical music gave the room a heavy, dense, depressing feel.

"You, OK?" Genny inquired.

"Oh, GG," Claire said with a defeated look.

"What's up, boss?" Genny tried to generate a smile from Claire.

"I'm overwhelmed. I want to shut everything down and research this project. I got other shit I must deal with!"

Genny was taken aback.

"No, nothing with you. I have many administrative things to handle. Sally can help with some. It's a lot of things." Rubbing her upper lip, she said, "The last few days have been such an exhilarating joy ride. Things that I want to do and will do. I'll be honest: I'm just a little deflated."

"Doctor, this doesn't sound like you." Rubbing her medallion, she said, "I must tell you my dream." Claire gave her young friend an affectionate nod. She recalled the dream in vivid detail. Claire sat motionless, almost stunned.

Claire got a text message and anxiously and immediately checked it out. Sighing, it was only Ditmer. She told him there was no latest information or progress and that she would check with him later.

Claire turned to Genny. "That was an incredible dream. The part when you traveled over to my house is what happened last night. Prisha had to leave in a hurry; she could not contact me and left a note. Prisha left on, and I feel foolish saying it, a secret government mission, for up to three to four weeks. I'm sorry, Genny, I'm sad and angry with myself that I didn't take her call yesterday. Now I don't know where she is or when I'll hear from her again." She was getting emotional.

Genny put a reassuring hand on hers. "I understand. I'm sorry. You know I'm here for you."

"Thank You." Claire regained her composure and confidence, getting right into the dream. "That is much more than a dream, Genny. Would you like to meet this gentleman?"

"How weird is this? But yes!"

Claire paged Sally, and she immediately appeared at her desk with a steno pad.

"Sally, this is a top priority; then we can get on with the day's agenda. This gentleman." Claire took a moment to write down the information and confirm with Genny that it was correct, then handed it to her.

"Sally, you know our contacts over at the UMass Boston Campus. Pressure them until they give us our man or his contact information."

The pitbull growled and then licked her chops. "Done!"

"Have him call me, and I will explain to him what's up. Thank you, Sally." The conversation ended, and Sally was on it.

17

Canal Street

When you are an aspiring archaeologist and the caller ID reads Harvard University School of Archaeology, you answer.

"Hello, Doctor Chevrolet. How can I help you?" He was as polite as possible, hoping this was not some robocall.

"Is this Lucas Johnny Chevrolet, professor at the University of Massachusetts in Boston?"

"Yes, the one and only. How can I assist you?" He was pleasant.

"Hi, I'm Sally Pedroia, administrative assistant to Doctor Claire Marie Randolph-Mishari, the School of Archaeology Academic Director at Harvard University. She wishes to speak with you on archaeology matters. Is that possible?" She was efficient.

"Yes, I would be more than happy to accommodate the Director," he said, his smile almost breaking his jaw.

"Please hold on, doctor. I'm going to put you through. Please hang on; thank you."

It had only been about fifteen minutes. Claire and Genny were still talking about research avenues. Claire thanked her for breakfast. Sally paged Claire.

"Dr. Chevrolet on line 2."

"Thank you, Super Woman!" Sally was pleased.

"Hi, this is Doctor Randolph-Mishari; thanks for taking my unsolicited call."

"Oh, my pleasure; I'm familiar with your body of work."

"Hope you like."

"Believe me, it is the best and the top of the field. I have read all your works."

"And I just ordered a copy of your book." He was astounded. Genny had informed Claire when she researched him.

"Doctor, what's up? How can I help you?"

Genny was following the conversation all the time, rubbing her medallion.

"Are you free this afternoon?"

"I don't want to sound obsequious, for you, yes."

"Claire laughed." She was getting good karma from Lucas. "Well, are you willing to meet my associate, Doctor Genny Giuliana Cantalupo?"

"That name has a familiar tone to it. Yes, I would." Smiling.

"There is one caveat."

"I knew this was too good to be true." Chuckling.

"No, there is no catch here. I want you to meet her at The Four's Restaurant on Canal Street in Boston."

"What? Doctor, you are putting me on. I was going there for lunch today."

"I'm not surprised the way this day has been breaking. Can you do one o'clock?"

"Yes, that will be great. Any heads up?"

"It is business, and we would respect your view or opinion in this matter. Privacy is of the utmost importance!"

"Yes! Sounds intriguing."

"Great, by the way, it's our treat!" Claire said.

"See her then."

"Thank you." Claire ended the call.

Lucas was blown away. He started researching Dr. Cantalupo, verifying with a huge exhale and a grin, mumbling, "Rico's granddaughter."

***

Claire finished the call. "Genny, meet him at the Fours at one o'clock. Let us talk about what you may discuss."

"I think just a basic introduction. If that goes well, I'll tell him about the dream leading into his relationship with Pa."

"Do not mention the disc! Feel out his current research; he may even give it out. None of this is underhanded. If we can trust him, we can arrange a meeting with the four of us, including Ditmer and possibly Charlie. We both should continue to research him before the meeting. There must be some connection here, I sense it. Figure it out. We can use as much trusted help as possible."

"I agree. Have faith in me. I'm more curious about his relationship with Pa and the dream." She rubbed her medallion.

"OK, expense it to the University, and leave a good tip." Claire laughed and felt better. She turned on her sound system. Genny hugged her and said, "Everything is going to be okay."

18

Return to The Fours

A dream, a medallion, a vault

The Fours Restaurant is located on Canal Street in Boston's North Station, West End area, a step away from the TD Garden. Its sports-oriented décor comprises Boston's finest collection of sports memorabilia. On a visit, it is not unusual to run into sports figures or out-of-town dignitaries. The downstairs is dominated by its magnificent, mahogany classic horseshoe, pub-style bar, and equally traditional dining area. There is also an upstairs dining room and kitchen.

Genny was about to enter her old college stomping grounds. She stopped and peeked at the menu on the outside marquee for the luncheon specials that she knew she would never have. A flood of memories, the great times, the games, the championship nights, the lunches, the dinners, and the times when it got so busy that she pitched in to help. Opening the door, the Four's appetizing aromas enveloped her, and delicious scents with a touch of alcohol.

Entering the foyer, she was greeted by the upstairs receptionist, who gave her a big hug. The owner then came over and gave her a tight squeeze.

"Oh my God, Genny, we have missed you. You look great." The owner was distracted and directed customers to their tables.

"I hope you have time to talk?"

"We will, but I'm looking for a guy named Lucas. Do you know him?"

"If you mean Doctor Chevrolet, he's a regular. Nice guy!" He seated another customer; a regular went straight to the bar. "He's over in the corner." Pointing.

"Thanks." She hugged him.

"Whoa, what do we have here?" The manager got up from his table, where he was ordering supplies, and embraced her. "The ghost is back in town!"

From behind the bar, the tender shouted, "Royalty is in the house! Lady, I'm pouring you a tall, slow, dark one!" Smiling, she flipped her thumbs up.

The regulars were chatting with another bartender down at the corner of the bar. They all raised their glasses and saluted her.

Out of the kitchen, checking on the commotion, the chef smiled at his old friend and said, "Johnny Kelly, no bread, extra supreme sauce on the side with veggies." Smiling, she nodded.

A happy distraction occurred as she walked over to Lucas, who was taking it all in.

He went first with the greetings. "Hi, I'm Lucas," he said, extending his hand.

"I'm…"

The chorus replied, "Genny!" She thought momentarily about how life was so good yet still so good. This is no longer part of it, feeling sad about how life changes.

"I'm Genny," she replied. She then asked the bartender for a booth.

"No, not that, GG!" He joked.

"Of course." He was laughing.

They were seated at a private table, looking out onto Canal Street and the outdoor tables.

They chatted briefly about her entrance, and the chef brought their food. Lucas ordered the special, and the server took over their drinks.

"Always good to see you, Missy." The server pleasingly said in his Irish brogue. "Just point, and I'll take care of you." He left.

They had some privacy. Lucas could see that she was carrying a copy of his book.

"You don't mind skipping the title formalities?" He asked.

"Not at all. This Doctor thing is getting boring after three days." Smiling.

She was closely examining him. He had golden bronze skin, bluish eyes, and an angular visage accenting his well-groomed, longish, dirty blonde hair. He was tall and handsome, but she could detect cigarette smoke.

"I am a well-acquainted follower of Dr. Randolph-Mishari. So, I assume you are the same," he said.

"I've known her since before my entrance into Harvard University. She counseled and guided me through my four years. She more than helped with my application to Cambridge University. We have gone on digs together. I collaborated closely with her in my three-plus years while working towards my doctorate. She has taught me everything about my science that I could know. We are now associates, and more importantly, I consider her a close, dear, and trusted friend."

"Wow, that's one big statement." He sipped his Guinness.

She chuckled, sipping her stout, and then took a bite to eat. She started rubbing her medallion. It caught his attention, but he said nothing.

He casually stated his resume and digging experience, especially in the Yucatan.

"Lucas, you get around." She liked his energy and the excitement in his eyes when he told his stories.

"Lucas, I almost do not know where to begin with this. I know you."

"I feel like we have met before." She continued.

"I don't know," he said. I don't think our paths have crossed professionally."

"Oh, I left one thing out. I took, or went to, a colloquium at Cornell a few years back on Mesoamerica Archaeology and Art."

"Shit! I took that; the classes were small and had two sections." He was excited. "I don't remember you."

Then, in her schoolgirl giggle, rubbing her medallion, "The Ancient Alien Conference at Ithaca College. You asked the question. Something about the soul, free will, and alien host." I remember.

Smiling, "Wow!" was his only response.

"But I know you from somewhere else." She told him the dream in detail in a solemn voice while rubbing her necklace.

"Yes, Genny, your grandfather," pausing as he ate and drank while digesting the dream, "was a mentor to me. I had no academic training in archaeology; he held my hand. He even helped me get this job in Boston. He often spoke of you." He had her attention, and a sad look graced it.

"First things first. I guess you're here because of the dream. Well, that was no ordinary dream. You were astral projecting or astral traveling. As a scientist, you may not believe this, but experiencing it, you may." She gazed at him, rubbing her medallion. He continued. "It's an out-of-body experience, 'OBE,' and usually intentional, conscious, or subconscious. You enter your subtle body; it is like a quasi-type of material in which you are neither solely physical nor spiritual. This is called the astral body, traveling throughout the astral plane, realm, or world. It is like your soul goes on a journey. While traveling, you experienced the Akashic records, a compilation of all knowledge. Believe it or not." He stopped and finished his drink and dinner, as did she. "You're a deep meditator?" He implied. Nothing was said for a few minutes. Both were in deep thought.

"How do you know this stuff?" She inquired.

"I'm a nerd!" They both laughed.

"Tell me about Enrico?" She looked him right in the eye.

"You have your Pa's eyes." Genny blushed.

"I did reach out to your family when he passed." He was sincere.

"I think I recall, but I am not certain." Genny winced.

"Doctor Enrico Virgili, my angel, the nicest person I have ever met." Genny felt a little sad, wondering why she had never heard of Lucas; would other relationships suddenly pop up?

"He took me under his wing. I'm a physicist with a doctorate from one of the best programs in the world, but I love archaeology. He was the same way, a doctorate in history, but an astounding archaeologist." Genny listened. "Genny, it is not just archaeology, but what it has to do with revealing our true past. No offense, but the scientific community is so caught up in its' bullshit beliefs that the truth becomes difficult to dig out."

"No offense taken." Sipping her stout, while a white mustache formed on her upper lip, caught a smiling Lucas.

"You went to Harvard and Cambridge. I'm certain they're not giving courses on the Pyramids being built with advanced technology."

"No, not really." Wiping her mouth, he quickly continued.

He went on for at least ten fascinating minutes on Ancient Astronaut Theory.

She interrupted, "Theory! That is the drawback! Theory! You understand, Lucas, that with all our scientific advancements, we can't take a goddam clear photo of a UAP or USP. We cannot get a consistent handful of facts. Making all these great arguments and presentations, then saying this and that is possible, and then they say, not giving names, ancient astronaut theorists, say 'yes,' You deserve credit for finding contradicting factual data, but nothing to attach it to." She was very calm.

"Genny, this is true, but I feel there is more to history than what we are taught, and it won't change until we unveil incontrovertible evidence, proof, or whatever to change the status. Let's get back to Rico." She was smiling.

"Just cause I said it, don't mean that I meant it." She quoted a favorite Adele song and made a funny face.

"What?" He was confused.

"I'm saying, tell me more?"

"Rico and his research were at the forefront of Mesoamerica, a land of the gods. He had authored papers, maybe even a book, but never published them for fear of academic ridicule. We would communicate using pseudonyms and secret words. In his collection, he had artifacts that could tip the human timetable. Genny, I was with him the day an elder, over a hundred years old, shaman greeted your Pa and placed that medallion around his neck with the words 'The possessor bears the weight and the truth of man, lost in the god's riddle.' The priest died an hour later. Here you are rubbing it as though a genie would appear." He laughed, and she giggled.

"Listen, Lucas, I might be on the same page with my reputation as Pa. My mind and imagination are more Graham Hancock than you would know." Defiantly stated. "Now, where is all of Pa's research at the University? Do you have it?"

"Wow! When your *mentor* called today, I never thought it was going here. I didn't know what to expect. Maybe you were interested in my book or the course I'm teaching. You and the Doctor are invited and should visit."

Genny had no idea that the conversation would lead to Enrico's research. "Lucas, where's the research?" with a stern look.

"Genny, nice look, but I do not know. He once told me he had a secret vault. Your medallion has a companion disc, which I've never seen, supposedly of alien origin. It was never evaluated or confirmed."

"Can you describe it?"

"Only from conversations. He said it was shiny metal with a bluish tint, with ancient and alien glyphs. Go ahead, say it, crazy."

To Lucas's surprise, she became more interested in the disc and its whereabouts.

"Did he get it with the medallion in the Yucatan?" She motioned to the server for two more Guinness. He brought them right over.

"As the story goes, the Shaman's family summoned and purportedly presented him with it the following day. Or they just told him the story. They said they belong together."

"Would this be in his vault?" she asked, taking a slug of stout. He shrugged his shoulders.

Switching the subject, she asks, "Lucas, how's your new novel coming along?"

"You know these things take time, research, etc."

"I only read a few chapters of your book on the way over. It is interesting, and I picked up a copy for the Doctor. Can I ask you what your latest work is about?" She gave him a flirtatious wink.

Lucas laughed, "Of course, writers always want to talk about their work." Lucas was a raconteur, and Genny did not need to buy his new book because he had just read it to her.

"My Lucas, fascinating, Knights Templar, Catholic Church, abortion, souls, wow! It's getting late, and I want to ponder this vault possibility. Let's exchange info. I want you to meet Doctor Randolph-Mishari in a casual setting. I think you will enjoy her and her perspectives."

"Where are we going with this?" He was confused.

"When I came here today, it was about the dream and your connection with Pa. Now that we've talked, there may be more to the story. We must keep this between us."

A sealed lip zipper gesture brought a closing smile and a clicking of glasses as they downed their stouts. They shook hands, and there was an energy, then Lucas left. Genny took care of the bill and chatted briefly, promising to return soon. Once outside, finding a bench, taking a seat, a little buzzed from the stout, called Claire and filled her in.

Genny was intrigued by the vault and then, as though hit with Thor's Hammer, came to a stunning realization. Pa shared archaeology experiences, the medallion, the vault, the house being a surviving joint tenant, Lucas Johnny Chevrolet, and the disc, which all made sense. If it does exist, the vault may be in or around the house!

19

The Medalion Tested

Genny took an Uber back to the University, thinking about her Pa and his vault. She wanted to understand more about him, let alone what he was working on, feeling that she may be or hold the key to a master plan. Unable to stop rubbing the medallion, she had an idea. The traffic was terrible, so she texted Claire to wait for her. Claire would be there upon her return.

***

The Museum was starting to close for the day. Genny went upstairs in a flash. Sally, still working, picked up her head and said, "She's waiting for you."

Claire was at her computer, focused. Genny took a seat in front of her desk.

"What a busy day. Where do I begin? I want to meet Doctor Chevrolet. Set dinner up at your place on Saturday, nothing special. This vault matter must be solved. It's on you. Read his book and fill me in." She was rattling off commands, and Genny was hesitant to interrupt her. Claire continued, "Today has been out of control, and tomorrow looks the same! Yes, and I haven't heard from Prisha. Yes, I am a bitch!" She cracked a smile. Genny was relieved.

"Doctor, is Ditmer still in?"

She texted him and said he was leaving shortly.

"Tell him we're coming over. I need something tested."

"What do you have?

"My medallion!" she said with a chill crawling down her back.

Claire was intrigued, an insightful, progressive thinker who needed not ask why.

She sent Ditmer a message that they were coming over. He was ok with it.

***

Genny took off her medallion, feeling naked, and handed it to Ditmer. He examined it and asked if he could also test the necklace.

"Don't hurt it." Genny squeamishly replied.

Ditmer snipped a piece of it and said he would stay and start the analysis.

Charlie Zaspa was the last employee heading out the door and was stopped by Ditmer.

"Do you have plans, Charlie?" She shook her head no. "We could use your help. Are you in?" Nodding yes. "Set up a photo shoot for." Pointing to the medallion, "This."

Ditmer's facility was the ultimate high-tech, enabling the University to do all its lab work in-house.

He carefully scraped off metal shavings for a deeper examination. Then, hurriedly swept them into a small tube, leaving several shavings behind. Like a helicopter parent, Genny cleaned the area and put the metal shavings into a paper towel. Without thought, she put them into her pocket and later into her backpack. Ditmer then brought the medallion to the X-ray fluorescence (XRF) equipment and set it up for analysis. He asked everyone to put on a set of goggles, a lab rule, and then he flashed a beam into the medallion. To his surprise, a momentary brilliant flash of light rebounded from its surface. "Now that is different. That beam oddly appeared, not from the surface, then departed."

He got his readings and discovered they were the same as the disc. The medallion was oddly warm.

"You didn't damage it?" Genny was concerned.

"No, no, no, it's fine." He handed it over to Charlie.

She immediately started taking images of the necklace and medallion, using different lighting with magnification.

"Ditmer turned to Claire and said, "It is the same material. Only this time, it released a tachyon particle beam."

Claire, in her classic pose, gave a big "Hmmm!"

Genny rubbed an invisible medallion.

"Ditmer, get me the results as soon as you can. Charlie, please email Genny and me the photos. Top secret, ok." They agreed.

"Saturday night, make yourselves free. We are having an informal dinner at Genny's. Use Uber and invoice my office, or better, I'll send a car. There will be a special guest: Doctor Lucas Johnny Chevrolet. I want you there to listen and ask questions. If you have time, research him. Thank you, and we'll speak in the morning." Pausing, "We are a team!" They nodded.

Genny had printed Lucas's name and additional info onto a piece of paper and handed it to Ditmer. Charlie handed Genny the medallion. It was warm.

Claire and Genny went back to Claire's office. Sally had left for the day. Soft classical music played to the museum's silence, and the flowers scented like a funeral parlor. Claire poured a bourbon; Genny declined, stating she had two drinks at lunch and was driving, but she took a small glass.

"Claire, there is something here, and I do not think it's by accident. I must find Pa's vault." They both got emails from Charlie.

Claire opened the file, and there were glyphs and images. It was a strange-looking image that looked like a classic alien or ALF on the face of a silver dollar. Genny went to rub her medallion but stopped.

"Another mystery, but I like the direction." Claire was confident.

They finished their drink. They were both eager to get home.

20

Birk's Law

It was Saturday, a hot late spring day in Utah. Prisha just received the good news that her team was so far ahead of schedule on their project that she needed to return to her office. The team was apprehensive, fearing that they would go home early. That was not the case. It was only Prisha.

As she packed, her thoughts drifted to her former assignment and how she was not forthcoming about its true objectives. Beebe Schwartz and Prisha had a secret agenda outside of their daily objectives. They were feeding confidential information to what they believed to be NASA, but were unsure. Prisha never shared this information with anyone other than Beebe Schwartz. She felt a little bit guilty.

The Skinwalker Project was going well. In a brief time, Prisha became friendly with the staff. They appreciated her knowledge, insights, and effectiveness in managing a team. They were by no means prisoners. They would roam, explore, take scientific readings, etc. While working at the mesa, the site of most significant interest in the wormhole theory, she found a piece of metal. She showed it to the Skinwalker team, who identified it as a piece extruded from the mesa. They had several samples, and she was welcome to examine it and forward her findings later. She placed the item into her bag and kept it as an archaeological gift for Claire.

She was flying out immediately in an Air Force jet from Dugway Proving Grounds, scheduled to leave at 2:30 pm (Mountain Day Time) MDT and arrive at 2:35 Eastern Standard Time (EST). She said her goodbyes and a thank you and boarded a helicopter, immediately heading to the base. She was eager to get her phone back. Communication at the ranch was a total blackout. On arrival, a staff sergeant, a woman, introduced herself as her escort to the flight. Prisha asked for her phone but was informed that Director Birk would return it to her in Boston. Saying nothing, she followed the sergeant, but inside, she was fuming and knew her days were numbered at the agency. She wanted out and to be with Claire.

On her arrival in Boston, she was taken to the JFK Federal Building, led inside, and proceeded up to her office. The office door was locked. She had no key, only her bag with a few things. Her luggage would be shipped the following day by cargo transport and delivered to her home.

It was Saturday, and it was close to four in the afternoon. Her floor was vacant except for one person. The thought of seeing him physically made her sick, but she overcame it and started towards his office. She could smell his stinking cigar.

She entered his office, and there he sat like the devil himself, a cigar in one hand and a drink in the other, under that surreal poster. She approached him, and he greeted her with a smoke ring. She waved it off.

"How was your trip?" He said with the intent to rile her.

"I want my phone!" she demanded.

"I want my phone, I want my phone, I want my phone…Wham, Wah!" He mocked her and rubbed his eyes, gesturing like a baby.

"Listen! I am out! I have had it!" she screamed. He continued mimicking gestures like Jack Nicholson in *The Shining*. Prisha backed off and got nervous. Her only thought was to get away from this madman.

"I'm out, I'm out… Is mommy coming to get you?" He continued, took another drink, walked behind Prisha, and closed his office door. She watched his every move as he walked back to his desk, putting his hand under his desk. She could hear the door lock click, which made him smile.

"You quit, yeah, sure, you quit." Continuing like a madman.

Prisha was very frightened, visibly shaking, when he began a tirade.

"Sir, you are drunk; please let this go for now." She pleaded.

"Sir, you are drunk." Mimicking her, "You miserable fucking left-wing liberals think you're saving the world. You're fucking killing it!" His caustic, inebriated, delusional rant continued.

"You quit nothing!" He screamed.

"Don't you know me by now? Don't you understand? I own you!" He was calm.

Prisha was frightened and had nowhere to go.

"Don't you realize I track your every step, every breath. I know when you shit! Yeah, you quit. You, that fancy doctor wife of yours, and her little girlfriend have all been under this evil," pointing to his eye.

"What is that little group up to, that big slob German scientist and his little girl Charlie? Not to mention that fucking radical Chevrolet who's been under watch for years." Prisha knew nothing of their plans.

"Yeah, you quit! As Pilate says, in my hands, your life is, so be very careful." He approached her and blew a smoke ring into her face and hair. He then pressed his thumb into her bindi. "I always wanted to do that."

She backed off, screaming. Laughing, he grabbed her by the arm and slapped her across the face. She was bleeding. "Did that hurt? Let me kiss your boo-boo!" He jestingly tried and was forcefully pushed away, accelerating his violence.

He approached her with the look of a psychotic madman. Grabbing her arms and throwing her across the room and onto the floor, hovering over her in an insane whisper, "Why did you have mommy come and get you? Don't you know how bad that makes me look?" As he tugged his suspenders, she kicked him with such force that it cracked his groin and cut his hand on his suspender. He exploded into a rage. His drunken eyes were rolling around their sockets, and cigar juice drooled from his chin.

Prisha, in an instant, got up, grabbed a bronze bust of Richard Nixon, and cracked it over his head. He fell to the floor like a slaughtered pig, bleeding from his forehead. She sprinted to his private elevator. The door was open, and his security key was in place. She went express to the parking garage. Fearing security, disheveled and bleeding, she cautiously exited the elevator.

She stealthily moved to a side exit leading to a path, which took her to a flight of stairs and crossed Congress Street. Looking back, she thought she saw security. Fixing herself as she mingled with the tourists at Faneuil Hall Marketplace, she entered the building, traveled through the crowded hall, and came out at the back entrance.

Quickly crossing Commercial Street, heading towards the waterfront near the New England Aquarium. Without a plan, she walked into the Aquarium T station, stepping onto a long descending elevator. She could hear a train approaching, but had no time or money, leaving her bag behind, to buy a boarding ticket, Charlie Pass, and walking through an open gate. It was crowded, a busy tourist destination, and had easy access to and from Logan International Airport. The transit worker saw her and did nothing but shout, "Fucking rich people!" Then, he continued playing with his phone.

She hurried to the platform not reading any signs, caught the train. It was crowded, and she was pushed into the middle of the aisle. The train left immediately. Looking at the stop indicator, she realized she was going in the wrong direction. The next stop was Maverick Station in East Boston. She got off, alone, physically hurt, in an unknown world, not frightened, and tried to get some bearings. A street map was on the wall, and she recognized Sumner Street. She thought Genny's family store was on Sumner Street, but where? She exited the station onto Sumner Street. It was crowded; buses and cars were blowing their horns in frustration. She asked a woman if she knew of any local Italian markets on Sumner Street. She said she did not, but she was sure there weren't any points in one direction. The lady gave Prisha a funny look as Prisha thanked her.

She started walking in the other direction. There were stores, apartment buildings, and restaurants, but she did not see a market. She crossed the street and asked an older man. He said yes, up about a quarter of a mile on your left. He had an Italian accent.

Then he said," T'Avios, good subs." Yes, T'Avios, she remembered.

"Grazie!" She nodded.

"Prego." He smiled at her and then continued on his way.

Finding her way to T'Avio's, she approached a young girl who was closing the store for the night. It was close to six.

"We're closing soon." The young girl was polite and could see that Prisha was hurt. Come inside, and I can help you. Inside, she handed Prisha a wet towel to wipe herself with and a bottle of water. Prisha, in all her pain, thanked her.

"I'm looking for the owners?" Whispering.

"Uncle Mike and Auntie G went to an anniversary party. Left a bit early today."

"Did you say, auntie? Would Genny Cantalupo be your cousin? "

"Yes! Are you part of the party?"

"No, but maybe?" Trying to be clever. "Do you know where she lives?" Prisha did not want to ask for her phone for fear of involving her with Birk.

"Let me lock up a second, and you can help me bring this order." Pointing to trays on a stand by the door, "over to her." Prisha smiled for the first time today, feeling a bit lucky, but her face hurt.

The doorbell rang.

21

The Vault

The following morning, Claire's team held a conference in her office. Ditmer was to give the analysis of the medallion. She sat patiently as Ditmer, sweating and breathing heavily, fumbled through his report.

As usual, the room was accented with soft classical music and fresh flowers.

Still in her classic pose, Claire had Prisha on her mind.

Genny was fantasizing about Lucas. She devilishly tried to get rid of all her lustful thoughts that were flowing like a breached dam leaking around her head.

Charlie Zaspa was thinking about what she was having for lunch.

Ditmer began. "I have examined the items. The necklace is dissimilar to the material we found on the disc, dating to a much more recent period. I need a bit more time to figure it out. On the other hand, the medallion is constructed of the same materials as the disc but has an active, unidentifiable element. This is what caused the tachyon burst." The group listened attentively.

Continuing, "Charlie took some exceptional images of the medallion. An image on one side will only appear in the infrared and ultraviolet range under lighting conditions outside our normal range of sight. Genny, let me see your medallion?"

"No!" She was abrupt. They all gave her a curious look. She guffawed, removed the item, and handed it to him.

"Thank you." Ditmer gave her a quizzical look, examined it under a light he had brought from the lab, and shone it on the medallion. You could see an image. The male or female image was unidentifiable in our computer base but looked human. Changing the light intensity, the image seemed to move. The room was still and intense. He began sweating again.

"Charlie experimented with her photography and, on a hunch, took a video—something we did not do with the disc. When I play the video under normal light intensity, nothing happens. However, when I change the spectrum of light, the image moves and changes, etc. When I go to the highest point in the spectrum of my light, the image rises into a standing position. I can only get to a certain point." Disappointingly sighing.

The medallion sat on the table like something out of Star Wars. They all looked in amazement. Genny went over and took her medallion and put it on.

"The other side held no surprises other than a series of similar unidentifiable glyphs, which were also found on the disc. The light did not affect it."

"We are everywhere but nowhere," Claire stated.

"I would like to meet on Saturday at Genny's. A professor, Johnny Lucas Chevrolet, will be our guest. Here is a quick background: He came to Genny in a dream and exists. She met him for lunch, and his books and research align with what we have." She took a sip of wine.

"Ok, Ditmer, since you and Charlie live close to one another, I will arrange a car to pick you up Saturday around three-thirty in the afternoon. We will meet at Genny's for pre-dinner cocktails and chat with our guest, Doctor Lucas Johnny Chevrolet. Dinner, informal, will be at six pm. For the next few days, think of any theory, research, or whatever; use your imagination, and think outside of what you have been taught. Your input is essential to our progress in research, or just authoring a paper. Ok, thanks. I will text you if I need anything."

Charlie and Ditmer left to discuss the project.

In an almost parental tone, Claire turned to Genny and said, "GG, you're getting possessive of your medallion."

"It's," with a joking funny hissing, "My Precious!" Genny grinned. Claire shook her head and smiled.

"Any word?" Genny quickly asked.

"No, thanks." Claire continued. "Genny, we must figure out this vault thing as soon as possible. Over the next few days, review all your grandfather's records, photos, and personal belongings. Examine your house for a vault or a clue. If nothing comes up, go to the building department to see if he has taken out any permits. Go to the Registry of Deeds in Suffolk County, Boston, or online and examine the records. If you physically go there to ask for help, their staff is good. Even hire a freelance title examiner for the day. Explore all your possibilities."

Genny nodded. "I'm familiar with those places, and I know people."

"Make sure everything is set for Saturday. I will call Lucas and make the arrangements." Genny was slightly disappointed that Claire was making the call, but nodded approval.

"Go home and get started, but stay in touch with me."

"What's your plan?" Genny asked.

"I'm calling a goddamn US Senator or two and getting Prisha back!" She said with authority and misty eyes.

"This will all work out?" Genny optimistically said.

"Yes, it will!" They affectionately hugged like family.

22

Saturday at Genny's

Claire arrived early, around 2 o'clock, on Saturday afternoon. She had her driver take her, and then the driver would pick up Ditmer and Charlie at a determined time. Claire was prepared to spend the evening as an option.

On her arrival, she discussed Prisha's situation, having called and pressured two US Senators and four US Congress members, and called the Vice-President's office. The consensus is that they knew nothing but would do their best to rectify or pressure the parties of concern. All of these politicians had ties and roots in the Randolph family. They had obligations. One US senator did say the situation was a "clusterfuck." Nobody knows who this person, Morgan Strassa, is, nor do they want to push it. She also noted that Stanley Birk is, quote, "Someone you don't fuck with!" This made Claire quite uneasy. She thanked them all and offered her continued support.

After a few glasses of wine, the subject of the vault came up.

"The vault? Any progress?" She asked Genny.

"None! I checked this house from the basement to the attic. I checked the garage. I used a metal detector in the yard. The City of Boston's building department had no records, and the Registry of Deeds produced some interesting information, but nothing led to a vault. I went through and read all his papers and photos. I reached out to some of his associates, but nothing for me to go any further. I have nothing, Claire; please feel free to spy around and use your genius to spot something."

"Don't worry. We have time. It's only been about a week. The finding is so exciting; we want to solve it immediately. Let us slow down and be happy with what we have found. We will uncover the answers. It may take weeks, months, or years. Let's go with an adage from my mentor, who once used the initialism PFD, Positive Forward Direction."

In her classic pose, sipping wine, she had Genny's full attention. "That is GG; every day, if we try to move even an inch closer to our goal, we have had a successful day." She would further say, "Everything is cumulative and, at some point, will be complete. I have followed those principles." She sipped her wine. "Do not get me wrong. I am privileged, but my mother always told me to have goals and work hard towards them. Shit, I'm full of philosophical bullshit today. It must be this wine, truth serum." They affectionately smiled.

Claire started examining artifacts, paintings, ceilings, and walls. She walked down into the basement, where a wine press and cellar existed. The place was damp and a pleasant wine-scented must. She admired the old photos of Italy, the vineyards, wine presses, barrels of wine, and a very happy-looking family. She could find nothing in her search. She was not that concerned. Thinking about it over the past day, she concluded that our lives might change quickly and radically if this is real. This may not be a good thing. She knew they had something spectacular, and they should control the timeline. She was wondering how this Chevrolet would drive and laughed.

"What's so funny?" Genny asked.

"Nothing at all. It's the wine." Raising a toast.

Genny was setting her dining room table. She placed cheese, meats, olives, crackers, etc., on various charcuterie boards. In Claire's honor, she played soft classical music, and the infuser spouted lavender. She set up an area on the patio where they could talk while capturing the city's beauty and the harbor.

Claire sat outside, taking it all in.

Ditmer and Charlie arrived a few minutes early. They were warmly greeted and entered "a museum in itself," as Ditmir admirably stated. Sitting out on the deck, they discussed the possibilities and directions of the project. Claire explained that they might be moving too fast and have something extraordinary, and we should slow it down. They all agreed, except Genny, the new kid on the block. She was starting to freak out about the medallion and its possible effect on her.

"I'm excited about this quest. It doesn't matter what comes about. It's a rush, opening your mind to the minds of the people or beings that produced these objects. I do not want to give up on this medallion and disc. This," rubbing the amulet, "has become my crusade! Of course, I will agree with your decision, but that is how I feel. I am sorry, but this is who I am."

"No, GG, not giving up, but slowing a bit."

Claire felt proud and accomplished for her role in Genny's growth. She raised her glass, and they all followed: "Doctor Genny Giuliana Cantalupo, a true scientist with the heart of a lion and the spirit of a goddess."

"To Genny. Hear, hear!" they toasted.

The doorbell chimed.

23

Good Vibrations

Lucas Johnny Chevrolet, the sandy-haired Adonis, walked in. Genny's heart leaped up, spiking her erotic thoughts.

He was introduced to the group of scientists. Genny poured him a glass of wine. He asked about the vault, and she had no news.

"Would you like a tour? Maybe you will see or identify something?"

"Great, yeah." He smiled. A smile, she perceived as flirtation.

She showed him around, and when he was in her bedroom, she said, "I liked your Stones."

He shot back an almost embarrassed look. "Of The Gods. You creep." She quipped.

He laughed. She slapped him on the hand. She felt a tingle. His interest piqued when he was in Enrico's room. He looked and touched everything, reaching for a feeling or a vibe, like a lost loved one, trying to remember them.

"Any ideas?" She inquired.

"I'm no Edgar Casey!" Lucas made a detective-like face and sent Genny into hysterics. Inexplicably, she held his hand. The tingling sensation returned. They became magnetically locked.

Their breathing increased. They gazed into one another's eyes and entered an infinite universe. Their surroundings became blurred and out of focus. They entered their souls' portals. Genny heard her name, and what seemed like a second was minutes. And forgotten.

"Let's get back to the party." In a serious tone, pausing, said, "Lucas, you must convince these scientists, people, of what you think and believe. Then, if you do, you will be told something you may not believe in and possibly change your life.

"Try me!" Emphatically.

"Maybe?" She winked.

"Possibly!" He replied.

"Now, who's the creep?" Genny quipped. Both smiled and joined the party on the deck.

24

For Whom the Drone Tolls

Lucas addressed the group as though it were a factual, **detailed** lecture and told it like a true storyteller. Claire and the others were quite impressed.

"In summary, I say this with no defamatory way of impugning the classic archaeological work of Doctor Virgili, he had other interests that were contradictory to the standard beliefs or professional expectations of a scientist in his profession. I was his disciple. I told you the story of the medallion. The Doctor's belief, theory, or whatever you want to call it, was outside his training. I touched upon the ancient civilizations, megalithic structures, and so on. The Doctor believed that an unknown species, aliens, advanced at some point deep in the past, altered our DNA and continued to adjust it over millennia.

He had a theory that with all their technology, these beings kept failing, and they would try again. He believed there was disagreement amongst these aliens about how to proceed. He was a scientist, a devout Christian, and a fervent Catholic. He thought Christianity, specifically the Catholic Church, was made guardians to protect life. A life that starts at conception, but no proof of this has arisen.

He had a theory that the Knights Templar had found damaging evidence that could destroy Christianity, especially the Catholic Church. In 1307, Pope Clement V conspired with King Philip IV of France to eradicate the Templar order.

The Doctor also believed evidence could be found in Avignon, France, where the Papacy moved from 1309 to 1377. He said he had proof or evidence that could lead to the truth, documentation stored and hidden in his vault. We cannot locate his vault. He mentioned it shortly before he died. He also contended that he had an alien disc." He described the disc in detail. "To my knowledge, no one has seen this. I'm led to believe it may be a story. My new book will contain these theories. Thank you for your time, and please read chapter 13 for the next class." They all laughed and cheered.

Claire took the floor and asked Lucas politely and professionally if he would not mind going inside while she discussed it with the team.

"Absolutely!" He sat drinking wine and eating cheese, while thinking and watching Genny.

They concurred that Lucas could be helpful in their endeavor. His work would complement their findings, and they agreed to invite him onto the team. Genny, the schoolgirl, was excited.

Looking up, they could hear an electronic drone hovering above them.

The thought was that there must have been some accident in the harbor, or someone was goofing around.

"Let's take this inside!" Claire commanded.

Once inside, they asked Lucas if he wanted to join this group, explaining that they were highly secretive.

"Do I get any hints?" He shrugged.

"It's yes or no!" Claire forcefully stared into his face.

"Well, working with you," bowing, "Doctor Randolph-Mishari, would be an honor beyond my dream beliefs. Yes, do you want some blood?" Genny giggled; too much wine.

They each took turns showing Lucas what they had. The disc was still at the University, but they had all the photos and reports. Lucas was more than blown away to the point of speechlessness.

The doorbell chimed.

25

Prisha's Return

"It's the food!" Genny said. Claire opened the door.

"Prisha!" Claire hugged and kissed her. Prisha held onto Claire like a drowning child. The house was abuzz. The young cousin brought the food that Genny's parents had prepared and placed it on the table. Genny slipped her a hundred-dollar bill and told her to have a good time tonight. Genny hugged and thanked her.

"I will!" She hurried away with a happy face.

Claire was visibly shaken by Prisha's condition and wanted to take her immediately to be examined. Prisha told her she was okay and they could go shortly, but first, most humorously, she said that she hadn't eaten anything today. The food's aroma had taken over her stomach, demanding satisfaction.

The table was set. Claire clung to Prisha, wanting to know what was happening and insisting they leave.

"I'm ok, Claire." Prisha, stained in blood and smelling like a cigar bar, sighed. Claire was becoming extremely uneasy and impatient.

Prisha knew the team and was introduced to Lucas.

They horrifyingly listened to Birk's behavior and how he warned her that they were all in his sights. They winced at her battle and encouragingly laughed when she clunked him over the head. Her adventure and how she ended up at Genny's was ingenious and fascinating. They all sadly looked around the table. Prisha was in physical pain, and Claire could not take it any longer.

"OK. The party is over!" Claire called for her car. "You can all take an Uber home on my account. Please be careful."

Claire continued to minister to Prisha's injuries. Genny had given her sweat clothes to wear. Claire's car arrived.

"I will contact you on Monday. Let's sit on this for a day. I must think." They were all in agreement. Claire and Prisha left.

They all pitched in to clean up. There was small talk about how badly they felt about Prisha. Genny kept on catching Lucas staring at her. She would get lost in a fantasy of another world.

Ditmer and Charlie shared a ride. It arrived; they thanked Genny and were off.

Lucas's Uber was not far behind. They were standing at the door, and Genny held his hand, pulled his face to hers, and kissed him. He kissed her back.

"You're welcome to stay the night." She kissed him again and did not want to let go.

The shared ride pulled up. "This may not be the best timing. My body is saying yes. My mind is saying take a guaranteed rain check." They had a mystically strong connection.

"I can live with that." She hugged him passionately and gave him a goodnight kiss that felt familiar and would linger. When he got into the car, he almost got out. He was worried about the day's events, knowing Birk's past encounters with him and his type of government, Nazism, believing that he may be the focus of their investigation. The drone freaked him out; he desired to stay but feared that the wrong people might get hurt.

Genny watched the car fade to black and then secured her home. It was still early, and she considered taking a nap or just getting ready for bed. She finished her glass of wine and floated to her room, dressing comfortably. Lying in bed, she rubbed her medallion and fell into a deep, happy sleep.

26

De Molayed

Part I – The sweep

The sun was up, and the morning dew graced the manicured lawn during its short visit. The circular driveway of the lavish Wellesley estate was a traffic jam of government vehicles. The doorbell was rung, followed by loud banging. The dogs were howling in their kennel. The President of Harvard University and his spouse were rudely awakened. The president reached for his cell phone, but there was no service. He pulled a gun from his night table drawer and walked down the ornamental winding staircase with his wife clinging to his shoulder. He reached for the door.

"Yes, how can I help you? The police are on the way." He roused.

"Sir, I have a search warrant. Please let us in."

"You have nothing, and I will speak to my attorneys!" He growled louder than his dogs.

"Sir, you have sixty seconds before we forcibly enter."

The President's wife headed back upstairs as he pulled the gun from his robe. The door was knocked down with a battering ram, and the president with it. The weapon rolled to the staircase.

"Sir, I have an order to search these premises." He showed him the warrant.

"You have nothing!" He got to his feet and knocked the order from the agent's hand.

"Gentlemen, search the premises. You know what we are looking for. Try not to be too destructive. Collect cell phones, iPads, cameras, and computers. Bring his wife down, but do not harm her."

"This is outrageous! You are going to hear about this!" The president was heated.

"Yes, sir, I hear about a lot of things. Cuff them, tape their mouths shut, and put them into the back of the van." They did.

Thirty minutes later, the convoy sped away.

***

Simultaneously, on a quiet country lane in Concord, Dr. Jeffrey Drayton was doing his morning workout when a convoy of government vehicles approached.

"What the fuck is this!" He raced to the front door to meet them. Before they could knock, he opened the door. "How can I help you?"

"Are you Doctor Jeffrey Drayton, Head of Management Information Systems at Harvard University?"

"Who wants to know?" Defiantly

"Yes or no, sir! I have a warrant to search your home." Showing him the warrant.

"Whoa, take it easy, boys. My wife and kids are asleep."

"It doesn't matter, sir."

"I'm calling my attorney." His cell phone had no service.

"Gentlemen, you know what you are looking for, plus all computers and electronics. Try not to frighten the children."

"Should we bring down the missus?"

"Yes, but she stays behind with the kids. We will leave a team with them until this action is completed. No outside communications!"

"Yes, sir."

Jeffrey did not put up a fight, and they bound him, placing him in the back of a van.

***

Cynthia Robeo was on a Skype call to Lagos, Nigeria, wishing her mother a happy birthday, when she heard a loud knock on the door of her Mattapan apartment. She was frightened but cooperative. They collected all her electronics and closed the screen on her laptop while her mother was still talking. They bound her and placed her into the van.

***

When she was taken into custody, Sally Pedroia was readying for a Sunday morning service.

***

Charlie Zaspa was saying her morning prayers when she heard a loud bang on the door of her Cambridge apartment. She was reluctant to answer it, and they knocked it down, forcibly handcuffed her, and her mouth was tightly taped; she was roughly taken to a van. The agents destroyed her place as they confiscated everything. Their joy exuded with an act of hate.

***

Exhausted from the past week, Ditmer slept; he did not hear the agents knock on the door of his Cambridge home. He was in bed when they stuck a search warrant into his face. He knew all about the tactics that his family faced in Germany. He did not resist them, but his heart ached as they destroyed his home. They took him away.

27

De Moylayed

Part II – The Medallion

Lucas was meditating in his small North End apartment when they came. He knew, he sensed it, and hoped that it was only him. His radical views and papers, pointing out prominent public and government dignitaries as conspirators in hiding truths, had always kept him under constant surveillance, threatened, and even manhandled on occasions.

He let them in and was immediately violently handcuffed, then he was forced to watch as they destroyed his apartment and took everything.

"Get everything, clean his Cloud, the works. Wipe him from the face of the earth." They did.

They threw him into the van.

***

Claire and Prisha had returned from the University infirmary. Prisha was okay but had a severely cut lip that required stitches. The brutality of this man momentarily shattered a strong, independent woman. She was shaken and looked to Claire for support.

Early the following morning, a loud, rude knock awakened the quiet South End brownstone. Claire went to the window and saw a convoy of government vehicles. Her thought was that they had come for Prisha for assaulting Birk. They both went downstairs and inquired who was there. They identified themselves as government agents and had a warrant to search the premises for illegal artifacts from Belize.

Claire took a deep breath and let them in.

The agent identified himself and handed her the order. A local judge signed it, and she made a mental note of it.

Claire gave the agent a stare that meant that this was personal.

"Gentlemen, search the premises. You know what we are looking for. Do not upset anything. If something is moved, place it gently back. Any damage will be at your expense. Take only phones, electronics, and computers."

They did as Claire and Prisha stood in their nightclothes, not knowing what was coming.

"Sir, we are all set."

"Handcuff the Indian girl and bring both to the van." The lead agent said.

They proceeded towards Prisha, and Claire stepped between them.

"If you touch her or lay a finger on her, all you endear, cherish, or hold valuable will come down upon you. I promise you!" Fiercely.

They knew Claire had power and backed off.

"Ladies, you must come with us. Please do not let us use force!"

They were allowed to dress and walk to the back seat of one of the SUVs.

***

Genny was in dreamland when she heard a loud knocking on her door. She checked her cell phone but had no service. She excitedly thought that Lucas had come back. She rushed to the door and, in a sweet, innocent voice, said, "Yes."

"We have a court order to search your home. Please open your door."

Standing in panties and a Taylor Swift tee shirt, innocently said, "I have to put something on."

The door crashed before a stunned Genny. They entered, not showing any paperwork. Then there was this smell: cigar smoke drifting through the door. It was Birk!

Fear struck Genny as this massive man with a bandage across his forehead barged into her home, smoking a cigar and stinking of alcohol.

"You know who I am?" Blowing a smoke ring.

Genny shrugged.

"Just in case you don't, I'm that prick, Stanley Birk." He smiles, chews, and drools on his cigar.

"You know what I hate?"

No response from Genny.

"Come on, give it a try?"

Her impulse was to crack a joke, but fear prevented it.

"I hate fucking liberals! I fucking hate left-wing radicals!" His eyes rolled like a madman's.

"Cute panties!" He smiled.

"Not a bad set; he checked her out." She had nothing to cover herself.

She was scared, thinking about what he had done to Prisha.

"Why don't you make life easy for yourself and give me what I want?" Spit flying.

She said nothing and started to shake.

"Gentlemen, proceed to look for the item. Take everything, destroy everything." They began a search-and-destroy mission.

Genny began to cry.

"You want a baba, sweetie!" Rubbing his eyes like a baby.

"You have something, ha, more than something that I want." He stared at her medallion. "I think I may take them."

He reached out, touching her medallion, and accidentally brushed her nipples. She pulled away in fear. He then jokingly attempted to rip off her panties." Pulling further away, she screamed a scream that could be heard a block away. The men stopped and looked.

"Continue!" Birk commanded.

Genny's heart was pounding.

"Don't do that again!" He put his face to hers and blew smoke into her mouth.

She spat into his face.

He went ballistic. "You fucking liberals. You spoiled bitch!"

The men continued to search, dumping out backpacks, bags, etc., ignoring the crime they were about to witness.

This enormous mountain of a man, an ex-professional boxer, closed his fist, reached his right hand as far back as he could, his eyes rolling in their sockets like a demonic roulette ball and in his best Sterling Hayden, while shouting "Fucking liberals!" Hit Genny with such force that it shattered her cheekbone. Teeth and blood flew from her mouth as she slumped to the floor. He then kneed her in the ribs, and they cracked like dry sticks. While Genny was prone on the floor, he removed the medallion. As a reflex, she made a faint attempt to grab it and whispered, "PA."

He laughed.

Barely breathing, she again faintly whispered. He smiled, then put his ear to her mouth, and she breathed, "FUCK-YOU!"

So enraged, he picked up her limp body and threw it through the glass patio doors. It shattered. She landed with a thud; a pool of blood oozed out like a tormented squashed tomato.

"Fucking liberal!" Brushing off his bleeding hand, the same one that Prisha damaged.

"We are all set here, sir. It's not here, but we have all the documents and electronics."

"Is she dead, sir?" Another agent asked.

Puffing on his cigar while admiring the medallion, he said, "I don't know." Then kicked her in the face. Sipping his flask, he commanded. "Throw her into the back of the van." He put the amulet around his neck and rubbed it; they were gone.

28

De Moylayed

Part III- The Reckoning

Sheila, the security guard who had volunteered overtime, was working the entrance when the government vehicles pulled up. They needed her for security codes, and they did not have the time, or they could risk making mistakes; they apprised her that what she was about to witness should never be brought to light. They questioned her and got all her personal information. They warned her that what was about to happen "never happened," as would her life. She began to panic and had an urge to check her phone. It was dead!

Convoy after convoy filled the parking lot. Agents with detecting equipment entered the museum and Ditmer's science lab. The destruction sounded like war.

A handcuffed, gagged, bleeding president and his wife were escorted inside the building. One after another, the captives would march upstairs to Claire's office.

Doctors Randolph-Mishari and Mishari-Randolph, unshackled, walked past a frightened Sheila on the way to the office.

A moment later, a van pulled right up to the door. Birk, blowing smoke and rubbing his trophy, walked past the guard and up the stairs.

The back door of the van opened, and two men pulled the battered, bloodied body of Genny and placed her on the floor right in front of Sheila. Sheila gagged and then puked. The agents laughed.

The group was arranged into a semicircle in Claire's office. Most of them, except Lucas and Claire, felt that they were being civilly violated. They could not wait to get free and pursue legal action with their political contacts, with no concept of what power is. The underworld opened, and the cigar-chewing, drooling Birk entered the room. The cigar's stench murdered the scented flowers. Not saying a thing and as cool as if nothing was happening, lifted a Grecian urn and used it as a spittoon.

"Nice handy piece," he chuckled."

Looking around the room, he felt great satisfaction, seeing the fear on their faces.

"Ah, my pretty little one." Walking towards Prisha.

"Don't go near her!" Claire warned him.

He rolled his eyes back and took an uncommonly deep breath. "Some birds' feathers can't be ruffled."

The university president glared at Claire. Why was she not bound and gagged? Claire returned the stare.

"You have all conspired to smuggle a sacred object from Belize. It has caused great concern to a certain agency in our government." He spouted bullshit.

"Succinctly put, you have something I want. I will get it, or no one leaves here until it is delivered." To Claire and Lucas's horror, he was rubbing the medallion.

A closer look at Birk showed a bleeding right hand and blood stains on his shoes, suit, and face.

"I'm not fucking around; people are going to get hurt!" He said something into a headset. The crashing and banging sounds in the museum ceased. The sound of dragging feet thumping up the stairs on the way up to the office could be heard and stopped just outside the entrance. Birk stepped out and said something to his men. He was enjoying life. Claire feared the worst.

"Ladies and gentlemen." In his best ringmaster impersonation, "Let me introduce to you from East Boston, exhibit A, the one and only Doctor Cantalupo." He nodded and then stepped out of the center of the semicircle, and two men threw the once beautiful, delicate flower Genny like a sack of shit into the center of the circle. Her partially nude body landed like thick, wet mud. Thoughts of any legal action were now gone. At gravity's mercy, Genny lay prone in a crucifix-like position out of an Alex DeLarge dream in *A Clockwork Orange*. Her face was disfigured, her bones were protruding from her shoulder and her chest, and shards of glass were sprinkled about her body. Her breathing was like a wounded deer's final gasps. She lay near death.

An uncontrollably emotional Lucas, still bound, went to her aid and was zapped by a stun gun, screaming and falling in agony to the floor. Prisha cried while squeezing Claire's hand. The president and his wife, Jeffrey Drayton, Cynthia Robeo, could not bear to look. Charlie Zaspa held Ditmer's handcuffed hand as tears poured down their cheeks. Sally just wept.

Claire was in a trance when Birk rolled those crazy eyes, billowing smoke, shouting at the top of his lungs, "Where is the fucking disc!" Echoing through the museum.

Claire broke ranks, went to Genny's side, and covered her with a blanket from the divan in her office. She was locking eyes with Birk. "Call an ambulance now! Follow me!" He did both.

They entered her private lab, and she hit a button. A secret compartment opened. There was a safe. She opened it and took out the disc. He marveled at it while rubbing the medallion. He took a picture and sent it out. A text returned. "Done!"

Birk got on his headset and said one word: "Yes!"

You could hear footsteps scurrying and vehicles screeching away. Birk slipped the disc inside his suit out of sight and walked towards the door, stepping on Genny's body.

Agents began uncuffing and cutting the wires of the captives. An ambulance could be heard approaching. Claire and Prisha tried to minister to Genny. As Birk was leaving, "I love quoting movies, even though I fuck them up, but get this, you may think you know who we are, but I know who you are, P.S. remember Genny." Smiling, he blew one last smoke ring, then crushed his cigar on the Persian Rug. "This never happened!" He laughed, hurrying to his vehicle, almost knocking over a paramedic rushing to Genny.

A gym bag with all their phones, now activated, was left in the doorway. As the paramedics worked on Genny, the president and his wife left, caring less about her. He began shouting and publicly admonished Claire with a tirade of obscenities and said she was finished. Claire, who held back her emotions, was now holding Genny's hand as a cataract of tears raced down her face. She looked up at him with that look. He left. Dr. Drayton, who was worried about his family, apologized and left. The rest remained for Genny.

29

De Molayed

Part IV- Aftermath

The paramedics were squeamish at the sight of Genny. They were not getting any life signs. "Do you want to call it in?" one said.

"What?" Said Claire, her focus becoming fanatical; "get her to the fucking Brigham and Women's. Do not call her death in! She will be met with an expecting team on arrival." Claire made calls as she rode in the ambulance. Lucas and Prisha went together and met Claire at the hospital. Ditmer and Charlie checked on the lab. Sally checked her desk. Cynthia went home. They took Genny, who showed no life signs.

Claire held her all the way, caressing her broken forehead and whispering words to hold on to life. There was no response, but her body was still warm.

An awaiting medical team whisked Genny away. They tried to stabilize her, taking her to an operating room. Hours passed without a word. All had opinions on what was happening.

Claire, Prisha, Lucas, and her parents, Michael and Ginerva, waited and prayed, each with positivity, guessing why there was a lack of forthcoming information. Doctor Isenberg, a friend of Claire and her family, approached. Claire could see from his tired, sullen eyes that this would be bad.

"Is she alive?" In a grief-stricken, rattled voice, her dad, Michael, quivered.

Dr. Isenberg closed the door to the waiting room.

"I am being honest, yes, barely, on life support. Your daughter has suffered trauma I have never seen before, even in Pakistan." They all took deep breaths and clung to the word alive.

"My Genny is strong." Her mother cried on her husband's shoulder.

"Yes, doctor. Please continue?" Claire was calm but wanted to cry on Michael's other shoulder.

"This is graphic, and we are working on this as we speak. The right side of your daughter's face has been pulverized. Her entire torso has been shattered. There is trauma to her head, neck, and spine. Her sternum caved in and broke. The ribs attached are broken and splintered in a compound nature. One splinter has pierced her heart, where it now remains. The damage from the glass is extensive. She is on life support, and we are doing everything possible to save her."

They were all crying. Claire pulled the doctor aside and asked him bluntly if there was any hope. He gritted his teeth and said, "There is always hope, but we need prayers, and possibly the most humane approach may be." Claire would not let him finish the sentence.

"Doctor Isenberg, you know my family; Genny is part of it. You have carte blanche financial to do any procedures that may save her life."

"Doctor Randolph-Mishari, we will. As we speak, I'm assembling a team; I've been contacted by…" He stopped.

Speaking to the group, he continued, "The greatest danger is the swelling in the brain."

"Can we see her?" Michael asked.

"Sir, you do not want to have this memory of your daughter. She will not know you are present, and a team is working on her. It would be best if you did not."

Her mother cried, "Should we call a priest?"

"Yes." He sadly replied.

Lucas spoke for the first time, sniffling, "Do we have a time frame?"

"The next 24 to 48 hours are critical. Let me not kid you; this is only the beginning. She may have other internal injuries we have not found or diagnosed. This is complicated and tragic. I will do my best, as will my team. I must get back."

"When will we hear from you again?" Michael sighed.

"My associates will update you every two hours in one fashion or another. Thank you."

"Thank you." They replied as he disappeared through the doors.

Lucas was whimpering, and Prisha went to console him.

"I've only known her for a few days, and it feels like a lifetime. This is all my fault."

Claire interrupted, "This is no one's fault! This was good science taken over by bad people."

They all sat and waited.

30

No More Hope

Claire's brain was on fire. She was informed, saddened, and felt a sense of responsibility for the destruction and hurt caused to her associates and friends. While they waited for word on Genny's condition, she called the attorneys who cared for the Randolph Trust. Claire was the heir and beneficiary, but she only dealt with specific aspects, and now, she wanted more control.

An hour had passed since Doctor Isenberg's report. Claire informed her trust's attorney that they set up an immediate restoration fund. She also wanted a detailed list of all politicians, charities, and businesses, national and international, that they have an interest in. She wanted to know who depended on Randolph's support. Claire specifically wanted the list to be typed on a standard typewriter—no receptionist, secretary, or anyone other than a partner in the firm. The list will be delivered to her office in her care or to Doctor Prisha Harshita Mishari-Randolph. The package is to be labeled as personal and confidential. Only Doctor Mishari-Randolph, Ms. Sally Pedroia, and I can receive the package. The person who typed it must deliver the package. It was agreed.

Two hours had passed, and Genny's condition was getting dire. Her brain wave activity was erratic, and her internal bleeding was not under control. She was bleeding to death. They all prayed.

Claire was all business. She confided in Prisha about her direction and the letter. She explained that this may sound harsh, but she wants her to, hopefully, temporarily take over Genny's office and teach Genny's classes during the fall semester. Claire said she would help her prepare for the classes and find an associate position in her field at the university. Claire's phone vibrated. The law office informed her that a bottomless fund had been set up and linked to her account. Claire thanked her attorney.

The following two-hour report was bleak. Genny's chance of becoming brain-dead was almost guaranteed if she didn't succumb first.

Ten hours later, an exhausted Doctor Isenberg sat the group in a small room, one of those rooms in which the door is closed and the doctor has deadly news. The Cantalupos hugged and wept. "My beautiful little girl," Ginerva whispered. Prisha hugged the destroyed Lucas.

Claire said, "Give it to us straight, please?"

"My heart breaks in these situations. There is no hope for her." Looking at Genny's parents and her proxy, "You must consider pulling the plug."

Claire got up and left the room. In an uncharacterized display of public emotion, she started banging the hallway walls, crying, "No! No! No! Please, no!" Sitting on the floor with her head tucked between her legs, sobbing as if she had lost her daughter. Her phone began to vibrate, and not caring, she dropped it and landed face up. It was her US Senator. She answered it.

The Senator could tell that Claire was grieving by her hello and said, "Claire, I know your situation. I know what you were just told. A group has been monitoring your situation. You have friends, and Morgan Strassa has enemies in the government. I can get you help, but none of the procedures have been done publicly; they are primarily research and experimental.

"I don't know. I would say yes, but it's her parents' call."

"You have to act fast!"

She reentered the room with renewed hope. Doctor Isenberg looked at her. He sensed what was about to come. She explained the situation. Ginerva got hysterical: "Oh my God, my baby!" Michael hugged her and nodded his head in approval.

"Yes!" She told the Senator.

He was quiet and then said, "She will be transported immediately. A team of Air Force doctors will assist Doctor Isenberg in preparing for her flight," Pausing "to Nevada. A special Air Force medical jet will take her to Mike O'Callaghan Military Medical Center on Nellis Air Force Base. Time is of the essence; the plan has begun. Doctor Isenberg and you can only accompany her. Start now preparing. You'll be leaving shortly."

"My God, outside of Area 51!" Claire had no more words.

"Yes!" Get ready.

"Thank you. We'll be in touch." Claire took a big breath.

"No, thank you for all your family has done. Bye." The conversation was over.

Time was short. Claire explained the situation. The Cantalupos were not happy with the plan but had little choice. Claire hugged Prisha and kissed her, telling her how much I love you and what you mean to me; Prisha reciprocated. Prisha had access to all of Claire's accounts. She told her to make sure the Cantalupos were ok. Take care of Lucas; let him stay with us until he knows what he will do. He has little funds, so without him feeling like a handout, give him whatever he needs. Prisha was coming out of her fear.

"We want to see her!" The Cantalupos insisted. It was their right, even though they advised them not to. They all wanted to see her. Doctor Isenberg looked at Claire and shook his head no.

Lucas, who was quiet and had no rights, wanted to see her.

The priest who had administered her last rites also shook his head no.

They were informed that a military transport team had arrived.

Genny's family and friends headed toward the intensive care unit. They arrived and were allowed to enter. Ginerva took one look and collapsed. Michael knelt at Genny's side, crying, and held her hand. "I love you." He kissed her hand and went to his wife's side. Prisha looked at Claire and wept. "Our poor baby!" Claire squeezed Prisha's hand.

Lucas looked on. The site was horrific. Half of her face was missing, her body was deformed, she had no shoulder, and you could see her broken ribs. Her body had cuts and bruises everywhere.

The transport team arrived. Everyone was asked to leave. Within fifteen minutes, they were out the door and on their way to the airport with a military escort. Doctor Isenberg informed his family of the situation and his departure.

Prisha took care of the business at hand.

The jet was off to Nevada.

31

The Cost of Victory

Birk **returned to his office later that evening, bringing great pleasure to him**. He enjoyed beating Genny, but wished he didn't lose his temper. "Fucking liberals," he drank and puffed away. Reliving and relishing the moment: he wished and fantasized that he had done the same to Claire and humiliated her in front of all those fucking liberals. He chuckled at his fancy. Then, reason caught him. "What the fuck is wrong with me?" He grabbed at his head as though a swarm of bees was in his skull. "When did I become an animal?" He put his head on his desk, knocking over his drink; the alcohol burned his bloodied hand. The drink spilled on the overturned photo of his family. He lifted it and looked at it, and smashed it into the desk, screaming at the top of his lungs, "FUCKING LIBERALS!"

Pouring another drink and puffing away, he picked up his phone. It was Morgan Strassa.

"Birk," the electronic voice inquired.

"Yes."

"We have the disc and the medallion."

"That was the objective," Birk replied.

"It was fucking messy!" Morgan Strassa was perturbed.

"Do you know what's happening now? You don't! Senators and Congressional leaders are up my ass!"

There was no reply.

"You were given authority and power, but not like the Gestapo. This was an important mission, but you must know how to handle the people you are destroying. You can't let them handle you. Birk, this is a Pyrrhic Victory when it should have been a blitzkrieg!"

"I don't understand. I was told to make this happen at all costs. Don't make me your scapegoat," a drunken Birk replied.

"Who the hell do you think you're talking to! You have to take this shit standing up!"

Birk was quiet and knew that he had overstepped.

"Mr. Birk, you can be replaced, and your memory will be reduced to ashes." Pausing.

"Do you understand me?"

"Yes, I apologize. It has been a long couple of days. I'm not thinking straight now." He was sincere.

"You're still the best man for the job—my handpicked Director. Your tactics are good, but try to realize certain people's power and the consequences that may follow. We'll figure this shit out. You're good. Keep an eye on that Skinwalker Project."

"Yes."

"So, we are good." After a long pause, he repeated, "We will continue to watch over your family." The call ended.

He picked up the picture on his desk, stared deeply into it, and cried.

***

Monday morning's breaking news reported that the Callahan Tunnel had to be shut down for several hours due to an early morning car accident. Doctor Genny Giuliana Cantalupo (Graduation Photo), driving a late-model Jeep Wrangler, lost control of the vehicle, flipped, and exploded into flames. (Stock photo) The recent Harvard doctoral recipient was celebrating with her friends. She was taken to a local hospital and listed as critical. Authorities say alcohol and speed appear to be factors. There were no other vehicles involved. There are no updates as of this broadcast. In other news…

32

Restitution: How Deep is Your Fund

Over the next few weeks, the government started to return the private belongings of the aggrieved group. Their lives would never be the same.

A report was leaked, and the president of Harvard College was under siege. Sexual allegations were made against him when he was an undergraduate student at Princeton University 35 years ago. He vehemently denied it, but the female and male accusers signed affidavits and were willing to testify against him. Excessive press constantly covered the story until he was forced to resign. His career was finished.

*****

Doctor Jeffrey Drayton received a 50% salary increase and a two hundred and fifty thousand dollar bonus from the Randolph Foundation. He never did another favor for anyone.

*****

The Foundation compensated Sally Pedroia for any home loss and gave her a 50% salary increase. She was also awarded an all-expenses-paid vacation anywhere in the world and fifty thousand dollars in cash. She remained loyal to Claire.

*****

Cynthia Robeo could not return home. The Foundation covered all her losses. She was put up in a luxury suite owned by the Randolph Foundation, with all expenses paid for the rest of her life. She also received a 50% pay increase with a promise of promotion. The Foundation also awarded her fifty thousand dollars and gave her family in Nigeria a generous monthly stipend. She remained loyal to Claire.

***

Charlie Zaspa was a victim of a cultural hate crime. Her belongings were destroyed and replaced by the Foundation. She received a 100% pay increase, a promotion, and two hundred fifty thousand dollars in cash. She formed a close relationship with Ditmer.

***

Doctor Ditmer Winkler, a widower, was also a victim of a seemingly personal crime. The Foundation replaced his losses. He received a 100% pay increase and two hundred and fifty thousand dollars in cash. His home was destroyed, and the Foundation paid to demolish it, rebuilding a bigger and more modern home with a fully equipped lab. In the meantime, he and Charlie were housed in luxury suites not far from the University for as long as needed. They would give their lives for Claire.

***

Sheila, the security guard, never returned to work. The following day, she packed all her belongings and moved home to Presque Isle, Maine, never venturing further than Aroostook County. When Claire learned about her ordeal, she arranged for her to take classes online at Harvard University to become a certified elementary school teacher. The Foundation sent her fifty thousand dollars in compensation. She also received a five-thousand-dollar-a-month pension from the school, funded by the Foundation.

Although she was grateful, she wished Claire good luck in her endeavors. Claire chuckled when she heard this.

***

The Museum suffered an immense loss and was closed for the summer. Insurance covered much of the damage, but the Foundation picked up the rest, making much-needed improvements and granting additional millions for expansion and further finds or acquisitions.

The science lab was also a victim of a vicious crime. The University, insurance, and mostly the Foundation fitted and expanded the facility to be a futuristic paradigm of cutting-edge science, the best in the world.

***

The Foundation, which Claire now controls, has a 100 billion-dollar Trust and 250 billion dollars in worldly assets. Extant before the American Revolution, it had a stranglehold on governments and global businesses. It is relied upon and respected around the world.

33

Broken

In a week or so, Lucas Johnny Chevrolet's life was crushed. He was a victim of a personal belief crime. He was persecuted for seeking the truth. A truth that jeopardized other people's beliefs. What is real when the truth is denied, hidden for personal agendas? Is the truth worth seeking if it's going to hurt innocent people? Sometimes, you question what is even real. How can I prove that I'm real? Do I exist beyond the realm of my thoughts? Am I insane? What drives me? The thoughts of a broken man returning to his family home in California. All that he had worked for was destroyed. His novel, notes, and records were erased from the cyber world. None of his possessions were ever returned. His apartment was uninhabitable. He stayed with Prisha and thanked her, and she arranged for his transportation back to California.

He knew Genny for only a few moments, but a force inside knew she was his soulmate. Seeing her in that state, the pain that she suffered was his. He returned home. His parents had never seen him so depressed and suggested he stay at their lodge in the mountains. He did.

Prisha arranged a 25-thousand-dollar line of credit on a card for him and a twelve-thousand-dollar-a-month stipend contingent on his staying in touch and working with Claire. He had no problem with this arrangement and was uncertain about his return to the University. His old Ford Bronco was still in the garage; his father had kept it running. He took it to the mountains, going off the grid, going dark like his heart and soul. He wanted to be alone with only the thoughts of Genny.

He was lying by the lake on a starry, moonless night, pondering his existence, looking into the sky and its reflection on the lake. Thinking how near, yet how far, there must be meaning.

There was an old typewriter and a ream of paper, and he started writing Dear Genny, Dear Genny…. until he fell asleep in his chair.

34

Reconstruction

Arrival at Area 51

Nellis Air Force Base in Nevada is a short distance, 80 miles from Groom Lake and Homey Airport (KXTA), Area 51. The two shared testing areas along the salt flats are ideal for long runways. Area 51 is highly classified. Both Nellis AFB and Area 51 are close to Las Vegas, Nevada. Both are veiled in secrecy, though Nellis AFB has recently become more accommodating to the community. It has opened its medical center and emergency services to the civilian population of Clark County, Nevada.

The US Government has publicly acknowledged Area 51, but it remains a top-secret military area. The world's most advanced flying machines are constructed and tested here. Area 51 has continued to become the focus of conspiracy theories on UAPs and extraterrestrials. Theorists claim that the alleged crafts from the Roswell, New Mexico incident in 1947 were brought to Area 51. The crafts and their biological remains have been allegedly examined and reverse-engineered, creating our modern-day technology and medicine.

***

They landed at Nellis AFB in a whirlwind. The flight was only a few hours long. Claire was at the side of a hyperbolic chamber where Genny was transported. Doctor Isenberg and the Air Force Team of physicians monitored her.

A high-tech ambulance equipped with a lift and hookups for the specially designed chamber greeted them. A staff sergeant quickly interviewed them as they arrived at the medical facility. The sergeant gave them passes, wished them good luck, and requested that they cooperate and do whatever they were asked, no matter how unreasonable it may seem. They agreed.

The ambulance pulled into a covered bay, almost a tunnel, backing into an emergency medical trauma entrance. Claire, Doctor Isenberg, and the sergeant were dropped off at an entry guarded by Military Police (MPs). They proceeded and were led down a long corridor, walking to the echoes of clicking heels, then greeted by an Air Force Medical Unit. The chamber resembled a futuristic casket, gliding silently with its escort, accompanied by pallbearers, proceeding down a long, lonely cathedral aisle. They reached an oversized steel-locked door with posted guards. The guard handed the sergeant a clipboard.

"Doctor Isenberg, please examine everything you see here and note it here?" She pointed and handed him the clipboard. He examined it as the steel door opened; on the inside, there were additional guards. The medical team sped away with Genny and escorted Claire. Doctor Isenberg was halted in his attempt to follow.

"Your journey has ended, doctor, as well as mine." The sergeant informed him.

Doctor Isenberg was confused but said nothing.

"You can finish the form on the way back to the airport."

He complied and then handed it over to the sergeant.

She smiled and showed her personality for the first time, "You'll be home for dinner, Doc. Transportation has been arranged for you at your airport destination. The United States Air Force thanks you for your service in this matter. It is confidential." She left him. His jet departed.

Claire realized that the doctor did not make it through the steel door. She said nothing. It was another long, cold-feeling corridor; the walls and floors were polished dark green, almost black granite. Looking up at the ceiling, it was triangular, right-angle in shape, with small windows like portals, whereby light could enter. Along the wall, motion sensors provided subdued LED lighting, triggered as they moved down the corridor. There was no furniture, benches, or anything. The place was void of fragrances and cold, with no obvious ventilation. The medical convoy turned into an area with four commercial-sized elevators. A guard was waiting at the opened elevator door. The chamber was placed into the elevator. The door closed as they descended at an incredible speed. Claire felt she traveled several hundred yards a quarter to half a mile. She did not ask.

The doors opened, and there was a Times Square business vitality. People and vehicles were traveling, appearing to be moving helter-skelter. Claire took it in and said nothing. They were led to an area. It was like a train platform, but not as large. Genny's chamber was loaded and secured into the vehicle. The passengers were buckled in. The pilot quickly stated that they may experience gravitational force, but not to worry.

Claire looked around. Above the door, a bronze tag read "Musk Industries." She smiled, knowing her Foundation had a financial interest in them.

The vehicle quickly accelerated, reaching speeds of over 300 miles per hour. Traveling through a trackless tube or any other type of connecting means it comes to a stop. The ride took about fifteen or sixteen minutes. Claire could see that Genny was stable. She almost thought that she detected her breathing.

The doors opened, and they were met by additional security. The chamber was loaded onto a vehicle designed for it. The Air Force personnel were scanned before they were allowed to board their awaiting transport. They left.

Claire was scanned, and her phone was requested. Security assured her that it would be returned at some point. She was then taken to meet the facilities director. She said nothing.

They were deep underground in Area 51.

35

Doctor Percy Martin James

Claire was taken to the facilities director, Percy Martin James, MD, Ph.D., who received his doctorate in biological engineering from MIT and his medical degree from Harvard University. Percy was a prodigy, a genius boy, receiving his BS at MIT at seventeen. He was an athletic, handsome African American who had written over fifty papers on groundbreaking biological-medical procedures.

Claire entered the office with a smile.

"Old friend." She hugged Percy. Their friendship began when he was at Harvard Medical School. He was visiting the Peabody Museum with his husband, and she had just returned from an exhibition. They talked and became friends. Harvard University wanted to keep him on staff and tried to use Claire as a means to an end. It failed.

"This is starting to fall into place."

"Yes, Claire, we don't have time to chat. You don't know how good it feels to see a friendly face. The Senator brought your situation to me. When he told me it was you, I was on board. This Morgan Strassa scent is starting to stink, and I wouldn't say I like it. I don't know who or what it is. We don't have much time. The President doesn't know about this place, but Dr. Randolph-Mishari is welcome."

"Will I get my phone back?"

"Yes, you're not a prisoner, but everything you say or do will be monitored."

She nodded, "Ok."

"I must go with the team. This is our plan, but we have no details currently."

"I've examined her charts over the last few hours and set up and scheduled procedures. We want to stabilize and restore her brain function. Her heart must be reconstructed and fortified. Her sternum, ribs, and clavicle must be rebuilt. Her face and teeth must be restructured. We have phenomenally advanced procedures. We will graft and bleach her skin and then balance the skin tones, matching the perfect coloring coded in her DNA. This sounds overwhelming, and we have the technology here. One procedure at a time. Have faith in us, me, Claire!"

She knew Percy was a genius and light-years ahead of his field, so she had confidence in him. He got up and started to leave.

"Wait!" Claire said.

"Will I see her? I have to report to her family."

"Do not worry. It will be taken care of."

Claire hugged him. "Thank you."

Percy smiled as he was leaving.

36

The Reconstruction of Genny

Procedure- Restoring Brain Function

Claire could make monitored phone calls and observe the procedures on a closed-circuit system. The procedures were performed in a room that was more like an advanced science laboratory than an operating room, filled with unfamiliar scientific equipment. She could not see Genny's covered face and body, only an exposed area of her head. Doctor James and his staff wore high-tech scrubs; no parts of their bodies were exposed.

Today's procedure was to restore Genny's brain function, control the brain's swelling, and clear and strengthen the entire central nervous system, displayed on a life-sized monitor. Another monitor projected a magnified schematic of her brain.

She was injected with a dye, which passed through her systems. It turned multicolored based on the area it was going in and its healthiness. Her brain was approaching failure.

She was hooked up to a machine that sampled and extracted her DNA. The results appeared on another monitor. Doctor James and his staff fed the information into an analyzer, which prepared a solution to match her DNA. The solution had an organic metal base. It was injected into Genny. They watched as the multicolor schematics slowly turned green. Her brain was changing at a much slower rate. Dr. James reinserted the connection and only increased the potency in her brain area. The brain's schematic slowly turned green. You could feel the excitement of the staff.

Genny was disconnected from the machine and brought to an observation room.

Dr. James entered the room where Claire was observing. Unmasking himself, he was elated.

"We will know in a few hours how effective the procedure was. It went well. She has a strong will. Her body absorbed the chemicals better than…" Stopping in mid-sentence.

Claire was feeling better. "Can I see her?"

"No, she is in isolation, continuously being monitored. I am confident that in a few hours, we will know its effectiveness."

"What was that procedure?"

"I'm sorry, Claire, that's classified and is only used if the patient is deemed terminal."

Claire nodded and said nothing.

"Claire, this procedure will enhance and strengthen her central nervous system. Her brain activity will become extraordinary." He was excited. "There is the possibility, if she survives, and I have confidence that she will, that she will develop an eidetic and photographic memory. Genny may also experience hyperthymesia." He almost couldn't control his sense of achievement.

"So, she may be able to recall her past experiences?" She asked.

"Yes, but it may be on different levels, but it will significantly improve."

"Also, she will have increased pineal gland activity. These possibilities include a touch of telepathy, precognition, telekinesis, and all abilities associated with, I hate to say this, the occult. This may not happen, probably won't, but it is possible. We still must proceed with her other major injuries."

Claire just listened to this science tale and thought of her poor Genny.

"So, in about two hours, as I said, we will test her autonomic and involuntary nervous system functions and go from there."

Claire just listened.

"She will remain unconscious, but she will be able to breathe on her own. If all goes well, in about 12-14 hours, we will work with the heart. We have it stabilized and safe, but want to repair it. My staff will need rest and to make the necessary calculations. We have the DNA sample in the analyzer to be ready." In his excitement, he did not realize he had overstated the procedure.

Claire thanked the doctor and asked him if she could make some calls. She was taken to a secure area, contacted Prisha, and asked if she was doing okay. She was then given Genny's status to pass on to the family and asked her to be aware of a package from the law office. Claire also reviewed some business, including restoring and fixing Genny's home. "I love you! And will call tomorrow." Prisha returned the sentiment. Claire's allotted time ended.

37

The Reconstruction

The Heart

Time was lost at the facility; it was a twenty-four-seven operation. Genny was being prepped for the second part of her reconstruction, the heart and the vascular system. Everywhere blood flows will be affected positively by this procedure. Every tissue in her, except the skeletal system, will be, to some capacity, renewed and enhanced. Any disease in her body will be purged. This was all contingent on patching the hole in her heart.

Like the day before, she was filled with fluids; dyes displayed every tissue in her body with a color grading. Her heart had a failing grade and was shown in bright red. You could see the hole and the damage from the splintered rib.

Her DNA, taken by the analyzing equipment, was fused with an organic metal chemical. The team examined their figures and injected them into her bloodstream. You could see veins, arteries, and blood vessels miraculously clean, purge, and open their ways. The solution made its way to the heart, and you could see that the heart wall was healing and strengthening. Copious amounts of fluids were being transfused, chemically bonding and blending with her blood. The heart pumped stronger than ever, and the fluids reached every capillary in her body. Genny's brain and heart were alive and well. Their electrical activity readings were met with applause.

After an hour or so, Dr. James declared the procedure a success, and they returned Genny to isolation.

With mixed emotions, Claire watched the procedure in astonishment, knowing that this was Genny's only alternative.

Dr. James entered the room with boyish excitement. "Claire, that went better than expected. She is going to make it! There are no guarantees for skeletal reconstruction. I do feel confident."

Claire once again didn't engage in what was really on her mind. "Thank you, Percy. What is next, and when can I see her?"

"You won't be able to see her for a few days. Trust me, she is fine. Unconscious and by her brain activity is in a happy dream state." Claire was pleased to hear this. "We're looking at 12 hours for her body to adjust and recover. We will then begin a two-part procedure. In the first part, we'll mend her chest and shoulder. We will then let her body rest for six to eight hours. She will be left in the lab and still connected to the devices during this time." Claire was intense in her classic pose. "The second procedure will be restoring her face, cheek, nose, eye socket, auditory canal, and teeth. This procedure can only be performed with the new fluids in her body. It's the pinnacle of the research here."

Claire gave a huge sigh! Dr. James didn't know how to read it and said nothing.

"You will be allowed to make your call. Thank you for your patience and cooperation. I know it's difficult not to be able to talk more about this, but we will upon successful completion." He left, and Claire was taken to her communication post.

38

The Reconstruction

The Shoulders, Sternum, and Face

Genny's chest and shoulder were displayed on the big screen. Clean-up work in both areas had taken place. You could see the fractures and missing bones in both. Once again, her DNA was mixed with the advanced solution, injected into her shoulder, and directly into her sternum.

Claire watched in amazement as they both slowly grew bone and became better than new. They then injected the fluid into several bones, strengthening every bone, muscle, ligament, and cartilage surrounding function and any past injury. You could see that the monitors' lights were all green. Part one was a success.

When the first procedure ended, Claire's monitor was turned off, and she returned to her quarters and had something to eat. It was brought to her. She was treated as a special guest, a courtesy that was noticed and appreciated. Trying to rest, but could not. She had no writing materials and couldn't keep notes. Meditation, a practice she learned from her student, Genny, kept her focused. Hours later, she returned to the viewing room. When the monitor turned on, a photo of Genny's beautiful face filled one of the large monitors. Claire sighed. Other monitors had anatomical representations of Genny's face and head, something out of Leonardo DaVinci's notebook.

The doctors began their procedures. Her body was in a secure standing position, her mangled head supported and exposed. The sight was grotesque. Visible were areas where bones had been removed, and her damaged or missing teeth. Her face, which had the same diagram and a grading system used in the prior procedures, could be seen on another monitor. She was injected with the fluids fused with her DNA. This time, it was encoded with a matrix of facial images.

Nothing was happening. Dr. James decided to remix a new DNA sample, leaving out the image matrix. He believed Genny was strong and didn't need any facial enhancement; her DNA was strong. She was injected.

Instantly, bones were forming, and teeth were growing. Every feature of her face was healing and glowing. Her hair was shining. Her face was developing like a dark room, photographic negative. Claire got the chills, whispering, "God!" Genny's reconstruction was miraculous. You could see the return of her beautiful features, but her skin was in a bad state. All the removed glass fragments left tiny, now barely visible scars. The final procedure would target and remove them. Her tattoos would receive a protected coating and enhancement.

The facial reconstruction procedure was an overwhelming success. Dr. James had made a scientific breakthrough that would never appear in any journal, and added new data to his research.

Dr. James entered the room and explained to Claire that everything was going better than planned. Before she could speak, he said, "In twelve hours, we will complete the project. In a day or two, Genny will be up rehabbing. I must get back to the lab." He left. Claire was astounded by the procedure. Thoughts that this is advanced biogenetic engineering: the science of the gods. She had concerns for Genny. She was allowed to make a call. Then, returning to her room, she took a nap.

It was day four, and Claire was wearing down. Today was a skin-healing and bleaching procedure.

39

Life

Genny, the girl Claire knew and loved like a daughter, lay naked on a cold-looking slab, unconscious, but her beauty, once again, breathed with life. The room was different, with just one monitor and its grading system. Genny was placed on an invisible glass table. It was like she was levitating. She was injected with a similar fluid of her DNA and organic metal. The doctor waited as he watched it travel through her system. They placed special glasses over her eyes. Then the staff all left the room. Then there was a light show. Multicolor lights were flashing, like the famous Encounter movie, the monitor rapidly turning all green. The lights stopped. The scientific team reentered the lab. The procedure was finished.

Genny was more beautiful than ever. They covered her body with a blanket and took her to the recovery area.

The team shared a champagne toast. Claire could see them. Their joy and success sadly reminded her of what she and Genny experienced when they learned about the disc. Yeah, some Nobel Prize, she thought.

Claire was waiting for the doctor.

Arriving with energy and a smile. "Doctor, it was a success!" He declared.

"Now what?"

"Genny will be under observation for the next twenty-four hours. We need to get as much information out of this as possible. You do understand this is quid pro quo. Then we will wake her up. You will be at her side. Then, she will be in rehab and tested for the next ten days," He repeated. "You will be at her side at every moment."

Claire was happy with the prognosis.

"Percy, what is the purpose of this kind of operation? Is it going to help the public? I don't mean to sound too curious, but I'm blown away by what I have seen. I am a scientist at the top of my field. I cannot explain this to anyone because they wouldn't believe it."

"Claire, first and foremost, I need your trust. Even with Genny, she will not know the full details of her procedures. She will be different, smarter, and better at virtually everything she does. Her senses will be sharp."

"What are you saying, Percy?"

"You were brought here by a group of people fighting an intergovernmental war. Our funding comes from one of these sides. You have friends on this side. We are a military operation. Use your imagination. This was her only hope. She is herself, flesh, bones, thoughts, free will, soul."

"It doesn't matter, Percy. We're going with it. It's done. You have my word, my trust, and thanks. One last request."

"That may be?" Raising his eyebrow.

"Let's have a coffee and catch up on some good old times?"

"Done!" They finished their talk and would meet for coffee.

40

Rebirth

The Soul's Voyage

Genny traveled in a psychedelic unconscious state as she was being rebuilt. Whether it was the new fluids circulating her system or an adjusting consciousness, from hyper brain activity, creating thoughts and dreams, vibrant, bright, intense Pop Art colors in a cubistic maze that would bring grins to Andy Warhol and Picasso. She traveled at the speed of light and passed by snails.

Her past came to life—she relived moments, sensing, feeling, and tasting them. The dead were alive; they spoke as though no time had passed. She was being baptized and could taste the priest's salty hands.

Holy Communion, the bland flavor of the Eucharistic wafer was burning her mouth, to the words: "Body of Christ, Body of Christ, Body of Christ echoed through the pathways of her mind in a slowly fading, continuous loop as contorted and exaggerated pictures of the crucifixion pulsated to the beat of a disco strobe light.

Her Catholic confirmation was relived with the gently floating, fading, sky-written message: "God is in all of us." It was in multiple languages, intersecting in strange patterns. She casually looked away, turned her head, and came face to face with a

Sumerian Gala priest, speaking, spitting, and frothing like a mad dog in his native language. She knew the translation: "The Holy Spirit is within all of us."

Revisiting Pa's hometown in Perugia, Italy, she was introduced to all her dead relatives, stretching back to the Roman Empire, all sharing the same name and tomb. Perched in their sarcophaguses, funerary boxes, pine boxes, and caskets, and speaking in Italian, Latin, and Etruscan, pointing, giving directions like an insane, amphetamine-crazy orchestra conductor.

In France, at Avignon, she met Pope Clement V while he was giving Judas Iscariot a piggyback ride; silver coins rained upon them, covering them, as a faint "I'm sorry!" could be heard through the din of the clanging coins. Both were quickly covered and gone.

It was an endless reel of dreams and travel. Talking with a being dressed in an ancient tribal gown featuring many feathers and a matching feathered headdress. He was standing on top of the medallion with an oar in his hand. He spoke to Genny in English and asked her if she wanted to go for a ride. "I have nothing else to do these days," was her response, and she got aboard the medallion. She was welcomed aboard. There were no introductions; he said, "I knew you, but you may know me." Standing, he began to paddle. She asked him where he was taking her. He said, "Nowhere, but I'm showing you the stars." Pointing to Orion's belt.

"Oh!" She replied. He paddled slowly, but they were moving at a tremendous velocity like Willie Wonka's steamboat. There is a planet like Earth. She could hear screaming as she watched the planet break apart. One ship escaped.

She was on the craft, and there was a small crew, row upon row of electronic storage devices, and strange beings as part of the crew.

It was a blur. They traveled back to Earth, and visions appeared in the sky in the early days of Earth.

-Cavemen, Neanderthals, all forms of early man.

-Giants, floods, and earth crust displacement.

-Antarctica, cities under the ground, and conduits with moving vehicles below the Earth's surface.

Churches, religions of the world, mass murders, wars, and the atomic bomb.

In a moment, it was over.

"That's your lesson, your beings, now your past. Time to leave." The dream was over, and another would begin.

41

Return to the Living

Genny 2.0

On the sixth day, Genny was resuscitated. She looked around, and Claire was at her side, along with Dr. James and his staff.

"Welcome back, Genny. I'm Dr. James. You had a bad go at it, and we got you back to this point, which is an excellent point!" he said emphatically.

"Where am I?" She turned to Claire. Claire turned to Dr. James.

"Your injuries were near fatal. Your only chance of a full recovery was here. We are a military hospital near Nellis Air Force Base, just outside Las Vegas." He smiled. She was satisfied with the answer.

"We will show you the magnitude of trauma we all faced over the next few days as you rehab and get stronger."

"I feel good. Where are my parents?" Concerned, needing a glass of water. The staff started removing the intravenous tubes.

"This is a secure military base, and they were not allowed to make the trip. Dr. Randolph-Mishari has been with us and kept your family apprised of your condition. To ease their anxiety, we will try to arrange a video chat later this morning. The call will be monitored with a delay for security reasons."

Genny looked at Claire.

"It's alright. Everything went well," Claire reassured her with a tightening grip on her hand.

"Doctor Cantalupo, you will be monitored, examined, tested, and begin physical therapy over ten days. When you return to Boston, Dr. Isenberg will be your physician, and he will follow a rehabilitation program we are setting into place. You are in Claire's temporary care until you can sustain yourself." Genny was surprised by the first-name basis. "I'm going to leave you two, Claire and Genny, alone to catch up. We are in the process of completing your dietary requirements over the period mentioned. The room is monitored." He informed them. The doctor and his team departed.

Claire hugs Genny. "GG, I thought we lost you!"

"I remember. Strangely, I feel I can remember everything. I should get hit in the head more often." Genny sounded like her old self.

"You don't have to talk about it."

"I do, Claire. It's important to me. It's coming back to me, but what did they do to me?" Claire nodded. Genny began her recollection of the event.

"The gathering ended shortly after you left with Prisha for the emergency room. Ditmer and Charlie left very distraught over the Birk's incident. Lucas stayed; I tried to convince him to stay the night. I wanted to be with him." Claire gave her a funny smile. "I kissed him and melted in his arms. He couldn't stay but gave a guaranteed rain check. I went to bed and was awoken by a thunderous knock a few hours later. I checked my phone for calls, but it was not working. I thought it was Lucas and rushed to the door. It was the happiest moment. Then it happened. They knocked the door down! Birk got very physical, and I felt he was getting sexual with me. Touching, implying he was going to have me. He tried to rip my panties off and then threw me to the floor. He blew smoke into my mouth." She begins to cry but continues, "I spit into his face. He hauled off on me and destroyed my face. I could hear and feel my bones break. I fell to the floor, and his knee crushed my chest. I remember I was almost out, he drooled in my face, and I said *Fuck-You!* I must have hit a nerve because he picked me up and threw me through the patio door. He did not violate me!" She burst into tears. Claire hugged her with so much love that the tears slowly turned to sobs and sighs.

Genny video-chatted with her parents. They had no idea how to set it up and went to Prisha, an expert in these matters. Genny reassured her parents; Claire did the same with Prisha. Both said, "See you in ten days." Everyone was happy, yet everyone missed one another. Over the ten days, Genny spoke with her parents on a few occasions. Claire called Prisha whenever she could.

Genny and Claire created a code, speaking to each other in a hybrid Sumerian/Akkadian dialect, hoping it was not translatable. They also spoke in Sanskrit and Mayan. Claire explained to the staff that Genny would teach at Harvard University without writing materials, thinking this was good practice. No one questioned or disagreed with her; it was all being monitored.

It was the end of day five of rehab, and everything was going great. Genny continued to dream every night and was told it would be normal. It was explained that we all dream all the time, but can't remember them. Genny now remembers everything, conscious or subconscious. Also, at the end of day five, Claire and Genny would eat in a dining area. Genny was around and about, feeling better than she had ever felt.

"I'm not right!" Genny said to Claire in Latin.

"How?" asked Claire in the same language.

"I've never been this smart. I can figure out anything. My mind moves so fast—it's almost like a computer. I know things that I never knew before. I remember the names and seats of my preschool classmates. I remember the classes, going home, what I had to eat, and what my mom said. The events are now in full detail. Claire, it's freaky."

"There were going to be some positive side effects. I'm sorry, we had no choice." Claire avoided the details of the procedures. Genny had yet to ask.

"Oh, no blame here. Only thanks and love." Hugging.

"My reflexes are uncanny; I can run faster and longer, jump higher and further, swim like a shark, and I don't get tired."

Claire was hurting inside, knowing what they did to Genny.

"Genny, you were treated like a military casualty, with many experimental procedures that won't be available for decades. I've known Dr. James for many years, and he was confident this would work out. It was our only option. You were such a strong being, both physically and mentally, that it appears that these procedures have enhanced your abilities. As Dr. James explained, it's like when a professional sports player gets hurt. They get the best treatment in the world and, at times, are better than they were."

"I'm not upset, but these new abilities have surprised me. It's not like I'm some artificial life form?" Claire shook her head but wasn't convinced otherwise.

They finished dinner and were off to their shared room, both looking forward to going home.

In a foreign tongue, Genny asked, "What about Birk?"

Claire, in disgust, "Untouchable."

"Lucas?" Genny asked.

"Still no contact. He wanted to be alone while in California." She spoke half-truths.

***

The following day, Genny was tested on accuracy with weapons and various related military fundamentals; she was exceptional. It was explained to her that some of her procedures were meant for military personnel, and they wanted to test the results. Genny did not mind, enjoyed the challenges, and thanked them for saving her life. She saw the before and after photos of her injuries. The team and all of those working on Genny genuinely liked her. She was always charismatic, but now she glowed.

42

Astral Lovers

On the sixth night of rehab, Genny had an experience. Her body began to float. Looking down, she saw herself asleep and Claire in the adjacent room.

"Claire, Claire, Claire, look at me. I'm flying! Claire, Claire, I'm flying! Claire, look!" There was no response. Genny blew her a kiss and said, "I'll see you in the morning."

Her body floated up level upon level of what appeared to be scientific activities. The facility made a beehive look like an inactive, vacant factory. She could hear multiple languages, many of which she was familiar with, and others she was processing as she moved out of the structure. She floated high above a nonexistent building, looking down at a desert with sage and dust playing together.

She rose high with no fear, remembering her last experience.

Drifting over mountains, she stopped, hovering above a log cabin. Looking down and seeing through the roof and walls, the lonely, sad, tired Lucas was asleep at his typewriter. Whispering, she said, "Can Lucas come out and play? Come on out, Lucas, and play with Genny?"

He was fast asleep, and suddenly his eyes opened. Looking up, he could see a shining light through the roof. Still traumatized by his recent experience, he tried to get out of the chair, but his body was in sleep paralysis. He struggled with no success.

"Lucas, come play with me?" She inhaled, creating a halo effect that enveloped Lucas, lifting his naked body from the chair. He was floating and was not afraid. Slowly rising, feeling the cool mountain air on his flesh, he looked down to see himself asleep in his chair. Rising, he looked up to what appeared to be an angel. The closer he got, the more he could see the beautiful nude image of Genny magically removing the last grotesque sight of her.. Sadness filled him, for he thought she had passed, and this was her spirit returning as a dream. He had not been in the communication loop, in his dark state. The closer he got, the more her beauty intensified; energy was all about her.

She touched him like the fingers in the Sistine Chapel; they were magnetic and drew his face to hers. They embraced, and a mystical, sensual tingling filled his soul with joy.

"Genny, are you real? I was so worried. You are so cold?"

She kissed his lips, and fire traveled to his toes, his bones filled with song."

"Genny."

"Lucas."

"There are no clouds in the sky, and I came to claim something you owe me: my rain check."

Kissing her, he continued believing this to be a dream. They kissed and made passionate love high in the California Mountains' big sky, an ocean of stars as a backdrop. Genny's senses were heightened, lost in an enraptured state that gods dream of. Lucas was transported into this euphoric, carnal black hole, seemingly lasting for eternity.

During a copulatory vocalization, Genny kissed and whispered into his ear. "I know!" There was no response; Lucas was breathing heavily.

"Lucas, I know." The sexual engagement was ending.

"I know." She repeated.

"What is it, Genny?" Huffing and puffing.

"Pa's vault…I've been there."

Both standing in space, naked, holding hands, Genny gently and sexually slid her hands to his fingertips and then released him. He floated away like an astronaut untethered on a spacewalk. Watching him descend slowly to his body, she whispered, "Thank you for the rain check." She could see his smile, which remained after he reentered his body.

Genny awoke and savored the experience. She did not tell anyone about her travels to the astral realm or that it was just a dream. This was now hers alone.

43

Coming Home

The next few days went as scheduled, and they packed their few things and headed home.

Dr. James came in with security procedures, and they had to sign disclosure affidavits, subject to federal penalties. He gave them his personal contact information. "Genny, you'll have some changes-physical, cognitive, maybe more." Handing her a pamphlet, "This explains the side effects. You're part of something, spectacular and… unprecedented. You'll have weekly appointments with Dr. Isenberg and our staff."

They signed the papers, and Claire explained that Dr. Isenberg is a family friend and longtime personal physician. "At this time, our options are limited; he is a good and trustworthy doctor," a philosophical Claire softly told Genny.

Genny was happy to be alive, reliving her dream a few days back. The vault and Pa were the only things on her mind. She had yet to process the disc and medallion taken from her.

Upon their departure, Genny subconsciously rubbed her medallion. They retraced their steps back to the tunnel transit. Genny was experiencing a déjà vu but said nothing. Arriving in Boston on a hot summer day, Dr. Isenberg greeted them. In a private room, he introduced himself and was stunned at her physical condition. He had been getting updates but had no idea what was happening. He examined Genny and checked Claire for exhaustion, telling her she should rest.

Outside the secured area were her mother, father, brother, Ditmer, Charlie, and Prisha.

Her parents saw her on the video chat but were speechless at Genny's health and couldn't wait to take her home, where she would stay for a short time. Prisha hugged her and told her that Lucas was unavailable and living off the grid, but we would try to contact him. Genny hugged and kissed her, thanking her.

Claire grabbed Prisha's hand and then shared a passionate kiss.

"You look so tired." Prisha sadly said,

Ditmer and Charlie hugged Claire, thanked her, and said they were always there for her. They hugged Genny.

They went their separate ways.

44

Reset

Claire handed Prisha a note as they stepped outside the airport terminal. It read. "Don't say a word. I'm sending the car away. I think we are being tracked and monitored. Give me your phone." Prisha gave her the phone and a look of concern.

Claire walked up to her driver and gave her a note. It read."This may seem odd, but I need a favor. We are staying in the area for a while and have transportation to get home. Please bring our phones inside the house and be as discreet as possible. Leave them on the kitchen table. When you leave, say goodnight as though we were there. I'll be in touch with you. Thanks." She gave her the phones and two one-hundred-dollar bills.

"Done!" She drove away.

Claire hailed a cab, and they got in.

"Two International Place."

They arrived, exiting the cab, and Claire paid with cash.

"Thank you." They simultaneously said.

Holding hands, they entered Citi Group Global Markets, Inc., one of Randolph's financial interests. They walked over to a private elevator and were greeted by security.

"Can I help you?" he pleasantly asked.

Claire stepped up to the elevator, punched in a code, and opened the door.

"If you need additional help, I'm at your service." The guard watched as they entered the elevator. Claire punched another code, and the elevator descended several floors. The door opened to another security guard who surveyed the women. Saying nothing, Claire walked over to a steel door, punched in a code, and the door opened.

"If you need further help, I'm here to assist you." The guard pleasantly said.

They walked into a corridor lined with doors on both sides. Security cameras abounded. Behind a bulletproof partition, another guard watched their every move.

Claire stopped at another steel door, punched in a sequence of numbers, and then pressed her hand to a scanner. A green light went on, and then she looked into a camera that scanned her eye. After a series of clicks, the door unlocked and opened.

The room was plush and exceptionally rich-looking. There was a long table with chairs around. Talking for the first time since leaving the airport.

Claire asked Prisha to have a seat.

"I'm sorry about these precautions. It's safe to talk here. We are in a sealed vault, with no electric transmissions in or out. I want to get our security company to sweep our home for bugs and install electronic jamming devices. Get new phones and credit cards. Doing the same at work, and everyone connected with us. I want them all to get new phones or have the ones they have checked out." She sighed.

"Oh, Christ! I missed you so much," Claire sighed in relief.

"I missed you," Prisha said, then hugged her, and they kissed. They hugged in a long, loving silence.

"Prisha, let me tell you what happened." In their embrace, Claire told her every detail about the place, the people, the security, and the secrecy. She was explaining the reconstruction of Genny and her new abilities, her eyes watering, saying that she may never be the same, but didn't know. She was distraught.

Prisha cradled her and told her that she was familiar with Area 51, that she had worked with Beebe Schwartz in secrecy, and that she apologized to Claire for never mentioning it.

Claire went to one of the smaller wall safes, punched in numbers, then hand and eye scans. The door opened. It was right out of James Bond. She took out 2-banded rolls of hundred-dollar bills, ten thousand dollars. There were phones and what looked like identification cards, passports, and handguns. She took two partially charged phones and then grabbed a handgun. Prisha said no, and then she put the gun back. She handed Prisha a roll of bills and a phone. Claire explained her plan, and Prisha agreed.

Retracing their steps, finding their way to the street, and hailing a cab.

"The Four Seasons Hotel," Claire commanded.

On the way, they activated their phones. Claire placed a call and punched in a code; a voice answered, "How can I help you?"

"Company suite at The Four Seasons Hotel in Boston."

"Yes, code, please." Claire punched in a code.

"Confirmed, the suite is available and now reserved for Charlotte Saunders Cushman and her partner." Cushman was a mid-19th-century sapphic stage actress from Boston whom Claire had studied and admired.

"Thank You." Claire ended the conversation.

They arrived at the hotel. Claire paid the cab driver, and they thanked one another. The hotel's receptionist greeted them and then proceeded to the check-in desk.

"Yes, a reservation for Charlotte Saunders Cushman and her partner." With a snobbish attitude, Prisha guffawed at the reference.

Though amazed when she saw the reservation, the desk clerk hid it as she replied, "Ty Warner Penthouse is being readied; I'll arrange an escort for you."

"Now, now, dear, don't get excited!" Claire played with Prisha.

"Please send dinner and a bottle of Louis Roederer, Cristal Brut 1990 Millennium Cuvee Methuselah."

The clerk checked her computer and said, "Yes, we have a bottle and will send it up. Are you expecting guests?" The champagne was a six-liter bottle.

"Absolutely not! Upon dinner served and champagne delivered, do not disturb until 0700." Claire was in a management temperament.

"Of course, please sign the register?" Claire complied.

"Identification?" She asked.

"That I cannot. All was lost in thievery; hence, we are here till morning." Claire is playing, trying to do her best, Charlotte Sauders Cushman.

The clerk gave Claire a funny look.

"Miss Cushman, this is highly irregular." Giving Claire a concerned look.

"So is this!" Politely holding the girl's hand and placing five one-hundred-dollar bills.

"Privacy!" Claire winked.

"Privacy guaranteed!"

"Cross your heart?" Claire was getting silly. Prisha was laughing.

The clerk crossed her heart; Claire thanked her for her help.

A porter took them to their penthouse.

When they were out of sight, the desk girl grumbled, "Fucking rich people!" then grinned, slipping the bills into her purse.

The porter let them in and showed them around. The huge bottle of champagne on ice sat uncorked on top of a fully stocked bar.

Claire handed the porter a hundred-dollar bill, and they thanked one another.

They relaxed in the luxurious suite. They drank champagne and were getting silly when dinner arrived. They ate, drank, and relaxed. They kissed, showered, and kissed. Dressed in plush, soft Turkish robes provided by the Hotel, they sank into each other and the soft couch. They talked, drank champagne, snuggled, played, and then went to bed, where Prisha said, "Let's leave everything behind tonight." Claire agreed as they made passionate love until they collapsed into a deep sleep, folding into one another's arms.

Claire awoke and sat up, indifferent to the luxurious accommodations. Prisha, soundly sleeping, rested her head across Claire's midsection. Claire's mouth was dry, and she reached for a glass of water on the nightstand. Sipping, looking down at Prisha, thanking the universe for bringing them together. She caressed her soulmate's forehead and hair. Feeling that a higher power, twin flames, brought them together.

Prisha awoke, sat beside Claire, and reached for water on her nightstand. A morning kiss and hug, then Prisha said, "That was the best night; I wish it could last forever." Snuggling up to Claire.

"It could be love, but it won't. I agree we should live like this more often, and I promise we will." Claire hugged Prisha. "This excessive luxury is not who we are. I never want to get lost in this, only in you." There was a quiet and peaceful silence as they listened to each other's breathing. Claire was pondering her place in life. Prisha appreciated the warmth of her body. Claire was feeling her love. She picked up the phone and said to the desk clerk, "One more night is required here!" Claire could hear computer typing.

"All set; a third night may not be possible." Apologetically.

"No, that's fine. Thank You." Prisha smiled, snuggling closer and tighter.

"Prisha, I am privileged. You know that. Wealthy beyond belief, my family has more money and assets than some small countries. We have power. I have power, but I don't understand why I was chosen, born into all of this. People are born poor, starving, and lead miserable lives. Why am I so fortunate? I have you, and I feel love. You are in my heart and mind. Why am I so lucky?" Prisha snuggled and just listened as Claire continued. "My mother, who had me in her early forties, and my father, who was much older, always told me to be humble, generous, kind, thoughtful, thankful, helpful, and strong. I loved her so much and miss her." She began to cry. Prisha took her and held her close as her tear drops rolled down Prisha's breast. Claire stopped crying and got strong again. "I'm sorry these events have been unnerving."

Prisha said, "Sometimes I feel the same way. Why do I have so much? My feelings for you burn within me." They kissed. "I miss my parents, my home, and my family. We were not rich, yet not poor; they gave me love and support. I have not seen them in years, and I fear that I may never see them again. Time is a great eraser, and I'm fearful of it." Sighing, wanting to cry, held it in. They embraced.

"That champagne was filled with emotions." Prisha smiled.

"I will take care of business this morning, and we will enjoy the afternoon and evening, then return to business tomorrow. Prisha, I will put Sally on this: plan a vacation to your home during the mid-semester break." Prisha kissed her, and nothing was said for a long time.

After showering and eating breakfast, Claire took care of her business with the help of Sally.

They went to the gift shop and bought sweatsuits and other clothing only tourists would buy. Changing, going incognito for a walk in Boston's Public Garden, feeding the ducks and their ducklings, and then riding the famous Swan Boats. They then shopped on Newbury Street and had a late lunch and drinks at an outdoor café. It was a perfect day, a beautiful time before they would get back to work and face the darkness that man brings upon himself.

45

Homecoming

Genny would stay at her parents' home, her childhood home, until it was habitable again. The family home was just half a block up the street from the family store. It was a small duplex. Her family lived on one side, and her aunt's family lived on the other. The house was just around the corner from Genny's home.

On the short ride home from the airport, she agreed she would help with the store and take it easy for a while.

Genny had traveled the world for the past decade before moving into her Pa's home; she hadn't spent much time at home since high school.

Upon entering the house, she felt a rush of memories and could smell the cooking: garlic, olive oil, escarole, and cannellini beans. Genny smiled. "Escarole and beans?"

Her mom hugged her, "GG's favorite." Her dad hugged her, remembering how he had last seen his precious daughter, and thanked God.

Genny could sense and feel their love as if it were physical. It was a long day, and her mom reheated dinner with a loaf of DeAngelis's fresh Italian bread and a bottle of Chianti.

"Now I know I'm in heaven." Buttering a slice of bread and dunking it into the sauce, Genny asked, "How is Robert? He left in such a rush. Saw that I was ok and left?"

"He's fine. He said he wanted to stop in next week and spend more time here during a layover." Ginerva said.

"I miss him and look forward to spending time and talking with him. How's teaching going?"

"Summer break, and I help your dad in the store."

"Retiring soon?"

"Hope not!" Ginerva quipped back.

They finished eating, and her dad, Michael, said, "One more surprise." Pulling a white box out from the refrigerator, reading Modern Pastry.

Genny's face lit up like a Christmas Tree. "No, not that. Oh my god, I am dead!" Her parents didn't like the dead comments as Michael opened the box, and there it was, heaven on earth, ricotta pie. Mom got the cappuccinos. The Cantalupos were in a state of quiet bliss. Then Genny apologized, hugged them, said she was tired, and headed towards her bedroom.

Her room was frozen in time, holding the memories and spirit of her childhood, a placebo for her parents. Lying on her bed brought back memories as fresh as the food they had just had. Genny loved her family. A crucifix was centered over her bed as rosary beads from her first communion wrapped around her bedpost. A picture of the Virgin Mary holding the Christ Child sat atop her dresser. Genny, as she got older, thought this was all rubbish and bullshit. She would never remove these religious and cultural artifacts; she loved and respected her family. Thoughts on their devotion to God, Jesus Christ, and the Catholic Church were nothing less than undeniable faith. She could remember her grandmother going to church every single day. Genny laughed, thinking that she must have done something terrible. Life is so fragile, love and bonding are so strong, and holding on to every beat is a job for more than mere mortals. Genny now understood what faith was about. Feeling guilty, selfish, and a bit ignorant, she smiled at the late lesson.

Closing her eyes, she tried not to recap the week's events. Lucas and her dreams were pleasantly trapped in an endless loop. She was longing for him, awaiting a word. She whispered, "Come on, Lucas. Come home to Genny. Please!"

Working in the store and making submarine sandwiches was fun. One customer joked, "I knew these sandwiches had a secret, but I didn't think it required a scientist." There were jokes on how the help was finally upgraded, all good-natured regulars bantering.

Within a few days, she heard from Claire and was updated on what was happening. They continued to communicate in their artificial language. She was told her home would be ready shortly, and no one was in touch with Lucas. The Lucas part was not true.

Genny sliced her finger badly while cutting a tomato. She could see the bone in her finger as a very thick, odd, colored blood oozed when it should have gushed. She quickly took a video of it. The help was calling an ambulance when she stopped them, went into the ladies' room, washed it off, and watched it heal in real time as though it was reminding her who she is now.. She was no longer able to work in the store and wanted to return to her home. This would be her last night in her parents' home.

Dreaming of Pa that night, she knew her quest had just started. She remembered that she knew where the vault was.

The following day, she moved back home. Now, all her thoughts were focused on Perugia, Italy, her Pa's, and her family's birthplace.

Her life had changed forever. Teaching at the University paled in comparison to her quest. She whispered, "The truth is out there, fuck I'm going to find it on my life."

She fell asleep and dreamed of Lucas's kiss.

46

Family Flame

Lucas awoke in the chair at his typewriter, refreshed, rejuvenated, and in the bliss of restoration, not knowing why. The dream was soon blurry and chaotic, its evanescent chemistry vaporizing the night images. Though he could not recall it, there was a good feeling; he felt intense happiness when he tried. Genny, his soul whispered. He quickly packed his few belongings and took a pack of Gitanes, crushing them and throwing them into the wastebasket.

Lucas pulled into his parents' driveway. They were heading out to work. They were excited seeing him, as was he to see them. They briefly talked and agreed that Lucas was taking them to dinner that evening.

Entering the house, he retrieved his phone and checked for messages and emails. There was an email from the University that he could address later, but there was no other. He was sad and still in the dark, and trying to reach out to anyone was impossible.

That evening, he took his parents to their favorite restaurant. They teased him along the way as if he had hit the lottery or robbed a bank. Once inside, they had cocktails. Lucas did not order a drink and declared himself the designated driver.

When they settled, Lucas told them how much he loved them and appreciated everything they had ever done for him. This was unlike him, and they were concerned.

"Are you ill?' His mother asked.

"Are you in danger?' asked his father. And to their surprise, Lucas shrugged his shoulders and told them every detail of his experience. He usually kept most things from his parents. They were getting older; he could see the gray and age lines on their faces, never taking the time with them, and you never know. You don't want to die with secrets or a withheld "I love you."

The story shocked them, and his mother hugged him like he was still a little boy.

"Lucas." His father told a story of when he first met his mom. "I moved from Marseilles to Paris when I entered the Sorbonne. I had a small apartment near the school in my senior year, just outside the Latin Quarter. I was earning money as a photographer while studying for a bachelor's degree in art history and archaeology, but I loved taking pictures. So never feel bad that you are following your passion." Jean-Paul Chevrolet was a raconteur, a genetic trait. "One gorgeous day in May, a week before graduation, I was out taking photos of the beautiful blooming flowers in the area, exiting the Rive Gauche and crossing the Le Pont Neuf, admiring the Seine and the tourists loving the city. Landing on the Ile de la Cité, a short, beautiful walk, I approached the Cathedral of Notre Dame for photos. It was a gorgeous day. I was shooting the Cathedral, not paying attention, as I stumbled over this woman who was drawing."

"Yeah, I was completing my master's thesis at the Paris School of Architecture when this joker stumbled over my project, knocking it to the ground," Olivia said.

"Oh, it wasn't that bad, was it?" Jean-Paul scrunched his nose.

"Yes." Olivia smiled.

"That smile still makes me sigh."

"I helped put her drawings together and offered to take accompanying photos. She told me she could not afford a photographer." Pausing, I said, "That's no problem as long as you have lunch with me. I looked her in the eye."

"His blue eyes captured me. I felt a tingle, and I said yes."

"I took the photos, and quite a nice job, I must say. We went to a small bistro, ate, talked, and drank for hours." Jean-Paul smiled.

"He invited me to his apartment. I should have said no, but I didn't. We are still together, and I love him as much as I did on that warm spring day in Paris." They kissed.

"That goes double for me." Jean-Paul hugged her and his son.

Lucas never loved and felt such happiness with his parents.

"Lucas, my love." Olivia spoke softly, holding his hand, "Follow your heart."

"Always follow the truth." Jean-Paul held the same hand in a triumvirate, a symbol of support.

Lucas sipped wine in a toast to his family, saying, "I love you."

Lucas would stay home for the next few weeks, receiving a package and no other mail. It was a phone and a note in Latin and Greek with instructions. Knowing enough to translate it, it was a message from Prisha explaining the security precautions, and Genny was making significant progress. Please do not attempt to contact her; Claire will advise.

He felt a sense of relief and wanted to head for Boston.

Later, he was informed of his associate professorship in Archaeology at the University of Massachusetts, Boston; details would follow.

He was again reminded not to contact Genny; she believed him to be in seclusion until his return to Boston. This was all for security reasons because they knew this was just the quest's beginning.

47

Quiet Bonds

The recent encounter deeply hurt Ditmer. The destruction of his home was sinister and hateful. Since the passing of his wife, many years ago, of breast cancer, he has dedicated his life to his work. His son, Klaus, his wife, and their two children, twins, lived in Germany. Klaus holds a doctorate in Artificial Intelligence and Data Science, which he teaches as a tenured professor at the University of Stuttgart.

It's been years since he saw his family, and he felt a trip should be planned.

With no interests other than work, his body and health had suffered. Loving beer had created, as they say, a beer belly. He was now staying at an apartment furnished by Claire and her foundation, overseeing the reconstruction of his home and the lab at work.

Charlie was also hurt by the vicious personal attack on her. Her family was scattered across the country, and at times, her parents would pine to return to Vietnam, saying, "America is a land of opportunity with no soul."

She never married and had very few close relationships. Ditmer and Charlie's passion was in their work.

Living across from Ditmer, they drifted together. She helped him with the reconstruction projects and plans for both, convincing him to eat better, drink less, go on long walks, and talk along the Charles River, down by MIT.

Ditmer was much older than Charlie, but their common ground made age an observational prejudice. Charlie had nowhere to move to but was welcome to stay at the apartment as long as she wanted.

"My place will be ready mid to late October." Pausing, Charlie curiously listened as they walked. "You have become very important to me." He paused for fear that what he was about to say could make Charlie run away or put her in a very uncomfortable position. "You are welcome. I mean, I would like you to…" He could not get the words out.

"Live with you," Charlie softly spoke, and they stopped walking.

"Yes, that's what I'm trying to say."

"Can I bring my Buddhist Temple?" Smiling.

"Oh, course, God is welcome in our home."

She held his hand, and with glassy eyes, a feeling of salvation passed through her. Her loneliness and isolation had become intense since the incident; only Ditmer's spirit held her together. Now, squeezing his hand, it replied, "Yes!"

They continued their walk, but the world had become brighter, and for the first time in a long time, they both felt a sense of joy, walking at a brisker pace, admiring the sculler's race and practice on the river. It was a beautiful summer day in Cambridge.

***

Sally Pedroia is a character right out of a good book of fiction. Claire's Miss Moneypenny is competent, reliable, and dedicated. It is rumored that Claire tried to build a relationship with her long before she met Prisha. It is unknown what became of the situation.

Sally graduated from Miss Porter's School and received an associate degree from the Katharine Gibbs School as an Administrative Assistant in Science. While working at Harvard University, she earned a Bachelor of Liberal Arts through Harvard University's Extension Courses. As Claire's assistant in the Museum setting, she earned a master's degree in Anthropology from the University's Extension Course.

Her passion for her job and eagerness to take on any project place her in a unique and needed position. She is well paid, equivalent to an Associate Professor. She is a spinster with a lustful eye for beautiful women and handsome men.

She rarely goes out, offering to stay home and write erotic, romantic fantasy stories under a pseudonym, which she publishes in a very successful blog.

She keeps her private life in a locked steel trap that never opens beyond her thoughts, finding satisfaction in her imagination.

The recent events have given her an adrenaline rush. All her items were returned with an attached ☺.

48

The Pigpen of Power

Director Stanley Birk was summoned to Washington, D.C., departing the terminal at Washington Dulles International Airport in his *Men in Black* attire and an accompanying umbrella on this hot, damp June morning. Urged to light a cigar in the non-smoking zone, he refrained, impatiently stepping to the curb. A late-model electrical van pulled up to him. An electronic voice said, "Please enter, Director Birk." The side door slid open. Birk, entering the vehicle, realized there was no driver. An envelope with his name on it was on the seat. Opening it, there was a cell phone with a note. "Activate when the vehicle drops you off." That was all.

Birk was under the impression that he was going to the Pentagon, as he had in the past. Not so this time, dropped at the gates of Arlington National Cemetery. The vehicle quietly departed. Birk opened his umbrella as light rain fell. The cherry blossom season had completed something he enjoyed with his family a few years back. Again, wanting to light his cigar, but could not.

His thoughts were, "Why am I here?" A sudden fear struck him as he activated the phone. A version of MapQuest appeared with walking directions.

He was honored to be among many brave Americans who died for their country. Following the map, he came across JFK's memorial, the president's family, and the eternal flame, which gave him a pleasant flashback.

"Dad, what does eternal mean?" His young son brought a smile once again.

Continuing, he walked a great distance and stopped, coming to the end of the developed cemetery. It was a secluded wooded area with a narrow, tree-covered path. Thoughts of Tommy being a "Made Man" in the movie *Goodfellas* crossed his worried mind. Travelling the path, arriving at an opening, there was a farm with animals, a farmhouse with a big red barn attached, and fields with crops. He was looking down at his phone, guiding him towards the buildings. The place smelled like a farm. There was an old wooden sign: *Once the property of George and Martha Washington, and later General Robert E. Lee.*

He was directed into the barn and greeted by the stench of pigs and horseshit. Led to a recently used stall with fresh dung on the floor; there was a director's chair with his name on it. Director Stanley Birk sat in the chair, with the smell of freshly excreted animal manure lingering like cigar smoke.

The phone vibrated, and Birk answered it," Yes!"

"Director Birk?" The computer simulation replied.

"Yes!"

Morgan Strassa began by getting right into the meeting without any pleasantries: "I was harsh on you when we last spoke. What I said was true; your means could use a little polish." The electronic laughter was spooky. You did a remarkable job recovering the disc and the medallion, now in safe hands." Pausing.

"We have placed you in a position to do a job that cannot fail. This makes you a conceived villain. You have to learn to control your urges for the success of this endeavor. You are the right person for this mission, and I appreciate it, but I will come down on you if one thing goes wrong." Birk sighed.

"Mr. Birk, you do understand we are the good guys. There is an old expression that says the truth hurts. We keep the truth from children and loved ones to avoid hurting them. If the truth were ever revealed about what we are doing, it wouldn't be believed, but it could destroy the world's religions and economy. It just can't happen! Do you understand?"

"Yes!" He didn't.

"For the next twenty to twenty-five days, you are going into a specially designed program to help manage your drinking, smoking, anger, and stress. Beebe Schwartz will be filling in for you. Do you understand?"

"Yes!"

"Upon your successful completion of the program, we are not looking for a fucking angel, but improvement. A weekend with your children will be arranged."

Birk was excited. "Yes!" Thinking now, I get whacked.

"By the way, Birk, we have made powerful enemies. I will keep you posted." The conversation ended, and instructions were texted. The butcher puppet exited the slaughterhouse.

Directed to a nearby road, the electronic, driverless vehicle picked him up and drove him to the Walter Reed Army Medical Center in Bethesda, Maryland, which was not a long ride, where he was expected.

49

Return to Work

Skinwalker Souvenir

Claire returned home for the first time in almost two weeks. She played soft classical music, prepared, and arranged the flowers they had picked up at the florist on their way home into vases.

"Prisha, the house looks wonderful; thank you!"

"I live here too," Prisha said; Claire grinned sheepishly.

"Do you want to come to work with me in the morning? I'm going in early. You don't have to be there until later in the morning."

"Sounds good, later."

"I'll take my car. You can Uber, and we can ride home together." Prisha agreed.

Claire entered the dining room. "What's this?" On the dining room table was a piece of metal. Picking it up.

"Something that almost cost me my life." Laughing somewhat.

"What do you mean?" Examining the object.

Prisha walked into the room. "Souvenir from Skinwalker Ranch. I found it near the mesa, and the Skinwalker team let me keep it for my analysis. I brought it home for you. My version of a souvenir."

"This is mine to keep?" A child's joy exuded.

"Yes, dear, a toy for my baby." Prisha smiled.

"Thank you, Prisha. I appreciate this. You don't know how much." She hugged Prisha.

"I think I do. I know I'm your second love to your work." Joking.

"You're never second in anything, but this excites me." Claire smiles, finger over her lip, glasses on her nose.

***

The workday started early. Sally was informed of Claire's schedule. On Claire's arrival, she could smell the freshly brewed coffee. With a bouquet, she approached Sally with a good morning and a big smile.

"Thank you, Doctor."

"Thank you, Sally, for getting Prisha situated." Then, peeking around her office, she said, "This place looks great!"

"Everything is as good as before, even better. Your office is all set; Prisha has been using Genny's office. How is she doing?"

"Good, she's with her parents. We'll see her soon."

"That's wonderful." Sally getting back to business. "With the incentives you offered the contractors, everything is way ahead of schedule with the Museum and the Lab. The Museum will open on September 1, and the new exhibits will be displayed. Work will continue, but it will be open to visitors. The Museum director, who was, and I do mean, shattered by what happened, is more than happy with the progress. The lab is functional and will be completed in a few weeks, around the semester's opening."

"That's good to hear. Did you receive that envelope?"

"Locked in the safe. You can reset the password."

Claire poured a coffee, "Let me get settled, and then we have business to discuss."

Loving the challenging tone of Claire's voice, Sally was all ears. "Beep, and I'm in." Claire entered her office with a flashback of Genny broken on the floor. She put on her classical music. She was trained in the violin and cello and was in the mood for upbeat concertos. She placed the flowers in vases. When she came to Birk's spittoon, she took it out to Sally.

"Sally, donate or sell this, but I never want to see it again!"

Sally took the vase and smashed it into pieces. Claire was pleasantly taken by surprise.

"That was a Greek artifact." A befuddled smile.

"Claire, it's where it fucking belongs!" They both agreed and laughed.

"I need a few more minutes to get ready."

She went to the safe, pulled out the list, and reset the password. It was an extensive pamphlet with several pages of details on each person. Later, she would thank the law firm for its work. She beeped Sally to come in..

"How have you been, Sally?" Sally gave her a general idea of her life.

"How are you and Prisha?"

"Honestly, because of all of this, never better." She filled her in on Genny's procedure and condition, leaving out significant details.

"You understand everything we do from here on in is between us."

"Can you use a better phrase?" Flirting a bit.

"Secret, private, no one else to find out," Smiling.

"You can rely on me." In a sincere, reassuring voice.

"I know I can."

"Is Ditmer in today?"

"He and Charlie have been working daily, setting up the lab."

"OK, I'll check the lab in a bit."

Claire slipped Sally a piece of paper.

"This is the judge who signed off on the search warrants. I want to know everything about this person. Everything! Only you, Prisha, and I will know of this. Do not search with any of your devices. Go to the library and sign on with a generic public password."

"Ah! I like this." Sally replied. Claire smiled at her pitbull.

"Prisha will be in a bit later. You know what her classes will look like; give her a hand."

"She has been on top of it and putting together a course syllabus. I have her class lists. I'll give them to her."

"Good. Anything pressing?"

"Yeah, you have a meeting with the new president at ten."

"The first African American Woman President of Harvard University has such a nice sound. I will be there. Confirm if you must."

"Sally." Claire was as serious as she could be. "We are dealing with something of great importance to the government. Be discreet and be careful; we aren't going to get the medical treatment Genny received."

"I will."

"You are part of this small, important team and needed."

Sally nodded, loving the drama. She was returning to her desk when Claire asked, "Ghostbusters were here?"

With a huge grin, "They were here, and in your basket, you'll find their completed work order."

"The only copy?"

"Yes, the only copy." Happy, Sally went back to her work.

"Oh, Sally, one more bit before I forget,"

"Prisha and I were thinking of going to India for mid-semester break."

"If I may, the break is a bit shorter this year, though the semester ends a week earlier. The flight to India and back will take two days. Let me plan something for you over or around Christmas."

"That's why I can't live without you. Do it. I'll let Prisha know when she arrives. Thanks!" Sally returned to her desk.

Claire checked the list from the security company. It was satisfactory. She called down to the Lab. There was no answer. She looked at Sally's prepared agenda but could not focus and put it down. Her focus was on the need for some fine-tuning. When she walked out to Sally to ask her a question, she was not there. Claire knew where she went.

50

Uncovering the Signal

A Familiar Composition

It was close to 8 am, two hours before she met with the president; she took her bag and went down to the Lab. No one was there. The lab was looking spectacular, an Area 51 flashback. Knowing her way around a lab, she located the portable XRF analyzer. Examining it and familiarizing herself with it, she turned it on. There was a slight hum, and an LED panel lit up. She tinkered with it. There was a coffee cup on the table, and she aimed the machine at it and turned it on. Readings are shown on the LED panel. Claire knew the composition and was satisfied with the reading. Pulling out her souvenir from Prisha, she aimed the machine at it, and the LED panel illuminated with information. Claire did not understand it. The device enabled her to email the information, and she sent it to herself. She deleted the results on the XRF and returned the machine to where she found it. Claire was not tiptoeing around; this was her lab, but she was being discreet.

Returning to her office, she printed the results. Examining the chemical composition, she saw it had familiar signatures, but she couldn't be sure.

It was 8:45, and Sally had not returned. She called the lab on the university's phone. Ditmer's heavily accented voice answered.

He was pleased to hear from Claire and said he would be right up.

Charlie and Ditmer sat across from Claire when she handed Ditmer the XRF handout. He was surprised and wondered how she got that info. Everything had been wiped clean out of the system.

"Tell me what you think?" She inquired.

"Well, this readout is very similar to the disc we had. It also contains all the same elements used in space programs worldwide and elements found in stealth technology. Without seeing where it came from and recalling exactly what was on the disc and medallion, it's the same, but I believe it has more elements. If I only had the disc?" He stopped, recalling the horrible ordeal.

"I never mentioned this before." Charlie paused as the two looked at her. "I stored all my photos of this project in a secure foreign database. I have never mentioned it for fear of involving them."

"That's wonderful." Claire said, "But leave it be for a short time." Claire pulled out the piece of metal and handed it to Ditmer." He focused on it.

Voices could be heard coming up the stairs.

"Put that away!" Instructing Ditmer, and he did.

Her office door swung open to the pleasant faces of Sally and Prisha. "Excuse me! I didn't realize you were in a meeting." Sally said.

"If I may quickly. I was discussing the trip to India with Prisha."

"Whatever she decides is good with me," Claire responded. Prisha walked over to a chair away from Claire's desk and seated herself.

"Is it possible to meet around two o'clock today? I want to go over a few things we discussed this morning." Smiling Sally.

"Yes," Claire said, and Sally left, closing the office door on the way out, and returned to her desk.

"Prisha, pull up a chair and join us. Ditmer, you can continue."

He took the item from his pocket and examined it.

"Prisha explains to Dr. Winkler what he is holding. We have no secrets here. We are a team, and as our colleague Dr. Chevrolet says, we are seeking answers to find the truth." Claire stated.

Prisha detailed her experience in Utah, the wormhole theory, and the objects in the mesa. Charlie and Ditmer listened intently.

"You do understand where we are at. Our lives are in play here. I'm all in. I want to expose those who did this to us. I want to destroy Stanley Birk! I want to find the truth. You can back out. I do understand. Prisha and I are scientists and, for personal reasons, want justice. There is a war within the government, and we have many friends and an equal number of enemies. I don't know who or in what direction we will take. We are going to move slowly and under the radar."

Ditmer turned to Charlie when Claire and Prisha picked up a romantic connection between them, and he said, "I'm in, whatever it takes." Charlie repeated the sentiment.

It was nine thirty a.m. Claire told Ditmer to hold on to the metal, explaining what she had done this morning and telling him to do "whatever you feel is safe with it."

Charlie was also eager to investigate the item.

"Prisha, discuss our trip with Sally. Whatever you say goes." She agreed.

"I may visit my son and his family in Stuttgart between semesters," Ditmer explained to Claire.

"We can talk about that later, but I have a ten o'clock appointment and a good fifteen-minute walk. So, meeting adjourned!"

Ditmer and Charlie could be heard whispering as they descended the stairs on the way back to the lab.

Claire collected herself, went into her private powder room, freshened up, and gathered a few things while chatting with Prisha. "Ditmer and Charlie?" Prisha quizzed, and Claire cast a pleasant and approving look. They walked to Sally's desk and gave each other a peck; Sally, watching, smiled. Claire was on her way.

*****

The meeting with the president couldn't have gone any better. Claire and her associates supported a tenured professor at the University. The president promised to support Claire and keep her informed of matters related to the University. They shared a splash of champagne.

*****

It was close to eleven; Claire called Prisha as she headed back to her office.

"Hey," Prisha answered.

"Pri, what are you up to?"

"I was just checking on the construction of the new office." An old storage room adjacent to Claire's office was being converted into an office. It was going to be Prisha's. It had access to the corridor leading to Claire's lab entrance. "It's coming along great; it should be ready before Genny returns."

"Oh, that is good news." Pausing, "Pri, I have an important meeting with Sally today and would like you to be present."

"Sure. What's up?

"Can't say now, it's a research project, private."

"Looking forward to it," Prisha replied.

"Pri, ask Sally to order lunch for us."

"Ok."

"I have some errands to run and want to visit our people in the lab."

"No problem, see you when you get here."

"Thanks. Love you."

"Love you too." The call ended.

Claire went on to her next appointment. Her manicurist and reflexologist were awaiting her.

***

When she entered the lab, it was close to one. There was a good amount of activity going on. Finishing work was being completed. New artifacts arrived and had to be dated and documented before being displayed. Charlie and Ditmer were sitting at a table finishing the lunch that Charlie had prepared.

Pleasantries were exchanged.

"Any changes?" Claire inquired as she made an obvious inspection of the place. It could be heard, "Looking great!"

"I was able to retrieve all the old images; it was difficult because all the passwords and passcodes had changed. I'll email them if you wish."

"Thanks, Charlie, yes, just to me." She sent the images.

"I did a thorough examination, and the results are as you found, with one exception. There are heat signatures like those found on crafts re-entering the Earth's atmosphere." He raised his eyebrows.

"Always something new, this is great. Sit on this for a while; keep it in the family." We'll stay in touch. They nodded.

Claire could be heard saying, "This place has been upgraded." Ditmer and Charlie excitedly discussed the new additions and innovations.

"Claire, I have no idea how much you spent, but this is one of the most advanced labs on the planet." He grabbed Charlie's hand. Claire was surprised at their outward show of affection, hugged them both, and was off to her office; it was close to two.

51

One for All

The Anagram Revelation

Sally had set up a little round table in Claire's office. Lunch was delivered and served elegantly, with floral fragrances and beautiful soft music.

Claire arrived and said, "Give me five minutes." Then she entered her office and saw the setup. She turned to Sally with a huge, affectionate grin and said, "Miss Porter taught you well." Though seemingly impossible, Sally blushed.

Claire checked her nails and freshened up a bit, then returned.

Sally and Prisha were seated. Flowers were placed on the table. Sally had poured tall glasses of Sauvignon Blanc and set a file on the table. Claire arrived and thanked Sally, then said to Prisha, "Now, this is who we are! Do you agree?" They grinned. Letting more of her school duties slip through her mind, Claire felt young and in love, enjoying the balance of being a top secret scientist and a pampered world of love and indulgences.

"Let me make a toast," she said, giggling like a college schoolgirl. Unus pro omnibus, omnes pro uno," they toast and then start in on their lunch.

"Claire, your nails look gorgeous," Prisha said.

"I made you a three-thirty appointment. If you wish."

"I do. Thank you, dear." Sally admired their love.

"Enough of this slobbering; let's get on with business," Sally said, sipping her perfectly chilled drink. She opened the folder with three reports, one for each. Claire and Prisha read as they continued to eat.

"I had to promise a favor to retired Judge Morton, who is on the faculty. I bumped into him. He gave me access to a retired judge's history and files kept by the government. It's a historical site. I said it was for a research project. So, it's like this: the judge who signed the search warrants was a Federal Appeals Judge appointed by President Ronald Reagan. He is old and no longer seated, but has never resigned, elected for life. He has remained inactive until this event. Privately, he is a bit of an enigma. He has been connected to an active alien investigator, a Strom Garasans. If he exists, this man is in his late nineties or better. He has been linked to Roswell, Area 51, a group known as the Mystic 12, J. Edgar Hoover, and a friend and associate of Ronald Reagan, as you can see in your report." Sally paused.

They looked at the list, and there was enough information to conclude that Strom Garasans had been around and possibly connected to multiple conspiracies if he was still alive.

"Great work. But how can we connect the judge to the person or person who wanted the warrants?"

"Holy shit!" Prisha gulped her wine.

"This sounds wild, but Morgan Strassa is an anagram for Strom Garasans." Flushed face.

"Prisha, you are incredible!" Sally got excited. Claire was verifying the possibility.

"Remarkable!" Claire sensed a breakthrough.

"It makes sense, now." Prisha took a deep breath. "Nobody knows who this Morgan Strassa is. If he is Strom Garasans, then he's old, possibly connected to life support, using the technology that Genny experienced keeping him alive and mentally fit."

"Yes, that's very possible and likely. His name sounds familiar. I may have come across him while doing research. He wasn't a good person." Claire said with a concerned look.

"He's been around for 75 years. What is he hiding?" Sally pointed out.

"Or better, what is he protecting?" Claire sat in her classic pose.

"They took all our evidence, possibly proof of an earlier or alien culture. They confiscated it without regard to any laws or stretching the limits of the law. We must be careful. There is a secret here. Is it Pandora's box?" Claire was unsure of her course of action, but the scientist in her wanted to go forward. The price will be something significant. She looked at Prisha.

"Sally, continue your research very discreetly. I say this because I believe that lives are at stake. You can back out, which will never change my opinion of you."

"I'm in, one for all, all for one." Sally stood up and put her hand in the middle of the table. Prisha rose and did the same.

Claire clasped them both. "Please, god, help us make the correct choices?" in a whisper.

Lunch ended. Prisha went to get her nails done. Claire and Sally chatted while they cleaned the place. Then Claire sat at her desk in a mental chess match, trying to figure out this puzzle, wondering if it was worth it. She concluded, "I'm a scientist and will live or die by curiosity." She pulled out her contact list.

52

Home Sweet Home

The House remembers

Genny returned home; the place was close to normal. Some artifacts had been broken, but the team from the Museum was able to restore them. Some furniture was replaced or upgraded; the patio and garage were restored. Enrico's room was back in place, and his documents were returned. Her backpack sat in the corner when she saw it last, the emptied contents stuffed back into it. The basement was cleaned and modernized. The wine press was replaced. The one saving grace was that her wines in the cellar were not disturbed. Genny had agreed to all the changes.

She unpacked the few items she had taken from her parents' house and wrapped her rosary beads around her bedpost. They were not for faith in God but her parents' faith.

Checking the empty fridge and kitchen cabinets, sighing, "Food shopping time."

She puttered around, putting on some Diana Krall and starting her infuser. Orange mist with a twist of lemon filled the air as she romantically danced to *Dancing in the Dark*, with thoughts of Lucas in her dreams. She was yearning for contact. Still communicating with Claire in their foreign language, Claire promised her good news soon. Genny wanted to start her search for him, but was convinced not to. She agreed.

She danced and tried to erase the memories of when she slept here last. It wasn't easy. She settled down, went to the computer, a new Apple iMac, excitedly hit the keys, and searched Perugia, Pope Clement V, The Papal Residency, Avignon, Philip the IV, and the Knights Templar. She wanted to leave immediately for her Pa's birthplace, but was hindered by doctors' appointments, and wanted to get in touch with Lucas.

She sent Claire a coded text message. Claire replied that the crew wanted her to come over on Friday morning for a little get-together and lunch; classes began the following Monday. She answered affirmatively and was delighted.

***

Checking the garage, she saw her newly upgraded Jeep Wrangler and grinned. "The reports of my demise!" Laughing, she had read them and had to reassure her old friends that she was still here.

53

Rehabilitation and Revelation

Genny's treatment location had changed. A wing of the old Soldiers' Home in Chelsea had been converted into a rehab center for the elderly. A few levels below, there was a beyond-the-state-of-the-art, secure medical research facility.

Genny entered the rehab center and was greeted by armed military security and then taken to the lower-level laboratories. The place was active, and there were many patients; all were amputees or severely injured, young servicemen and women. She was pleasantly greeted by many of them.

She was then taken down a long corridor to an elevator, down a few levels, opening into a sterile environment. Genny was placed in front of a receptionist, tucked away behind thick glass. In a bureaucratic tone, "Please fill out and sign this waiver." It was a nondisclosure agreement. She read it in a glance.

"You have to read it, ma'am!" The receptionist said.

"I did, but I need a pen?"

"My apologies." The receptionist handed her a pen.

The agreement said, "This is a highly secured research facility, and you must agree under penalty of federal law not to speak or reveal what you see or experience here." She signed the waiver and was let into a hall with many examination rooms.

Inside were doctors and technicians working on what appeared to be robots, AI, or artificial life forms. She began to feel very uncomfortable, a sinking feeling. Looking down at the end of the hall, Dr. Isenberg was waiting for her arrival.

"Hello, Genny? How are you doing?"

"Strange place, Doc?"

"Yes, it is a research, rehab facility, highly classified."

"Is this necessary?" Genny felt a loss of freedom.

"I'm sorry, just a bit longer. A few more appointments." Talking with little emotion.

They walked into a private exam room. A nurse asked Genny to lie on a padded table. Then, the back of it was cranked into an almost right angle. The technicians were ready to take her blood pressure and vials of her thick blood and prep her for an EKG and an MRI.

Genny wanted to leave and became very upset with the Doctor.

"This is bullshit! You should have prepared me for this!" Starting to get up.

"Genny, this is necessary. Please be patient. You went through a lot, and we must know if you will be ok."

Genny took a big breath. "OK! But you should have prepared me!"

"My apologies, I didn't have time. I didn't think that this was going to be this intense. Genny, you have ten more appointments after today, only one more like this; by Thanksgiving, you will be done for at least six months."

Genny was still dissatisfied with the arrangement and began rubbing her imaginary medallion, remembering her cut.

She lost faith and trust in Dr. Isenberg and told him about her cut. He looked at it, and there was only a faint scar. She showed him the video of the healing incision on her phone.

"Am I one of those fucking things out there!" She was highly emotional, and her blood pressure was elevated to a critical level; her heart rate was racing."

"No, Genny, please relax and take a deep breath, and I'll explain." He watched as her levels returned to near normal.

"Genny, you received transfusions that would enhance your healing. I'm giving it to you straight, as I was told, and read." He began to sweat.

"It was experimental, your only hope for life."

Genny was feeling chills.

"It worked and was only temporary, I was told. Your body has adapted to it and has become part of your vascular system."

Genny didn't know what to believe but felt as healthy as ever.

"Genny, this is new to your system. You experienced a rebirth. Notice how quickly a cut or bruise heals on a baby. That's you."

"Am I normal, human?"

"Yes, Genny, you are you, but you are a better physical and mental version."

"It sounds like a biological enhancement."

"It is, but you are you."

"Can I have babies?" Almost crying.

Dr. Isenberg, with a quiet, sad look, had no response.

They continued taking tubes of her strange-looking blood, an EKG, an MRI, and then a battery of physical and mental exams. It was an exhausting day. Anxiety reigned; she was so unprepared that she never knew what was going to happen next.

She left the facility tired for the first time in a long time. When she got home, it was dark. She was hungry, and there was no food in the house. She went to bed and slept; for the first time in a long time, she did not dream.

54

Echoes of Support

When Genny awoke, it was past ten, almost thirteen hours of sleep.** She was depressed and hungry. Calling her dad at the market.

"T'Avio's how can I help you?"

"Dad, I need food?" Speaking like a child.

"GG, what's the matter?" Michael said with anxiety.

"I don't feel good, Daddy?"

"Mom started work today; I'll be right over; your cousin will be in shortly."

"No, Dad, I went to the doctor yesterday. I'm okay, a little down, but very hungry."

"I'll send something over immediately. You sure you don't want me to come over?"

"No, Dad, thanks. If you can put a little box of food together, I'll send you a hug."

"Hang in there for half an hour, and I'll send you something." Michael felt her voice improving.

"I love ya."

"Love you too, GG." Michael could see the store backing up and had to go.

Lethargically, she sat in her armchair, looking at her backpack and other items. The thought of yesterday didn't sit well. All the steam going forward had vaporized. Lucas was just a pleasant dream in a world of nightmares. Sitting in total silence, losing track of time, the doorbell rang. Her young cousin, who helped in the store, arrived with a box of groceries and a hot breakfast. Genny invited her in, but she declined and had to get back to work. The cousins hugged. Genny had been close to her older brother and sister, but she was a late arrival, and Genny was flying through life as the young girl grew.

Genny ate and ate and ate. Her voracious appetite and consumption revived her. She put on some quiet music and put the groceries away as the feeling of gloom and doom returned.

***

Claire answered her phone. "GG, everything ok?" No longer using code.

"No, not really." Claire could hear the sadness in her voice.

"What's the matter, baby?" Genny told her about the cut and the extensive, surprising examination, which included racing against robots and playing chess against a computer.

"And they want me to talk to a shrink. Oh, yeah, Isenberg doesn't know if I could have a family." Crying, in a deep depression. Claire felt sadness and guilt for withholding information from her. Sometimes, the truth must wait; that was her thinking.

"Genny, this is hard now. It will get better. You have come so far. Please have faith in yourself and don't give up hope." Claire delivers the message using the strength of mentorship and friendship.

Genny sniffled, "Claire, please be honest with me. Am I a

fucking robot? Am I some freakish artificial life form?" There was a long silence as Claire searched for a truthful response.

"You are Genny!" Genny disconnected the call.

Claire sat worried and called Michael.

"T'Avio's," In a pleasant voice, "How can I help you?"

"Michael, it's Claire."

"Oh yes." His voice dropped.

"I need your help?"

"What's up?"

"In a discreet, inconspicuous way, could you have someone stay with Genny tonight? She's depressed. I don't think she should be alone."

"I know. She just called, and she was as sad as I could remember. She wouldn't let me come over."

"Think of something, please! Please make certain that she returns to the University tomorrow. We will cheer her up."

"I'll do my best. I'll walk over there with Ginerva and have dinner with her."

"That sounds good. Thanks."

Claire put everything aside and activated her plan a few days in advance.

Michael texted Genny and told her that he and Mom were bringing supper.

"K" was her text.

"Around six."

"K," Genny turned off the music and returned to bed.

***

Stanley Birk had completed his rehab. He wasn't the best patient, but he passed the standard set for him.

Upon his release, he was handed a note that said he would be taken to a private resort in Virginia Beach. He would spend two days with his family before being picked up and returned to the Pentagon.

The Birks had a splendid weekend. The kids wished to see him more often, and his ex-wife hoped she would never see him again. He was picked up and taken to the Pentagon.

***

Two armed military guards took him to a small room. It was soundproof; he could hear his head hum. One chair was placed in the center of the room. A familiar voice asked him to be seated.

"Mr. Birk"

"Yes."

"I hope your stay at Walter Reed was beneficial?"

"Yes." Wanting to light a cigar.

"I will restate: This is a difficult job. You are the best and most suited person for it. You must be smart, clever, tactical, and always in control of yourself. You can be fearful, extremely vicious, and sadistic, but you cannot; let me repeat this with emphasis: YOU CAN NOT KILL!"

"Thou shalt not kill! Thou shalt not kill! Thou shalt not kill!" Continuing in electronic brainwashing.

"Repeat it?"

"Thou shalt not kill," Birk spoke quietly, wishing for a drink.

"Mr. Birk, with emotion after me. Thou shalt not kill!"

"Thou shalt not kill." Birk was a little louder.

"Mr. Birk, you don't seem so convinced. We have until the end of time for you to get this right."

"Again!

"Thou shalt not kill."

"Again!"

"Thou shalt not kill." Finally, after more than fifty tries. Birk replied.

"THOU SHALT NOT KILL!" Thinking of killing himself.

"Excellent, Mr. Birk. It will be hard to convince the world that we are the good guys. Why do you think we saved that pretty pain in the ass?"

There was no reply.

"Please, Mr. Birk, do not let me lose my temper. I want you to think of what's going on here; you are acting like a fucking dimwit. Now, please take a moment and consider why we did what we did for this girl. Some people believe they have power, but it is only an illusion that I perpetrate. Now, why did we save her soul?"

"THOU SHALT NOT KILL!"

"Good boy, Mr. Birk, you'll be sent back to Boston from here. Beebe Schwartz will update you on your files and return to her Houston duties. Understand?"

"Yes."

"Mr. Birk, I only wish… that you and I would happily get along. I have responsibilities, and I apologize for being harsh, but it must be done. Enjoy your flight." They took Birk away.

55

Unexpected Delivery

Genny was in a deep dream state, in which she was being slashed and cut by robots, as they laughed, the cuts kept repairing themselves. The doorbell rang. Breathing heavily and sweating, looking at her phone, it was six o'clock; it must be her parents sighing, not even showering today, and finding her way to the door.

"Who is it?" she jokingly said.

"Pizza man!"

"What the fuck!" Whispering as she peeked out the door. There was a man holding pizzas with his back to her.

"You have the wrong address. It's not my order, thank you."

He spoke, and she replied, "Yes, that's my address, but I didn't order."

He mumbled a note: "Genny be right over, got tied up at the store. Love, Dad."

She checked her phone; there was a message from her dad, asking her to call him.

"I haven't got all day, lady!" The delivery person was getting impatient, so she called her dad.

"Hi, GG, we'll be right over." Michael knew she would check.

"OH!"

"Got to go, wrapping up a big order. See you in about twenty; start without us."

"I will not! I will wait!"

"Lady, I've got to go!" The pizza deliveryman was getting more impatient.

She opened the door, not looking at the deliveryman, took the pizzas, and was closing the door when the delivery person stopped the door with his foot.

"What, no tip?"

She turned, ready to apologize, dropped the pizzas, and leaped into Lucas's arms.

Life is so fragile; in a moment, a fraction of time, emotions and feelings can magically reverse. She hugged him so hard that he was losing his breath. He did the same. They kissed and hugged, staring into each other's eyes, crying as they held one another; the breath of their lives filled the other.

Lucas picked up the pizzas and placed them on the kitchen table. He held Genny at arm's length and just admired her. He really couldn't believe what he was seeing.

"My god, Genny, you look, look." Stuttering, the words couldn't come out. "I prayed for you. I prayed that you didn't suffer." Genny just stared at him.

Genny pulled him closer to her, closer to her face, and kissed him with so much love and passion that they fused into one. In a breath, Lucas said, "We have so much to catch up on."

"Would that your early evening NPT is telling me that the rain check is about to come… due."

"Clever gal." Smiling, "Morning wood…would, but the pizza is getting cold." Jokingly.

"Lucas, I want to share with you right now." Genny pulled Lucas into her bedroom.

'You mean a piece." Laughing.

"Lucas, I need you now. Please! I'm sorry." Her body was bursting with passion.

Lucas kissed her. "Genny, you have been the only thing on my mind these past weeks."

Hours later, the heated pizza was great. They talked. Genny hadn't realized she was being protected and placed outside the loop. Tomorrow, that would all change, and she fell asleep in his arms, returning to her bliss-filled dreams and fantasies.

Lucas got up to use the bathroom, got his phone, and texted Claire, "All is well. See you tomorrow." ☺

Claire loved the text.

56

Morning Light

Genny slept silently and a bit late. Lucas had stayed for the night. He washed his clothes before he went to bed. He was up early, showered, and prepared breakfast for Genny.

"I thought it was a dream." Telling Lucas when she got up.

"No, it's real and wonderful." Morning kiss.

"Shit, I haven't showered in two days!" She was a little embarrassed.

"Don't worry about that foolishness. Life is much more important."

"Yeah, I'll be right back. I'm cleaning up." She turned on some music and freshened the area with the infuser."

"Eat first?" But she was gone.

A little time later, she returned in a robe and with a towel wrapped around her wet hair.

"We have time. Let's talk," Genny said, munching on toast. She told him about her experience up to this moment, and he affectionately hugged her.

He then told her about his new position at his university.

"I think it's great!" She was happy for him.

"It is. It's a dream come true, but does not compare with you." He was sincere. She hugged him.

"Where are you staying?"

"Claire got me a furnished apartment until I can find something else."

"Where?"

"It's in Dorchester, not far from the University."

"Do you like it? Are you happy?"

"It's convenient and free. The neighborhood is a little bit sketchy, but not too dangerous. I'm within walking distance of the school."

"Where are you considering moving to?"

"Probably something a bit larger and more of a higher end. I want you to come over and feel comfortable."

"I don't think so!" She was adamant.

"What do you mean?" Puzzled

"Lucas, we've only known one another for a short period. I'm being honest. We've been through so much, and our relationship has moved at a quasar-like speed. I've had erotic dreams of you. I've watched over you while you were in the mountains. I have such a feeling and a bond with you. I feel I've known you from another life. I want to be near you all the time." Pausing. "Please, don't run out the door." Genny took a deep breath and looked into his dazzling, sparkling blue eyes.

Lucas started running towards the door, stopped, turned around, and grabbed Genny. Her towel unraveled, falling to the floor as she slipped out of her robe. They kissed as her naked, warm body pressed against his.

"Genny, this makes no sense. You come to me in my dreams. I think of you obsessively. I want to be with you always. I feel that I've always been with you. I don't know why. Cupid has struck me hard."

"I've noticed," Genny smirked.

"Genny, I've never felt this happy before. I love you!"

"I know how you feel because I love you." They kissed, fell to their knees, and embraced on the floor, making passionate love as though they were on their honeymoon.

Both breathe the bliss and joy of life; Genny said, "You live here now and always. Lucas Johnny Chevrolet, this is your home. I need you; I want you; I love you!" They kissed. "We are in this thing that has only begun as one."

"I'll get the Honda in tip-top running condition for you, and we can share everything."

Lucas flashed that beautiful smile. "Why, you thought I was leaving?" Genny playfully punched him. "That hurt." He wasn't joking. They agreed that they should shower again and meet their friends.

57

AGENDA

Reunited-Recomitted

New England Fall was in the air on this cool, breezy late August day. The meeting was scheduled for noon. Prisha was settling into her new office. Charlie and Ditmer were in the lab, readying for the semester and the re-opening of the Museum. Sally was at her desk interviewing candidates to assist her and Claire with the school workload. Claire was in her office, going through her list of connections, confidants, and political friends, trying to locate Morgan Strassa, aka Strom Garasans, with no luck, but not giving up.

Genny grabbed her old, faithful, worn, beat-up backpack and looked inside. Everything seemed to be stuffed as it had been when she had last used it. They left and headed for the University.

There was a comfortable silence as Genny drove the Jeep Wrangler, holding hands until the traffic no longer allowed it.

She pulled into her parking spot. RESERVED FOR DR. CANTALUPO. All the education and dreams of teaching and research, leading archaeological digs, and writing papers, the engines that pushed her, were now stalled. Stale in her mind.

Questioning who she was, what she was, and where she was going. She just stared out the front window of the car.

"Hello! Where are you? Come back to Earth, Genny." Lucas joked but worried about her.

Security greeted them without any issues, and they walked up to the offices. Genny was getting flashbacks of being carried up the stairs and how everything was blurred then, but was now coming into focus.

"Genny, you, ok?"

"I'm sorry, I just got a flashback."

The last candidate for the day walked past them and headed out through the Museum, which was open but not to the public.

Sally greeted them with hugs, and Prisha exited her office and did the same. They walked into Claire's office, and Genny felt queasy. Claire hugged Genny like a sad mother with her sick child, then greeted and thanked Lucas.

The soft classical music and floral delights created a pleasant and comfortable atmosphere. Steps could be heard coming up the stairs. Ditmer and Charlie gave their salutations and greetings.

"I'm so happy we all are here today." Claire was taking charge. "I've converted my lab into a lab and a small private conference room." They entered a continuing floral fragrance and soft music. The room was enlarged. There was modern media equipment and a new chalkboard. "Phones will not work here; quickly make arrangements with your party if you expect a call. The dampening field is better than the security of the President of the United States. Continuous tracking and monitoring of all electronic activity are performed. The room is free of all types of electronic waves. The computer has no Wi-Fi but is connected with a closed Ethernet cable. Nothing enters the computer unless a coded password accesses it; there is no email or anything. It's a real virgin. I've yet to use it."

There was a small round conference table for seven people. In the back of the room, a buffet table with healthy food platters, coffee, seltzers, and pastries, per Sally, sat. They seated themselves.

"Sally, you are part of this, but please take care of the university's business today. For now, I will keep you up to speed." Sally was leaving when Claire said, "No, Sally, wait. Put the answering machine on and an out-to-lunch sign on your desk. Lock my door and come join us." Sally was honored.

"Thank you, Sally, for the set-up," Claire said, and they all thanked her.

In her classic pose, Claire said, "The last few months have been the most dramatic and life-changing experiences one can have. Our lives have changed forever. The road we were traveling is a long-lost trail; events that have occurred cannot be changed. Look around; we are all scientists; we have been trained, and our special DNA pushes us to seek, search, and explain events. Our goal is to advance knowledge. We use science to advance science with new technologies. We are continually searching, looking for answers. I kid you not, this group, we are scientists and philosophers who seek knowledge and truth!" Pausing to take a sip of water, the group was getting so inspired by her words, Genny held Lucas's hand. Charlie looked at Ditmer as though Claire was talking directly to them. Prisha was so proud and in love. Sally was never happier.

"I am committed to the truth. I say this with my life, what has been taken from us is nothing but the 'Rape of the Disc and Medallion.' And I cannot let this crime go without impunity; it is in my gut. However, we must be methodical and cautious. I don't know what we seek. It may be something that we do not want to know. I don't know, but I cannot stress enough that I cannot continue this life with the thought of this mystery never being explored. Before we get into an agenda, please let us know how you feel about this. You can always back out."

"Ditmer, we have talked. If you like, please share with our family," Claire stated.

"I am a scientist, yes. I always search for answers and the truth. We have been wronged. I have been wronged. The world is filled with hate and prejudice, and it's easy to ignore if you're not the target, but when you are, it's painful. You think of your family, which makes you sad, but makes you want to fix it. By God, I'm so into this puzzle with my life." In his deep German accent, he concluded.

"Charlie, how do you feel about this?"

In her shy, quiet voice, "I repeat Ditmer's sentiments. I, too, was violated by hate. Ditmer and I have become one harmonious voice, and I will forfeit my life for this project. Hopefully not!" They laughed.

"Sally."

"I'm all in for the adventure. What is life without risk? I would risk my life for the people in this room."

"Lucas."

"The last few months have so much turned my world. I, too, was treated like a criminal. I thought they took everything I had, but I've found everything I ever wanted; here in this room is my life, and I plan to fulfill its destiny."

"Prisha."

"I know who and what we face, but I don't know why. I seek truth and have found and understand deeper love in this adventure. This feeling is worth my life. However, I do share Charlie's sentiment." They laughed approvingly.

"Genny."

"Well, kiddies, I think I've already given my life." The room got very still. "My rebirth has brought new visions and a lust for this quest. It's raging in my, possibly synthetic, bones. I'm so thirsty and anxious for the knowledge that we seek. I don't know what happened to me, but like my family here, it has brought me trust and love in you." Turning, looking at Lucas's face, and squeezing his hand, she sighed. He winced.

"OK, grab food or something. We're going to continue." Claire stayed in control.

58

Secrets, Samples, and Theories

"So, it is agreed that we are going forward cautiously and as discreetly as possible?" She perused the intense, serious looks on their faces and felt sadness and love. Claire was confused about where all this sentimentality emanated from, but of course, it was from her hollow, overly planned childhood, except for her mom; love then was a foreign and distant land. They all nodded.

"We just want to find answers. Our innocence has been ripped from us. We can't forget that, but let's try going forward with fresh perspectives. Love for the work we do! Try not to seek revenge for what was done. Which is difficult for me, but I will try." Again, the beautiful faces of her friends were filled with concern because of Genny's words. "We can share this challenge with this family and live with it with our closest love." They all smiled, even Sally.

"We have two new events to discuss today. Lucas and Genny, this is new to you. Sally, you are aware of what's going on," Claire stated.

"Charlie retrieved the disc and medallion images from a secured off-the-grid cloud. With great difficulty, she was able to download them." Charlie handed each a folder with the images in color and 3D of the disc and the medallion.

"We are familiar with these, so take them home, review, and study them."

"The second, Charlie, handing you the following images." After the folders were distributed, Claire explained how these images came about. She produced the metal sample and passed it around the table.

Lucas held it for a moment and, reading the data that Ditmer had prepared, asked, "Ditmer, does your analysis indicate that this is a similar foreign matter?"

"Yes, Lucas," Ditmer replied.

"You also indicate that burn patterns are consistent with those we find on reentering craft in our space program."

"Yes, I'm confident of that."

"So, you conclude that this foreign material is from space."

"The evidence points to that, but sometimes technology can fool us. Sometimes, you think we are advanced, but we discovered we were working with Troglodytes' tools years later. With the technology we have today, that is my assumption."

"So, this is part of a spacecraft!" Genny interjected. Ditmer shrugged his shoulders. Genny touched the metal and got a vibration from it. She did not say anything.

"Do we have a 3D printer?" Lucas asked.

Ditmer, with a proud smile, said, "The best on the planet."

Lucas got up and began to walk around the table. "I contend that the first disc was a set of instructions, planted, wanting it to be discovered. For what reason, I have no clue currently. Genny's medallion is some Rosetta Stone, mystery solver, or a map leading to an answer to a question I have no idea." He continued his circumnavigation of the table as they listened.

"This is going to sound crazy and almost deus ex machina, but." He paused.

"Expound, Lucas! We are dealing with things we have no idea of or control over. This is why we are here!" Claire spoke in a powerful voice.

"Two scientists, Robert Grass in Switzerland and Yaniv Erlich in Israel, embedded DNA with a blueprint into a plastic rabbit, and when they took a piece of the rabbit, the 3D printer reproduced it. It's a little more complicated than that, but that is the gist of it."

"I've read of this. What are your thoughts?" Claire stated.

Still circling the room, he walked over to the chalkboard, picked up chalk, placed it down, and then, in natural schoolteacher fashion, lectured on the possibilities of taking the metal sample, or part of it, as an advanced technology that may contain DNA and reproduce the item.

"What you say may be possible, but if it's large—and probably is—then what? Tell me more about your thoughts on this technology?" Prisha inquired.

"Prisha, my thinking is that the 3d printer has limits. It will tell you if, under certain conditions, it's possible. The printer will display an image of the completed item from my readings. So, if it just reads it, we can get an image. Of course, we have no idea if there is DNA in the matter."

"I know the Swiss Federal Institute of Technology Director in Zurich. We will have to buy two programs as an experiment because I'm certain one goes with the other. First is the process of interjecting DNA into inorganic material to understand how it works, and second is the 3D program of reading and writing that process. It will be expensive."

"This is why we are meeting. Ditmer, do it! It's a technology the University should have; anything beyond our budget, the Foundation will fund. If the school responds slowly, the Foundation will buy and gift it to the Lab. Just buy it; Sally will give you the information," Claire demanded.

Ditmer nodded. "I will get started immediately after this meeting."

Genny was excited. Lucas sat down.

"Any questions? We are going to explore Lucas's theory.

"Yes." Genny dug through her backpack and pulled out a small container and a wrapped paper towel, placing them on the table."

"What is it, Genny?" Claire inquired.

"Metal shavings from the disc and medallion when Ditmer took samples."

The room was blown away, astonished at this revelation.

"Lucas, Ditmer, if this works, how will the program reproduce the foreign metals?" Sally asked.

"I don't know," Lucas replied as Ditmer shrugged.

"Any questions? Let's take a ten-minute break."

"Sally, can you check the phones?" Claire whispered.

They all checked their phones as they exited Claire's lab.

59

Journeys Ahead

"I would like to close today with our statuses over the next few months. We have…I know I have reevaluated my life. Some matters must get done, and there are things that I want to do. The things I want to do are overriding what the world calls my responsibilities. I'm not being very lucid. I only want to spend time with people I care about and love." She searched for Prisha's hand.

"At the end of the semester, Prisha and I are going to India. She is returning home for the first time as a married gay woman. This may be very difficult. India has no same-sex marriage laws, but there is favorable legislation. We are not quite sure what to expect."

"I have spoken with family members, and they are cautiously optimistic. Chennai is not Cambridge. This is who I am, and hopefully, we will be received well." Prisha was confident.

Genny, always having a strong family connection, got emotional and sniffled. "If they don't love you, something is wrong with them."

"Genny, it's a cultural thing. You can be loved but ostracized."

"So, we are leaving at semester's end," Prisha said.

Ditmer said, "Charlie and I have grown very close since the incident. We will live together like a couple, a family. Over time, she has become part of me. We enjoy our shared moments and have so much in common. Sometimes, you don't see the beauty and look beyond it. When you do see it, hope it's not too late."

Charlie held his hand. "We are going to Stuttgart at the end of the semester to see Ditmer's family. I am fearful that I won't be accepted. I've always faced non-acceptance. It has never been a problem, but now a funny-looking Asian woman who is more than half your father's age and size may not be…" She paused. "I'm used to loneliness and isolation, but I do not want Ditmer to get hurt." She sighed.

Genny and Sally went over and hugged the diminutive treasure. There was silence.

"I'm going to Amsterdam at semester's end." Sally boasted, "Life is too short, and I need a good blowout!" They all laughed at the prim and proper woman letting it out, wanting to feed her lonely, dark side.

"Get a tattoo or two for me." Genny teased. "While you people are on vacation. I will be on a quest. Medical issues have delayed my departure."

"Genny, it's so good to see you," Sally interrupted, and then they gushed about how happy they were to see her looking so good.

Genny rubbed an ancient and unique gold crucifix that her Pa had given her, which she had in her childhood bedroom, replacing the medallion. "I'm going to Perugia to find Enrico's vault. I have a good idea and plenty of time to do research."

"Your office is open; check out Prisha's office before leaving. GG, research here; we would love your company. You can also organize for next semester." Claire stated.

"That sounds good. I think I will," Genny replied.

"Also, it looks good in the eyes of the G men," Claire laughed.

"Lucas and I will be living in sin at my home." Lucas made an embarrassing, funny gee-whiz face.

"I plan to accompany and guide my lustful companion on her trip."

Genny blew him a kiss. "Hopefully, it will include Avignon." She said.

"This sounds good," Claire went on. "Let's make a leap of faith. Genny and Lucas are successful or plan to go to Avignon. We should meet up with them."

Claire went to the computer and looked at a map of Europe. With a big smile, she said, "I got it. Monaco! We'll spend two nights in first-class suites, relax, and play with the wealthy. I promised Prisha a bit more luxury. My treat, kiddies." Picking up on Genny's remark, Claire was enjoying her new cerebral freedom.

"Let me coordinate all of this. Come to me, and I'll happily set up your trips." Sally was excited.

They all agreed, and the meeting ended. Prisha showed Genny and Lucas her office. All the accessories she was used to were magnificent. They wished her well and went to Genny's office. Lucas was quite impressed, and she showed him the passageway leading to Claire and Prisha's offices. Once back in her office, Genny kissed Lucas. "Let's go visit the store and Dad. Then we can shoot over to UMass and your office if you like. Then head to your apartment and pick up some of your belongings." He thought it was a great plan. It was a long and pleasant day.

60

The Past Present

A Man Reborn

Stanley Birk awoke refreshed, feeling physically energized for the first time in a long time. Free of alcohol and tobacco for close to a month. He found his way down to the complex's gym and did a quick, brisk, thirty-minute workout. He returned to his condo, showered, and headed to work. Stopping at Paci's Delicatessen for a breakfast sandwich and black coffee. Quickly eating the sandwich at a small table, he took his coffee back for a refill and then left. His gait was slower than usual, smelling the greenery and flowers as they would soon fade into the fall season. Children holding hands with their parents on their way to school, pigeons and other birds fluttering, escaping wily squirrels. Stanley felt young and alive.

Entering the Federal Building, he was greeted with great respect. Today, he thanked the guards for their service. He conversed, joked, and talked about sports for a few minutes. The guard at the elevator welcomed him back. Stanley told him what a fine asset he has been to him. The guard smiled.

Stanley didn't go into the elevator but went to a kiosk and made a purchase. He then took the employee elevator to his floor.

Getting off and passing his team, he greeted them with hellos and asked how it was going. They were surprised but pleased about the director's new approach. They had heard rumors of his rehabilitation treatment.

Tina was at her desk and was surprised to see the Director walking down the corridor.

"Good morning, Tina." An unfamiliar pleasant voice.

"Good morning, Director." Smiling.

Stanley handed her a bouquet and said, "Thank you."

"Thank you!" She was stunned; this was the first time she had received flowers at work.

"When you get a chance, I'd like to review last month's events. I talked with Beebe and said you can bring me up to date."

"Yes, sir." She was so excited about the flowers and looked for a vase. She knew one was in Prisha's old office, so she went and retrieved it.

Tina was approaching middle age. She had lived her entire life in the North End of Boston, selflessly caring for her parents until their passing. The niece of the head of a renowned Boston mafia family received the respect of a queen. Every political door was open to her. She didn't flaunt her access, but she was taken care of when her name came up—living quietly in her waterfront apartment, enjoying her work, and vacationing in Bermuda. Today was pleasantly different.

Stanley beeped her in. He was holding a stack of files, placing them on the edge of his desk. Stanley looked at her, maybe for the first time, and saw what a beautiful and beautifully kept woman she was.

They went over all the files. Stanley didn't get upset over how Beebe Schwartz ran his projects, but she was nowhere near as organized as he was.

"We'll figure this out, get things straight, no problem." He spoke.

"So, how have you been?" Never once in the time she worked with Birk did he ask her about her personal life.

"Do you want to know? Or are you just being polite?" Tina was frank.

Stanley smiled with a rugged yet good-looking face and spoke tenderly, "I'm interested." With a quirky shrug of his shoulder.

Tina thought he was brainwashed after the events, but if he wasn't, then he was charming, something missing in her life.

"Well, I still miss my mom, who passed a few years back."

"I'm sorry about that." He was sincere.

"It was crazy around here for a bit." She spoke.

"I apologize; I had problems, took them to work, and abused my fellow employees. I was a jerk!"

Tina thought, is this a transformation, a mask, or who Stanley Birk is?

"Director."

"Stanley, in this setting." He smiled.

Tina returned it.

"Well, I like this, Stanley." She said as he laughed.

"I do, too; I hope he stays awhile," he said as Tina laughed.

"Listen, this is a combination of business and pleasure. Are you free after work?" He pleasantly asked.

"I am. My boyfriend of decades left me for a younger woman." She got despondent and collected her thoughts, "I think if my father or uncle were alive, he wouldn't." She looked serious.

"Well, if you're not going to have me thrown into the harbor?" He knew the family history.

"No! I was joking. That's how I felt, but it would never happen." Laughing.

"I've had this hankering for clam chowder, and we could get dinner at the Union Oyster House out back here." Birk charmingly.

"Mr. Birk."

"Stanley," he said.

"Stanley, you can understand my hesitation; this transformation is so sudden."

"I agree with you that it is. Have dinner, and I'll explain the treatment."

"Ok!" She spoke. She was well acquainted with the restaurant within walking distance of her home.

"For now, business as usual." He smiled at her like a typical boss would.

Stanley thought about Tina for a few moments, then got back to work.

Tina made a cup of tea and thought about what had just happened. She wondered if he had changed or if she would end up in the harbor tonight. She laughed at her dark thoughts and got to work.

Nothing was mentioned until it was past five thirty, and employees left for the day.

61

Union and Oyster

Stanley came out of his office, full of energy and ready to go to dinner.

"We still on, Tina?"

Returning from the lady's room, smelling fresh and looking very attractive. "Yes," turning around and checking to see if anyone was about, "Stanley." They laughed, returned to his office, and took his private elevator to the garage. A small path led to a short flight of stairs, crossing Congress Street; they had arrived.

The historic Union Oyster House on Union Street in Boston has served customers for two hundred years. The building, which has roots in the American Revolution, is a National Historic Landmark. The restaurant is not fancy; it's all about the ambiance of history. The food is traditional and delicious.

They walked in and headed toward a crowded bar. At the end, two seats were open, and they grabbed them.

"Holy shit! What do we have here? Stanley the Boxer and Tina A. never use her last name." Frankie, aka Cheesecake, welcomed his old friends.

"Fucking Cheesecake!" Stanley hugged his old bartender friend.

"Still a fucking asshole, Frankie?" Tina spits out in a former North End accent.

They chatted for a few moments.

"What you having, Tina?"

"Give me a glass of Jack; I'm not driving." She winked at him. "Rocks."

"Stan."

Birk started to drool at the sight of the liquor, and he could smell cigar smoke on Frankie. "Cranberry, soda, and a slice of lime." His demons backed off.

"On the wagon?"

"Yup."

"We'll take care of you," Frankie replied. Tina sincerely patted Stanley on the hands; they seemed to be shaking.

"Cheesecake, we need chowders!" Talking loudly as the bartender served at the other end of the bar. Cheesecake flipped thumbs up.

Stan and Tina were enjoying the evening.

"I haven't been out since, well, the breakup. I don't want to talk about that, but I feel I'm over it, accept it, and want to go forward with my life." Birk confessed.

"Good for you, Stan. I feel the same way. I'm just sad that I gave up so much for that man, no marriage, no children; he led me on, fooled me. My friends told me to dump him over a decade ago. I was blind, but I'm happy." Pausing as Stanley listened intently to her story. "I don't know who I'm with tonight, but I like this guy."

Stanley smiled. "Yeah, I like this guy too," Sighing.

They ate and talked. Tina looked at Stan, thinking, "You never know what goes on in someone's head." Tina was feeling good.

They got up, and Tina would take a short Uber ride home. Stan said it was such a nice night, "I'll walk you home." She looked at him, not knowing his intent, but liked it, and then said, "I have a better idea." Stan looked confused.

"I'll walk you home." He smiled, and they held hands and walked to his condominium complex. Tina spent the night.

62

The Metal Speaks

Ditmer immediately contacted the Swiss Federal Institute of Technology. They said they would have to contact their partners in Israel and inform them of their intentions. The institute indicated that the transaction with Harvard University was a matter of formalities and found it encouraging that they could put their product into the hands of such a prestigious institution.

Early the following morning, the institute contacted Ditmer with the transaction details. They said they would invoice Harvard University, but Ditmer insisted they pay upfront. The deal was done.

Ditmer and Charlie received a voluminous email and were informed that FedEx, International Overnight Delivery, would deliver additional software.

They printed it out, syncing their equipment with the proper software. It was extensive and would take a few days to understand and set up. Claire was informed. She told them there was no need to rush; we were anxious, but nothing would change in a few days.

It was hectic. Classes had begun, and the new and improved Museum had reopened. The Peabodys would be proud.

Claire got a call from the university president. She and the head of the science department were informed of the donation, and they were thrilled. She joked with Claire, "Not bad for the first few weeks in the office." She thanked Claire and said she would send a personal thank you to the foundation. They never asked what it was for.

When they got the program up and running, it was midday, midweek. Ditmer texted Claire and said the program was set up. He wanted them present when they tested for the possibility of DNA in the metals, which would be after five o'clock.

Claire asked Sally, Prisha, and Genny to meet with her in her lab. Sally and Claire entered the room, greeted by Prisha and Genny, who were seated.

"My back door girls," Claire joked.

"Listen, everything is ready to go today at five. That is the DNA testing. We will walk to the lab separately, as inconspicuously as possible." They nodded their consent.

"Genny, get Lucas over here, somehow, discreetly, use telepathy if you have to," getting silly.

Genny, deep into research, had come in the last two days and was enjoying her time with the girls. She was scheduled for another check-up tomorrow and informed Claire.

"That's okay, but tonight could be a little late." Claire checked the time.

"That's ok. I'll get Lucas here." They went back to work.

***

They had all arrived. The lab was super high-tech. The 3D printer and its electronic components took up ample space in the back of the lab, which was once the main storage locker room; a more extensive, futuristic, technical storage area was added to the back of the building.

The 3D printer will create a three-dimensional digital model from the DNA. It then creates layers of material in succession, making the object.

Everyone had left for the day. Charlie set up chairs so they could relax and watch the experiment.

"As you look around, you will notice one of the world's best-equipped, most advanced science labs; I am proud to be part of it." They all listened to Ditmer with great interest.

"You understand this is just an experiment with a possibility of failure. I wanted you here, firsthand, to see success or failure." Ditmer looked at his audience, continuing, "My thinking as a scientist is as follows. We keep coming up with discoveries. Things that are right in front of us change as we learn or understand science. Our colleagues in Switzerland and Israel have made an incredible discovery; that's how science advances: one thing leads to another. You get ideas, and then you build upon them. Lucas said this might be God's act, leading us to discovery. Although very well stated, I do not think it's that, but rather sound scientific thinking." Ditmer never looked or sounded better. "Before we know for certain if these artifacts are from an advanced technology, I logically conclude that their science progressed the way ours does. I have confidence in this experiment."

They cheered him on. He laughed and proceeded to the 3D printer, placing the piece of metal on the table. He turned the machine on. A laser started to scan the metal. Ditmer programmed the machine to search for DNA or any material that could replicate the metal.

The machine was working; you could hear it thinking, for five minutes, nothing happened. Charlie made a few adjustments, rotating and turning the metal over, as Ditmer recalculated the printer. Nothing happened.

The group sat like they were in a movie theater, without popcorn.

"I'm sorry," Ditmer said when suddenly, an image appeared on the large six-foot LED screen. It showed the schematics of a curved panel with all kinds of markings that looked like measurements. It was in a grid showing where the piece fitted into place, like a piece of a puzzle, with other parts consisting of a larger assembled object. Then suddenly, all kinds of text appeared on the right column, assumed to be the materials used and their chemical structures.

They watched the sci-fi movie in breathless silence.

A message flashed that read, "Area too small. Lacking rebuilding elements. Replication possible, time 192 hours."

"This is amazing!" Lucas declared.

"I had confidence," Ditmer stated.

"It looks like a part for a section of some craft. Can you print everything out? There is no need to replicate the item currently." Claire spoke.

Charlie printed multiple pages and handed them to Claire.

"Well! What do you think?" Claire asked.

"Let's get copies to analyze it over the next few days."

"That's a good idea, but as few copies as possible," Claire stated.

They discussed the object when Claire said, "Charlie and Ditmer share a copy, as well as Genny and Lucas. Prisha and I will share this copy." Holding it up, "Sally, you do not need a copy."

They agreed, but Sally looked disappointed.

"Sally, you can review this copy in the office," Claire said, making Sally feel not left out.

In the meantime, Ditmer was setting up the disc shavings for scanning. The group settled down. The process was repeated.

The disc appeared on the screen like a spinning gyroscope; analysis of the materials and an incredible amount of information populated the screen. The 3D computer read, "Analysis complete. Complex alloys require additional time for replication. Replication time 46-48 hours." It listed the additional metals required for the project.

"We've captured the information. Do you feel any need to replicate the disc? Charlie has also supplied her images." Ditmer asked.

"We have all the information; the disc was our Nobel Prize." Genny was laughing while getting shuffled, flashbacks of her journey.

"We should do what we did with the Skinwalker piece, make copies, and study," Prisha said.

They all agreed.

Claire checked with Ditmer to see if the information would be stored safely in their network. He implied that it should be okay.

"Just OK!" Claire snapped at him.

"I'm certain it will be safe; we are just familiarizing ourselves with the new system." Ditmer felt assured that Claire was up on and aware of the safety protocols.

They all agreed not to replicate the disc at this time.

The process with the medallion fragments was the same. The printout had a long narrative. Replication would take 12-18 hours. They agreed to replicate it. Some information was missing from the 3D images that appeared on the original medallion. They would like to revisit the medallion. Ditmer and Charlie wanted to see how well the printer worked. Genny wanted her medallion, even a copy.

Claire told them to review the material and that we would meet on Friday at her lab. She wished Genny well on her doctor's appointment. Sally left, saying she'd see Claire and Prisha in the morning. Genny and Lucas headed back to East Boston separately. Claire and Prisha went home to the South End. Charlie and Ditmer attended the lab and worked on replicating the medallion.

63

Breakfast in Bed

Truth and Surveillance

Stanley awoke; Tina's warmth felt comforting. He gently lifted her arm, got up, and used the bathroom. He slipped on his workout clothes and headed quietly towards the kitchen, where he placed a note, "Down to the gym for a thirty-minute workout."

Returning to his flat, he noticed the note had been taken. By the bedroom door, there was a sticky note. "Breakfast in bed!"

Stanley entered and was served a warm breakfast. It was still early; Stanley showered and readied for work. Tina dressed and made a cup of coffee.

They rode down the elevator to Tina's waiting Uber. They kissed and would meet at work.

Stanley repeated yesterday's path to his building; it was still early.

He was sitting at his desk, sipping his coffee, enjoying his new full-of-life feeling. He began reflecting on his work. Knowing what he had to do and how he had to do it, he started feeling short of why. The discs, the medallion, were more of a mystery to him than all the parties involved, and he never thought of questioning his superiors. The power and impunity excited him. Now, with a clear, open mind, he wasn't so sure.

There was activity outside of his open door. The day was unfolding. He started going through some of the typical files. The belief was that he and his team were investigating UAPs to verify them and not to disprove them. Today, he was uncertain that it wasn't just the opposite.

Do your fucking job and stop thinking so much was his message to himself.

About forty-five minutes later, Tina, as attractive as ever, walked into his office.

"You're late!" Barking loudly and sternly, his voice could be heard beyond his office.

"That's one thing you don't have to worry about." Winking.

"No, you've got to get working, it's late!"

She was hurt and went to her desk. Sitting down, she noticed a bouquet of roses in a vase under the desk with a note: "Thank you for a wonderful evening. Got Ya!"

Tina floated into his office and handed him a file.

"Director, this is an urgent matter." He took the file, and she then returned to her desk.

Director Stanley Birk had two teams. The research team had all the visibility; the security team lurked in the shadows. He held a report from his security officer. It needed to be discussed, so he arranged a meeting with him and his team after work.

Stanley wanted to meet them at Grill 23 & Bar on Berkeley Street in Boston. When he called, no reservations were available, but after speaking with the manager, he got a reservation for two, for him and Tina. The team would meet in the lounge.

Later that morning, Tina came in with some papers.

"You busy tonight?"

Tina replied, "No."

"I have a meeting tonight with the security team. It should take thirty to forty-five minutes. I'm meeting them at Grill 23. Would you like to come?" She smiled. "You can't sit in on the meeting, but you can relax and have drinks and appetizers while waiting until the meeting ends. We have a reservation for dinner when the meeting is wrapped up."

Still smiling said it all.

The Director and the team leaders sat at a bar table and had drinks; Stanley had cranberry, soda, and lime. They told him that Claire and her associates were shielded with the most up-to-date security. The lead agent said, "They will continue to try to infiltrate their defenses, but it seems they have systems that evolve with every threat."

Stanley said, "They are frightened or are hiding something." He told his team, "They are no longer a threat."

"Has something happened in my absence? Why did you pursue this?"

"That bitch Schwartz has it in for them. We do our job." The agent explained.

"That Randolph lady has deep pockets and contacts. I don't think we should mess with them for no reason." The Director explained.

"Sir, as I said, while you were away, Beebe Schwartz asked us to keep monitoring them." Another agent added.

"Schwartz was always in contact with the Boss." A third agent added.

Stanley was taken aback but tried not to show it.

"She has worked with Dr. Mishari-Randolph, and she couldn't emphasize enough the brilliant mind she has, and her wife is her equal. She said they are true scientists and will always follow the truth. They have unlimited resources and could be a threat." Explained the lead agent.

"A threat to what?" The Director shrugged.

"Finding the truth!" The lead agent replied.

"Gentlemen, I don't live in a fucking cave, but please, between us. Will someone tell me what the 'truth' is?" They shrugged their shoulders. The Director sipped his drink and saw Tina sitting, drinking, and watching the news.

They all lifted their glasses.

"Listen, we are soldiers, and we will follow orders; I will be told what to do and will pass it on to you. We are a team. Some of you have received commendations for our recent work. So, let's continue, as a challenge, to break their security. In the meantime, assign a team to follow all of them. Take photos and videos, then evaluate what you have. We have the workforce for now, and they are not our main concern." Birk barked.

"Are we violating their civil rights?" A new, younger agent asked.

They burst into laughter. They were all in agreement, and the lead agent, in an ass-licking maneuver, said, "It's a perfect solution." They finished their drinks and left. Stanley joined Tina.

"Enjoying yourself?"

"I am. There are a lot of well-to-do people in here."

"Yup, Tina, but we are more important."

"I agree." She gave him a quick kiss and excitedly said, "See, see over there!" Not wanting to point, she directed her gaze.

"You're shitting me!"

"Mr. Wonderful, Chef Wonderful, what's his name? It's *Shark Tank*." Tina rattled off.

"That guy can be such an honest S.O.B., and I love him!" Stanley chirped.

"I love him too; he makes that show work!" Tina said.

"I agree."

"Did he just say to that man, 'You're dead to me!'" They laughed and then were off, seated for dinner. It was a wonderful evening; they chatted and had so much in common. Returning to Stanley's pad, they watched *Shark Tank*, the show where entrepreneurs' dreams are realized. They made love.

64

Enhanced

Genny's head was in a swirl, thinking of last week's appointment and figuring out who she was. She got to her appointment and went to the examination and testing rooms. Dr. Isenberg was nowhere to be found. A young, handsome man in an Air Force uniform greeted her.

"You must be Genny?"

"Nice guess." She rudely replied.

"I'm Dr. Briscoe, and I will be with you today."

"Where's Isenberg?" Cooly.

"He's not needed today."

Even though she didn't have total confidence in Dr. Isenberg, she felt safe when he was present.

"So, you're a captain?"

"Yes, I am." He smiled.

"And you went to medical school?"

"Yes, I did. Tufts University, right here in Medford. I was fortunate to qualify for the Armed Forces Health Professions Scholarship Program, HPSP."

"I'm familiar with the program."

He continued, "Then additional military medical training, and if you don't believe me, my degrees are hanging on the wall," pointing "right in there." He smiled, and the ice was broken.

"Did you get much financial assistance?"

"Yes, just about all of it. I have a military family background, which was a perfect situation." Dr. Briscoe explained.

"So, what's up, Doc?" Flirting with the young doctor. He was about her age or just a bit older.

"Today will not be like last week. I'm going to take your vitals. We are going to have a chat. Then, do a few mental and physical activities. Genny, they are like games." In a gentle manner, he then took her vitals.

Genny read his diplomas. "You're a shrink?"

"Kind of." Laughing, "Genny, relax and enjoy today; you are special, very special to us. We're not here to hurt you, but to check and make sure you are okay. You had such a traumatic experience, and sometimes these experiences take time for you to understand and adjust to."

Genny was relaxed.

"First of all, I want to apologize for last week. Someone should have informed and briefed you on what they would be doing. You have every right to be unhappy with the experience. If I'm here, that will never happen again. When you leave, you will receive a list of your upcoming appointments and what each will entail."

"You better be here!" Genny was pleased.

"Can we have an honest talk? Doctor to Doctor?"

"Oh, here comes the shrink talk," laughing. "Yes, we can." Genny was as relaxed as she ever was.

"You have heard this before, but I will repeat it." He had her before and after charts with photos in front of him. He didn't let Genny see them.

"You had terminal injuries, and the only course of action was with experimental procedures meant for military personnel injured during active duty. How do you feel about that?"

"I didn't have any choice in the matter. I'm frightened by my abilities and sensitivities. I don't know my body and fear I don't know myself."

"Genny, we are trying to learn exactly what your capabilities are. However, I assure you that you are you. What abilities frighten you?"

"My strength and endurance, without actively staying in shape, I have never felt better. I remember everything; I learn instantly, and my mind operates so fast that I can simultaneously talk, think, and do equations. Sometimes, I think I know what people are thinking. I never said it to them, and not that clear, but like hunches."

"You have been treated with an agent that cleared all the brain's pathways and accessed areas that are not normally used. They will become normal to you over time and will develop as you want to develop them. What are you sensitive to?"

"All of my senses seem enhanced, especially touch." She stopped.

"Sexually, you are extremely aroused. It's okay. We can talk about this."

"Doctor, it's like nothing I can explain or imagine; when I'm with my partner, every cell in my body is filled with joy and pleasure."

"This is not a side effect, but something you must control and live with."

"Oh! I can live with that." Smiling.

"The next question may be awkward, but it's important and I must ask you." Genny gave him a silly sideways look, and he then continued. "Do you or think about masturbating?"

With a goofy smile, blushing, "Nooo. I hope you don't use that as a pickup line."

"Sorry about that." They chuckled. "It's for the soldiers and their ability to keep their focus at all times." She was okay with that.

"If we could change anything, what would it be?"

"Doctor, the truth being told, nothing. My world has never been better. My only fear was that I was a robot, some AI." She got very emotional.

"Relax, Genny, just breathe and relax."

"To be truthful, some procedures and materials used to save your life are also used in experimental AI. I assure you that you are not a robot. You are Genny, physically better, smarter, but the same girl you were."

Genny was happy with that.

One last question for this session: "Do you still dream often?"

"I dream every night, last week after the exam, the exception, but I dream every time I close my eyes. I dream I leave my body, dream about the future, dream of the past, all in vivid color, and remember every detail."

"Does that bother you? I can prescribe medication if you want."

"No, doctor, I like my dreams. If you want to be honest, I will. Sometimes my dreams are so erotic and real, and when I awake, I'm out of breath from the ecstasy."

"Yeah, I can see why you would want to dream." He withheld his laugh, but Genny could see through him. Laughing, she liked Dr. Briscoe and felt she could trust him.

"So, do you have any questions, or if you think of things you want to discuss over the next few weeks, make notes or mental notes, and we can discuss them? You and I have seven more appointments. We'll meet like this for the next six weeks. You will have a complete medical check-up on the seventh, and your last week will be with me. Dr. Isenberg will supervise your medical check-up. Now let's go have some fun."

"Yes, one question, Doc, how is my reproductive system? I'm concerned about this. Dr. Isenberg kind of just blew it off. It did upset me."

Looking into her eyes, he said, "It is better than ever; all your parts are ready to go. If you want a family, then you will." She sighed and smiled.

Genny felt better, somebody she could talk to outside of her private life. Today was going well.

The doctor then took her and tested her for clairvoyance, psychokinesis, and telepathy. An assistant blindfolded her, and then she was placed into a maze with noise-cancelation headphones; she had to find her way out of the labyrinth, and she did.

"Genny, how are we doing?"

"This is interesting and fun." Smiling.

"One more test, and that's it today. OK, Genny?"

"Oh! Oh! The day was going too well."

"No. No. This will be fun. It's a swimming test. Were you not on the intramural swim team in college?"

"This is going to be fun." Reassuring her, "There's an assistant in the locker room," pointing, "who will aid you in getting ready."

Genny returned and was connected to waterproof wireless conductors all over her body. Then, she was placed into a small swimming pool, where she was to swim against various currents, all being monitored. She did it for close to half an hour. The test administrators looked at the doctor in utter amazement.

Genny enjoyed the workout and got ready to leave. She thanked Dr. Briscoe and said she looked forward to next week's appointment. He was also pleased with the day's work.

65

Puzzled Pizza

In her car, she texted Lucas, "Day went well on the way home. I will pick up pizza. Love ya"

Lucas replied, "Just leaving; I will pick up some beer. Love you."

They got home almost at the same time.

"Sierra Nevada, yum." Genny smiled.

"Pepperoni, I hope?" Lucas anxiously asked.

Genny flipped open the lid, and there it was.

Genny's house was updated. The patio was extended, and part was screened in, opening into a pergola. It sits on a precipice overlooking the harbor, feeling like being in Rome and looking out over the Tiber River. The screened-in portion has a spiral staircase leading up to an entry and out to an open deck, which can also be accessed on the second floor.

New England weather is fickle, and today it was warm. They took their dinner to the pergola, along with yesterday's printout. They conversed about how their days went, ate pizza, and drank beer.

Lucas spread the documents over the table.

"I'm starting to make connections with some of the symbols, and I think, with the information you had originally deciphered, that the disc is a set of instructions. I'm getting lots of hints from the metal schematics, using the symbols, I can figure out which are related to certain assembly parts, cross-referencing them with symbols on the disc," Lucas said.

Genny, tired from today's appointment, said. "It's just puzzled pieces."

"Genny, don't you mean puzzled pizza?" He held up a slice, and she came over, laughing, and took a bite. Then she kissed him and then returned to her seat.

"Lucas, it was a long day. Let's fuck this thing for a bit; let's enjoy the pizza, beer, sunset, and each other." He held her hand as the sun set over Charlestown.

***

Stanley and Tina kept their private affair an essential focus for the next few months. He would bring her a flower daily. Stanley was meeting and understanding his employees, and the camaraderie and morale of his staff were never higher. It was a very good time.

66

A Little Bit of Disc and a Little Bit of Data

A Final Gathering

Claire looked around the table at the faces of the anxious crew. She had received bad news that she didn't even have time to tell Prisha. They were going over their notes like enlightened college students. Ditmer was going to present Genny with the medallion. Claire inhaled and began the meeting.

"I'm enthused that we are going to share some interesting information. I can see it on your faces." Genny could read Claire's body language and see that something was wrong.

"We are on a scientific journey. Are we motivated by science or revenge? I know what I have said in the past. I look at your happy, beautiful faces; our lives and relationships have never been better. Is this quest worth changing all of that?"

Prisha stared at Claire, knowing something had just happened because moments before, they were discussing the medallion.

"Don't answer that question; let me tell you something. The local jurisdiction has no interest in or understanding what we are doing or what recently occurred. They follow orders. Someone high above them has an interest in our work." Turning to Prisha.

"Dr. Mishari-Randolph," Prisha, stunned at the title, "You have been compromised. Beebe Schwartz has sold you out. She was responsible for you not going to Houston, whereby you would have been the Director, and she would have worked with Birk. She is complicit with him and his activities and even has a closer relationship with Morgan Strassa." Prisha was hurt, but got no sympathy at this time.

"The good news is that this Morgan Strassa cannot penetrate our security. The bad news is that, as of today, we are all under surveillance, 24/7. This will be our last organized meeting. We will work independently if we decide to continue and report back to me, and I will disseminate the information again if we continue."

The room fell silent.

"I can't get a fix on this, Morgan Strassa, but I will continue. I think we are dealing with an issue that goes beyond our government. The danger may be too risky." Claire stated.

"For me," Genny said, "I wouldn't want anybody here to get hurt, but all that I have learned or ever been taught, the things I have sought, have culminated into this. I have no desire to do anything except to pursue this venture. We want to know and understand where we came from. Life has a meaning and a purpose. I think we are on that path. Somebody or something has put us on this track. I will do what you say, but I am seeing this through."

"Genny, I love you, and I say this because I care. This threat is real. We are onto something, and they appear to be using every means to keep us in place. Will they kill us and our families, do physical harm, cause financial disaster, or public humiliation? I don't know. Is this worth it?" Claire was all in but wanted them to understand what they were facing. Genny's spirit lifted hers.

"When we leave here today, behave in a normal fashion. This is our last group meeting!" She stopped talking, hugged Prisha, and whispered, "I'll explain later, don't feel bad. Schwartz is an asshole; she doesn't know that you know." Prisha laughed but was hurt and pissed off.

Claire continued as though she had not made the warning statement.

"Genny, I was happy to hear that your appointment went well."

"It did." She smiled.

Ditmer presented the medallion to Genny. She held it and passed it around the table. The printer worked with detail.

When it came back to Ditmer, he said it was replicated, except that no raised 3D images appeared or could be found.

"What do you think?" Claire asked Genny. Claire knew and was proud that Genny was about to go rogue, and her appointments only grounded her.

"It feels the same weight and looks, but it's not the same. I can feel it more now than ever before. Or I should say I can't feel it. There is no spirit or soul in it. It's a piece of metal. I think it would be dangerous for it to leave the premises." Genny stated.

"I think that is wise," Claire said.

"I would like us to share all we know as a group. Then, continue independently with our research. I'm going to Italy and following this through, even to visit my relatives." Genny continued, "I have plenty of time and resources to dig deep without suspicion. If there is a breakthrough, we can share it; we still work together and are friends. I plan to sit in on Prisha's classes and maybe guess lecture and the same with Lucas, but my focus is on finding an answer."

"Let's review the disc or whatever?" Claire asked.

Prisha spoke quietly and said Claire could speak for her. They had studied the items together, and she knew where she stood. She was still thinking about Beebe.

Sally said she couldn't make heads or tails of the items but would ask questions if something was made clear.

Charlie spoke for her and Ditmer, saying, "Translations are not our specialty, although we encounter many artifacts we can identify. Ask any technical questions, and we will try to answer."

The meeting was moving as Claire anticipated, except for wanting to assuage Prisha's hurt feelings.

67

Truth and Translation

Lucas stood up and thanked Claire for the opportunity at his university. Now, walking around the table, he started. "I'm also going to talk for Genny in the next few minutes. She was tired from her appointments and went to bed early. She likes her dream sleep." It was an inside joke. "We previously discussed your findings, which were eradicated, about the earlier disc research. I stayed up late, and the following is my analysis and theory of what may be happening."

"The disc was intended to be found and dated; at this time, I do not know why. However, it is a set of instructions. Backtracking, I used the writings with the Skinwalker metal and could identify characters matching descriptions in the schematics. I cross-referenced them with the disc and the medallion. Using this result and adding to your research, I was able to pick out phrases that read almost like the Ten Commandments, but with more instructions to be taught by someone like a missionary. My thinking, reading into this, is that they, an advanced early civilization, had advanced technical abilities and could and wanted to manipulate humans with fear. They wanted to be worshipped and considered, as the word came down, as 'Gods.' There are recurring themes: not killing one another, souls, free will, and tricky translation. These ideas were to be taught and passed on. I believe they stayed on until, I'll call it, religion became part of their everyday existence. Any questions?"

"Lucas, I'm glad you are part of this team," Claire stated.

"Me too; I mostly dream about you." Genny reached out for his hand.

"So, you think they are aliens, and they started human civilization?" Sally threw it out.

"Scientifically, I don't know. As a possibility, and being a scientist, I would like to get an answer. Sally, that is a rational deduction with some evidence." Lucas answered. "I was doing similar research before becoming part of this group. My new, now lost book was about this line of thought, with no concrete evidence but a lot of clues. These discoveries are like a missing link in my research. So, for me, it goes much further than just looking at the material before us."

"If I can continue with my theory on the medallion." Pausing, "I believe the medallion was not intended to be found. It contains much of the language as the disc. I believe it was a symbol with instructions passed down to a priest or a shaman, whom their people could identify as a spiritual leader. They, in turn, would pass the medallion on to the next shaman, or a ceremony upon their death, an election, or something, as we have studied in ancient cultures, and the medallion would always contain the 'word of God.' Just a theory. I also believe the original 3D image you experienced was verbal instructions from God to the shaman. That could not be replicated, and Genny felt it wasn't there. Just my observation. Any questions?"

"Lucas, that puts things into a context we can logically follow," Claire stated.

"I have one more request for Ditmer and Charlie. I noticed what appeared to be numbers and markings on the medallion, inconsistent with the other writing. Can you clean that up?"

"I believe we can. If you look at Charlie's photo, we can get a better, magnified image. If possible, I want to check these writings on the medallion and compare, maybe see if they were created at different times."

"That would be so helpful!" Lucas replied to Ditmer.

"I will get it to you one way or another later today."

"That's great, thanks," Lucas replied.

"So, for now, these formal meetings will discontinue, but we will work together and have safe areas where we can talk." Claire ended the meeting.

They talked and exchanged ideas before discreetly returning to their jobs. Lucas and Genny went to her office while Claire and Prisha remained alone.

"Prisha, you have a right to feel betrayed; try not to be upset. These people have been exposed; thankfully, you know who they are." Claire said, feeling the sadness and disappointment on Prisha's face.

"I'm more than a little upset, but shocked and hurt by the betrayal. I was used! It's Beebe. I trusted her. She was my friend. Yes, you had to bring it up with the group; we are transparent. To say I'm not hurt would be a lie. Who am I kidding, Claire? I'm crushed!" Prisha let out a sad sigh. "I work hard, do my job without an agenda, then people close to you hurt you when you're not looking." Claire gave her a reassuring hug.

"Pri, people suck; however, we know their agenda and will play it along those lines," Claire advised her. They continued their discussion and left early.

Sally returned to her desk and cleared her afternoon schedule to go food shopping.

Ditmer and Charlie were up to their necks at work. The Museum opened, and they helped tag and document new artifacts. Ditmer was assigned graduate students to help them catch up. Charlie worked on the images and got a good picture of what appeared to be numbers. Ditmer verified that the numbers and markings were much more recent than the other material. He glanced outside and saw that Genny's car was still in the lot. He quickly put a package together, along with an artifact in his hand, and walked over to the Museum, displaying the artifact as he walked. This was not an unusual activity. Sally was on her way out, and he handed the envelope to her, asking her to give it to Genny.

"What's up with this artifact?" Sally asked. He shrugged and left inconspicuously.

Sally whispered loud enough so he could hear her, "Thanks, Sherlock!"

Sally returned upstairs, paged Genny, and said, "There's a package on my desk. I'm leaving for the weekend. Have a good one." Genny thanked her and reciprocated; Sally left.

Genny got the package, and they reviewed it.

"Genny, these, what appear to be numbers, were scratched in at a later date," Lucas said,

"So, what's your thinking?" Genny asked.

"A shaman gave the medallion to Rico. This must have had some additional meaning. I only call these numbers because I extrapolated figures from the Skinwalker metal's schematics; however, they look like numbers, and I am unsure about the other markings. I think we or I can make something out of this over time."

"They look like numbers to me," Genny said and paused.

"We must be careful and stay within our routines," Genny said.

"I agree, by the way, you're coming or guest lecturing in my class?" Lucas said.

"Why you have a problem with that?" Smiling.

"Love it! And I cannot wait." They kissed and wrapped up their belongings. Genny had viewed every document and was confident she could recall it all. Lucas had dropped Genny off earlier that day, using one car to go to dinner without the two vehicles, but they got takeout and more beer.

68

Connections and Coordinates

Calm Before the Quest

The semester moved along without any hitches. They would meet and talk in the safe areas, but did not raise the attention or come under suspicion of Birk's men.

The key to unraveling the mystery was Genny's visit to Italy. Sally had made all the travel arrangements for the group. Everything was business as usual and going well, so the sting of their violation lessened, and the quest seemed to soften. The fall in New England and the joyous environment of a university campus made living pleasurable. Claire and Prisha were never happier, though some trepidation of possible rejection on their trip to India created subconscious anxieties.

Charlie and Ditmer privately got married and were living happily in their new home. They continued their long walks and healthy eating habits and had become complacent, but they also feared rejection in Germany.

Sally continued her very private life, revealing on her blog that she was going to Amsterdam and would blog daily, getting a tremendous response. Also, compiling her short works into a book and self-publishing with KDP (Kindle Direct Publishing) was a success, and she was making money.

The quest for Lucas and Genny was only beginning. Genny would visit and lecture at Lucas's University. They lectured as a team, and the school was thrilled at the response they were getting. Luminaries in their field would appear in their class, and they would later see reviews. They began to write a book on their research, but revealed it to no one.

Genny continued with her appointments, and they went well; she revealed her dream of being cut and healing, but said it has never reoccurred. The doctor was satisfied. Genny only had the primary physical and a last session with Dr. Briscoe, which she was sad about. He had become a trusted sounding board for her emotions. Over that period, Genny was tested as though she were in the military, using tactical procedures. She learned and enjoyed the art of survival and self-defense. The military was so pleased with her accelerated progress and understanding of the operation that they asked her if she would consider teaching at their facility. She told them she would think about it over the holidays.

For two months, Genny and Lucas spent days and evenings trying to crack the numeric code. One night, while sipping wine and smoking a joint, Genny sprang to her feet, surprising Lucas.

She screamed, "SERENDIPITY!"

"What?" Lucas buzzed and stunned.

"Lucas, I saw numbers configured like this in my tactical training." She took the numbers and made a few adjustments. "Do you see it, lover-boy?" She rubbed his thigh.

"No."

"Look very closely and think. What have we been looking at for weeks?" She squeezed his thigh.

"Maps. Oh, fuck me!"

"Later!" She smiled.

"They're fucking coordinates! You are a genius!" They hugged and jumped around like they just hit the lottery. They cleared the table, wrote the numbers in large print, and then used a secure search engine to see where they were. The first came back as a location in Avignon, Palais des Papes, the fortress of the Papal State in Avignon. The second location immediately popped up: Palazzo delle Canoniche, Perugia Cathedral.

"Ok, now we have something to work on," Genny said.

"Lucas agreed."

They got lost in this moment of discovery, drank, smoked, and went to bed to sleep on it.

The following morning, Genny got up early, did a yoga workout, and jumped on the spin bike, killing it. Lucas awoke to the sound of the bike.

Genny shortly joined him in the den, sitting in their customary spots on the floor. Sitting across from one another, holding hands, they started breathing in rhythm as they meditated. Electricity flowed from Genny to Lucas: the morning routine was spiritual. Finishing, Genny made them smoothies, and they sat silently on this Saturday.

"I think the Avignon location makes sense," Genny said.

"Perugia was a Papal Residence," Lucas answered.

"Yeah, but Clement the V wasn't buried there," Genny said.

"My thinking is that these coordinates may have been marked recently. We don't have the original to confirm this. Rico was given the amulet, and then he gave it to you. This has been passed down for millennia, and to you!" Lucas, raising the inflection of his voice, then deduced. "It's the vault."

Genny agreed because it was something to go on, and they wouldn't know until they were physically there.

"Soon enough!" Genny sipped her smoothie.

***

Director Birk and the agency operated smoothly and calmly during the fall months. His team investigated several unidentified objects and leaked those sightings that the department thought suitable to the press. The investigation of Claire's team continued, and no unusual activity or movement was noticeable. Birk's team would have difficulty figuring out what Claire's team was doing and if it was clandestine or covert because research, working with artifacts, and teaching were their professions. Their crime was that they came close to a secret truth during their everyday business.

Stanley and Tina's relationship grew. They took a short vacation to Bermuda under the guise of official business and planned a later trip to Bimini in the Bahamas. The thought of his kids was always present, but Tina made him forget about his ex-wife.

Birk pondered his past, the intentional and unintentional hurt he caused people, knowing there was nothing he could do about it but move forward and try to improve.

69

India

Arrival in Chennai

The Emirates flight from Boston's Logan International Airport, at 2305, to Chennai International Airport had one stop in Dubai. It flew twelve hours and fifteen minutes to Dubai, with a one-hour forty-minute layover there. Then, it flew to Chennai for a four-hour ten-minute flight arrival at 0240, plus a day later. It was an 18–20-hour journey over several time zones.

Sally had arranged to fly Claire and Prisha first class, Gold Frequent Flyer, on the Boeing 777-300. The accommodation was equal to flying in the best hotel in the world, with advanced technology, gourmet food and service, an onboard shower, and a spa.

On their arrival, they were greeted by a representative of the hotel where they would spend the next eight days. ITC Grand Chola, Chennai, was not a 5-star hotel; it achieved seven stars and is one of the twenty best hotels in the world.

Claire had Sally book the best suite for her and Prisha and a block of luxury suites for their family. The ride from the airport to the hotel was about ten miles, a half-hour, and would take them through the city's heart, where 4,700,000 souls densely resided.

Chennai, formerly known as Madras, is located on the Coromandel Coast of the Bay of Bengal in Eastern India. It is the capital of the State of Tamil Nadu. It is a major technological center known for the best modern WIFI in India. At one time, it was the home of the British East India Company. It has a diverse culture whereby the old slowly fades into the new. The climate is warm, 70-80 degrees in December.

Chennai and Tamil Nadu are considered the most liberal city and state in India regarding the acceptance of gay rights. However, members of the LGBT+ community are still battling discrimination, arranged opposite-sex marriages, excessive bullying, suicide, and family rejection. Until 2018, gay sex was a punishable criminal offense. There is legislation to pass a same-sex marriage equality law, with significant opposition.

Delayed at the airport, their early morning ride was at rush hour. Prisha viewed familiar streets with unanswerable thoughts floating about as the sun rose. Claire, who has traveled the world, was still amazed at the abject poverty that sat next to so much prosperity and how ancient cultures, an ox-pulled wagon, holding up traffic, as a motorized rickshaw was passing it, all worked together. Claire loved this contrast, but seeing young children begging for some coins was sad.

Prisha observed Claire's intensity from that classic pose.

"They have laws for beggars; I don't know how enforceable they are?" Prisha explained.

"That's interesting." Claire pondered as they sat in traffic longer than expected. Neither cared, as they enjoyed the culture and each other's company.

"Everything will be okay," Claire confidently assured, holding Prisha's hand, who quietly sat with a vacant, timorous expression.

Their limousine arrived. They were greeted like royalty, checked in, and confirmed all the reservations. Their family would spend two nights at the hotel. Claire was told that complimentary champagne and breakfast would be brought to their suite.

Their flight was so luxurious that sleeping on board was not a problem, and they weren't that tired. The suite was magnificent, with a breakfast veranda and a splendid city view. They had their breakfast and the day to themselves. Their families would arrive tomorrow for two days and nights.

Prisha's family home was a more than modest traditional courtyard home in the southern part of the city. Her dad was a successful leather manufacturer and exporter, religious, highly respected, and esteemed in his community.

Prisha had an older sister, Shreya, who was married and had three children. Her cousin and best friend, Anika, was married and had two children. Their families and Prisha's parents would be guests of the hotel and its luxurious amenities.

Prisha contacted her sister and cousin and planned to meet the following day.

Today, the girls would rest, relax, tour the city, and eat out.

They shopped, made special arrangements, and picked up gifts for their family. Then, they took a ride out to Marina Beach, where Prisha showed Claire some places she used to go. They planned a late lunch at a local establishment. Prisha was concerned about leaving the gifts in the car, so they returned to the hotel, had a late lunch there, relaxed at the spa, sat by the pool, and then returned to their suite.

70

Leather and Lights

"Tonight, I want to take you out." Smiling at Claire.

"By your look, it looks like fun." Claire returned her look with a coy smile.

They arranged for a driver to be at their disposal.

"Where to tonight, ladies?" Their chauffeur politely asked.

"*The Leather Bar*," Prisha replied.

"Not quite what you think, dear," Prisha answered Claire's curious look.

They drove in silence as Prisha's deep thoughts submerged into her lost world. Claire pondered the quest and how it was becoming distant, thinking Monaco could be the end or the beginning of something extraordinary.

"Tell me about this Leather Bar we're going to?"

Prisha smiled. "The bar is a tribute to the city's leather industry. I used to come here with my cousin Anika. Our dads are in the leather industry and thought it was great. It is, but it's people-friendly." Kissing Claire on the cheek, whispering, "a safe space."

Claire caught her drift, hugged her, and kissed her. The chauffeur saw it in the rear-view mirror and smiled.

They arrived and were graciously greeted and seated.

Prisha got childishly excited, saying, "It's Karaoke Night!"

"Oh, oh." Claire was skeptical, but they had fun with karaoke in the past.

"Two Espresso Martinis?" Prisha ordered from the waiter.

They sipped them while observing the friendly crowd, singing and dancing. Claire had never seen Prisha so young, happy, and full of life's energy. She welcomed it and waved to the waiter for two more martinis and two glasses of water.

"Let's dance," Prisha said as they finished their second drink. Claire nodded to the waiter; two more.

They danced like they were in Cambridge, having a night of relaxation, creating a fond, loving memory.

Seated, they finished their drinks and ordered cheese sticks and a plate of vegetables. They got back on the dance floor.

Both felt slightly shaky, yet they ordered another round of drinks as it was their turn for karaoke.

A woman came up to them. "Prisha?" It was an old grade school friend.

They hugged with meaning and happiness.

"Meera, this is my wife, Claire." The girl looked at Prisha with such warmth and whispered in her ear, "I'm so proud of you." Hugging her again with a kiss on the cheek. "So nice to meet you, Claire."

They were then handed the microphones.

"Prisha, let's blow this place away!" Claire spat out the words with part of her drink.

The room was adjusted to the upcoming disco tune—the disco ball and reflecting lights transported you back to the USA in the 1970s.

Abba's *Disco Queen* filled the room. They got up, belted it out, played with the lyrics, and invited everyone to dance. They were almost drunk, flirting frivolously and flaunting with one another. They were greeted with applause.

Prisha would never see Meera again.

On their ride back to the hotel, Prisha asked, "Is this who we are?" They hugged. It was the most fun night of their relationship.

71

Family and Fractures

Their guests started arriving, marveling at the hotel's luxury. The children were excited about the swimming pools and game rooms. The men were enthused to try the cigar bar. The ladies wanted to be treated like royalty at the salons.

Prisha couldn't be any happier to see the looks on their faces. They all warmly hugged her as she introduced Claire to them. Her sister Shreya and mom Lakshmi were in tears, telling Prisha she had never looked more beautiful. Her nieces and nephews politely embraced her, not knowing her. The men were cool to her. Her cousin, Anika, unnoticed by all but Prisha, did not approach her.

The meet-and-greet was served in Prisha's suite. To end, all went to play, have fun, and have dinner at six.

Claire told Prisha she had business at the front desk.

Prisha was seated at the table when Anika placed her hands on Prisha's shoulders.

"I was hurt you didn't say hello?" Prisha said and did not turn around.

Anika gently caressed Prisha's breast. Prisha lovingly and gently removed her hand.

"You used to enjoy that." Anika, as beautiful as Prisha, lovingly spoke.

"I still do." She replied.

Anika turned Prisha around and then affectionately kissed her on the lips.

Claire had forgotten a memo and was returning to the room when she saw the kiss. She got sick, felt a sinking feeling, and froze.

Prisha did not share the kiss and moved away from Anika as gently as possible.

"Prisha, I love you!" Anika was getting emotional.

Claire could hear the conversation.

"I love you, too," Claire heard, and a tear came to her eye. She was about to leave.

"As my family, my cousin." Standing up and looking Anika in the eye, she said, "I love Claire. You have no idea. She is my first thought in the morning and the last at night. I can't live without her and would never," raising her voice. "Ever do anything to hurt her!" Anika fell back. Claire couldn't love Prisha anymore and wanted to enter the room and hold her.

Prisha continued, "We were kids, we had feelings, we played, and I loved you, but time has changed all of that. You will always be a big part of my life."

Anika began to cry.

"You have two beautiful children, and Kabir seems like a wonderful man."

Anika hugged Prisha, sobbing, "I'm so sorry! I've missed you so much."

Prisha had no response.

"You were brilliant; you went to school and escaped life here. My parents knew who I was, yet they arranged a marriage. Kabir is a great guy and a terrific father, kind…but when I close my eyes, I remember you."

"I'm so sorry, my precious Anika." Prisha hugged her.

"I fear your father may not accept your arrangement."

The words landed hard on Prisha.

Claire backed up and made approaching sounds.

The cousins regained their composure as Claire entered the suite.

"Anika was just leaving," Prisha said.

"Nice to meet you. I hope to talk with you tonight."

Anika nodded and left the room.

"Claire, I have something to tell you. Anika and I, when we were young." Claire put her finger across Prisha's lips, preventing her from saying anything.

"We all have a past. I love you, now kiss me?"

"I love you, too!"

It was a loving embrace.

Prisha expressed her fears that Ajay, her dad, may not accept their marriage. Claire told her we can only hope for the best, and let's go forward with hope.

"Have you talked to your mother?"

"Only Anika."

72

A Watch and a Wound

They got ready for dinner.

Claire wanted to do everything she could to make this work for Prisha. Claire had wealth, and with it came power; Prisha knew this but didn't fully understand the full scope of it and didn't want to.

The dinner was a feast unlike anything the family will ever partake in again. Prisha's family was starting to wonder how wealthy Claire was.

The dinner went well. Ajay would not look at or talk to Prisha, so Claire talked about the leather industry with him. Claire does her homework. Ajay took her conversation lightly until it reached a level beyond his field of knowledge. She knew and understood the business and who the players were. He was impressed, but he played it quietly.

It was the Christmas season, and Prisha was acting like Santa Claus. It was not a big part of their families' tradition, but they were intrigued. The room was filled with poinsettias and candles. Claire arranged for a Christmas tree to be placed by the decorative fireplace and stockings, filled with gifts and goodies for each family member; wrapped packages and gift boxes abound under the tree.

Prisha was informed but left it to Claire, who worked with Shreya; she was all for it with the kids.

After dinner, everyone opened their gifts. Shreya dangled keys for a new Mercedes SUV. Lakshmi was showing off her unique jewelry. The kids had toys, games, computers, and phones. There were satisfying, grateful, and thoughtful gifts for everyone.

Ajay slowly and discreetly watched the joy that exuded from Prisha, which hadn't changed since she was a child.

There were no more gifts to be opened. Only Ajay did not participate in the ceremony. Lakshi convinced him to go to his stocking. There, he found a lump of coal, later explained, wrapped with a note and a smiley face in Prisha's handwriting.

"Santa wants to deliver your gift personally."

Standing at the back of the room, Santa Claus presented Ajay with a small box.

Not knowing what was inside, his family implored him to open it. There was a card that read, "I will always love you, PRISHA." Reading it but not looking up, he unwrapped the package. He knew the box. He remembers telling Prisha when she was a little girl that he will get one of these when he's very successful.

In his hand and eye was a Platinum Rolex Daytona 116502. His eyes got misty, and without a word, he left.

Prisha's heart sank.

The party ended as a great success, and the family was never happier.

***

The second day of celebration went well, with the absence of Ajay, who returned home.

On the fourth day, Prisha was losing steam, but they visited the archaeological sites of the seven Pagodas and shrines in Malappuram.

That evening, they had dinner at Shreya's and Hari's home. The kids were wild and joyful. Shreya loved her younger sister, and Hari was a pleasure. As the beautiful evening wound down, Claire was very abrupt. How can we make your life better? Shreya spilled the tea, and Claire said she would arrange for all her financial affairs to be taken care of and find Hari a more suitable position; Claire was reliable. When leaving, Prisha invited them to Nice, explaining they were only two days but could stay as long as they wanted. They were excited and said yes, and would find a babysitter for the children. Hari told them that they were always welcome in their home.

The following day, they relaxed around the pool and spa, had a few drinks, and then got ready for an evening at Prisha's childhood home.

They had a pleasant evening. Her dad asked her how her career was going, and the ice melted. He inquired about Claire and what she did for a living, and was surprised, thinking she did nothing. Prisha was always quiet about her relationship, not wanting to upset her parents. They knew of Claire, but the picture wasn't lucid; neither Prisha nor her parents pursued the subject. He was very impressed when she told him of her pedigree and college degrees.

At dinner, Ajay was proudly wearing the watch. Lakshi sat quietly all that evening; she loved her daughter and liked Claire.

They had decided to stay that evening.

Ajay asked Lakshi to prepare the guest room.

"That's ok. My room is fine." Prisha said.

"It's for Claire," Ajay said.

For the first time, Prisha said, "Claire is my wife. I love her as I love you. She will be sleeping with me."

Lakshmi was nervous.

"So be it." Ajay coolly conceded.

The room was that of a young girl. There were dolls and religious statues: Shiva, Parvati, Buddha, and Ganesh. The twin bed was barely big enough for one of them, but they had no problem and slept well.

After breakfast, they left. Her parents agreed to have dinner with them at the hotel before they left for Nice.

Prisha was hopeful that Ajay would bless their marriage, but she was realistic; it would be the hardest thing he had ever had to do. They returned to their luxurious hotel accommodations.

They relaxed and talked about Nice and Monaco and meeting up with their friends. They agreed that this was a pleasant break.

That evening, they took Anika out to friendly bars. She had a good time and wished them well. They told Anika to stay in touch and visit.

73

The Decision

Stuttgart, Amsterdam, Bimini, Rome

They were flying out in the morning. Dinner was at six; her dad wanted Italian, and that would be.

They sat and quietly ate dessert, and nothing was said. Ajay, emotional for the first time, looked at his beautiful baby in the face. "I love you more than anything. I always knew that this day would arrive. You must understand my position in life. I know you do. You will not be here, but I have to live here; I know it's unfair; I love you and miss you, but I." Pausing, his hands shaking and eyes watering.

Prisha's bottom lip was quivering, not wanting to hear what was next.

Ajay took a deep breath and said, "I cannot accept this marriage." Got up and slowly walked away. Prisha sobbed like a baby into Claire's arms. Lakshi began crying and hugging her daughter, knowing she would probably never see her again.

The restaurant got quiet as the drama unfolded. Ajay, almost to the door, hearing the sobs and the pains of loss, stopped and turned around, with a long, deep focus, like Tevye, in *Fiddler on the Roof*, watched and listened to his loves, crushed under the pestle of his decision, and began crying. He returned to the table, hugged the group, and said, "Welcome to the family, daughter, and hugged Claire." It was a moment, a very happy one.

Claire convinced them to stay for the night, and they returned to the suite. They talked all night. Ajay felt a world of relief and was his affable, enjoyable self. Claire was going to bankroll and expand his business. She was using every possible thought to keep the family close. Ajay could become the largest leather manufacturer and exporter in India.

The following day, they met up with Shreya and Hari. Lakshmi would watch the grandchildren. Claire asked them if it was all right to be away from the children at Christmas; they were welcome to come. Shreya and Hari laughed, "It's ok!"

India was good.

***

His son Klaus, his wife Hildegard, and their 6-year-old twins, Eric and Erica, greeted Ditmer and Charlie at Stuttgart International Airport. They, too, were on semester-ending break, both professors at the University of Stuttgart's science department.

During the long flight over, Charlie and Ditmer were quiet, both thinking of the possibilities of this visit,

Klaus and Hildegard hugged Ditmer as he introduced his wife, Charlie. They greeted her as though she had always been part of the family.

Klaus whispered to Charlie, "Thank you for taking care of Dad." Charlie melted with the gesture.

The children greeted their grandfather with homemade Christmas cards. They looked at Charlie and thought her funny, different-looking. It was explained to them that she was from another part of the world. They understood and liked her, and by the end of the visit, they called her Oma.

They had a joyous Christmas together. They went on sightseeing tours, and Ditmer and Charlie got time to spend together privately, like on a honeymoon. They left early in the morning, the day after Christmas, and his son and family promised they would visit them.

It was a long, relaxing, and contemplative train ride to Monaco. They could have flown, but they wanted time to digest their lives. They were excited to meet up with their friends and see Monte Carlo. During their ride, they talked about their visit and the disc, medallion, and metal.

***

In the comfort of KLM's Royal Dutch Airlines' World Business Class, Sally blogged across the Atlantic Ocean, arriving at Schiphol airport. She was chauffeured to the Anantara Grand Hotel Krasnapolsky, Dam Square, Amsterdam, a lovely suite, gifted by Claire, a tenth of a mile, walking distance to Amsterdam's infamous Red-Light district. Claire secretly knew the inner Sally.

Sally partied and partied hard, a pub crawl in Dam Square, Leidseplein Square activities, a boat cruise, a brothel tour, and a buyer at De Wallen, all the time blogging. Her blog was blowing up; she loved it.

Before leaving, she went on an architectural and archaeological tour, culminating in a visit to the Anne Frank House.

She boarded an early train the day after Christmas, blogging to Monaco, and she could not wait to set her soul into Monte Carlo. Her blog entry, leaving Amsterdam, wrote, "You haven't sinned, you haven't lived, until you spend time in Amsterdam. Details to follow, she showed a happy face emoji."

***

Stanley Birk and his team were investigating Unidentified Submersible Objects (USO), also called unidentified submersible phenomenon, near Bimini Island in the Bahamas. It was so close to Christmas and such a long, challenging year that he took a team and their families for a working holiday. He took Tina.

The investigation was successful, and they had time to celebrate Christmas in the Bahamas.

Early on Christmas morning, the Director and his security team were ordered to meet in Rome as soon as possible. Stanley had to leave, but Tina and the research team could wrap up the project and stay a few more days.

The Director got a flight, and he was briefed while in midair.

74

The Final Exam

Genny spotted Dr. Isenberg outside the examination room, approaching him and saying, "Hello."

"You're looking good, Genny." He replied.

"I've been working hard." Cooly.

"The report shows that your progress is outstanding. They are interested in you and want to keep you around."

"We've been talking about it, and I will make a decision the first of the year."

"It would be different; I think you would enjoy it." He smiled.

Genny deduced he was nothing more than a government pawn, a whore of sense. He would do anything to get paid well. Genny wondered if he wasn't double-dipping with the Randolph Foundation. He did save my life, she thought. Or did he? She was wondering if he wanted to pull the plug.

"I still want to teach." Wanting to get to Italy and do research.

"You can do both." Smiling smugly.

"I could, but you know, Doc, I like my time." Tipping her hand, saying she had no intention of working here.

"Let's get started." He gave her a basic exam, blood test, EKG, and MRI.

The results were back before she finished.

"You healed well. Your brain activity is ultra-sharp. Your skeletal system and surrounding organs and tissues are amazing. The procedures performed on you are futuristic. Almost with a robot or AI construction." He threw the deliberate dig; he didn't like Genny's arrogance.

"Whatever you say, Doc." Dr. Briscoe had strengthened her psychological defense system.

"Do you have any questions? Today is our last meeting."

"I should have brought some champagne." Sarcastically. He didn't like it.

"You have a battery of tests; I'd like to watch you perform?" He wasn't asking.

"Whatever you say, Isenberg." Genny had lost respect for the doctor for not taking the time to inform her of the first major physical and accompanying tests, and he seemed not to care about her mental well-being. She had no contact with him since the last exam.

Her parapsychology abilities were unlimited. The physical strength and ability she exhibited had increased over her last test. Her cognitive skills were computer-like, yet she was still the likable, funny Genny.

***

Lucas and Genny continued to study and research the Perugia area, trying to understand the history and the lay of the land. Genny had contacted a family member in Italy who could help guide them, and they could stay at his home. His one caveat was that there were certain restricted areas; he would show them and instruct them, but not go with them. They were ok with that.

Her grand-cousin sent them the agenda and showed them the restricted areas, the areas that interested them the most.

Genny's final meeting with Dr. Briscoe was bittersweet. He had become a security blanket. His straightforward truthfulness gave her the guidance she needed to figure out exactly who she was and what she could do. He was so upfront that he told her he was returning to Area 51 and reporting to Dr. James on her progress.

"Genny, are you still dreaming?"

"For the record?"

"No, just for me." She hesitated, not sure whether to share her thoughts.

"That's ok." He was sincere.

"No, I want to tell you. It's not disturbing but puzzling." Her body became quiet as she told him the dream.

"I was in a dark area, maybe a cave; it was warm, the humidity was high, and I was dripping sweat. I walked into a vertical rainbow of light. My body tingled, and I was feeling euphoric, not high. It was a feeling better than sex. I could smell my favorite scents and taste my favorite things. The music I loved played in multiple songs, and I could hear them all as if only one were playing. I could see the past, things that were only lost moments, like when you are doing nothing, as though my life had been recorded. Then this feeling of being touched, not just touched but being enveloped, no, it was coming from inside out. Yes, this feeling, an experience, was pulling itself from within me. It was like that astral projection experience, with greater sensual pleasure. A figure, an apparition, a ghost, stood before me. I did not recognize it, but when I looked into its eyes, I felt a part of me. It was happy, almost holy. It touched my eyes, and I awoke. I never felt more content, happy, or satisfied. Lucas lay beside me; I gently touched his arm, and while in a deep sleep, he lovingly smiled, whispering, addressing me in a foreign tongue; he called me something, my name, unrecognizable, which now I cannot remember. I remember everything, but not this."

"Off the record."

"Yes," Genny replied.

"Wow! That is deep, Genny!" He unprofessionally responded. Genny flashed a beautiful smile.

The session ended with a sad goodbye.

75

A Roman Pause

Genny, since her dream, became quiet and meditated more often and longer. Lucas noticed it. She said it was nothing, but she was thinking about their trip.

On the flight to Rome, Genny continued to be quiet. The closer she got to Europe, the more heightened her senses became. Lucas took this time to plan a few days of sightseeing in Rome before driving to Perugia.

Staying in a hotel in the heart of Rome's oldest part enabled them to tour on foot. Genny could feel the history, climbing out of her funk.

When they were at Circus Maximus, Genny said, holding Lucas's hand, "We have been here before. I can feel it. Lucas, I can sense, almost relive, this moment." He did not doubt her.

"Lucas, when we study history, we only see blocks of time, the story, and not the real moments. I mean the exact moments through someone's eye, not a historian, but as it is happening. Oh, I don't know. This is great." She hugged him.

The following day, she had the same experience at the Coliseum.

Genny spotted a tattoo parlor and decided she needed a memento. Although not covered in tattoos, she had more body art than the average person who gets tattoos. They were reminders of places and people that had meaning to her.

The tattooist, speaking in English, appreciated Genny's gallery and the quality of her images. Genny explained that much of her work was done by tribespeople, who were trusted and befriended in her fieldwork.

"You're becoming quite the illustrated woman?" Admiring and complimenting her. Genny smiled and asked for a tattoo on her inner left bicep. She handed her a drawing of the medallion; it had three Mayan characters inside of a small heart, translating LJC.

"This could be complicated?" Genny looked around at the artwork on the walls. Gave her a reassuring wink.

It turned out subtle but spoke to you; it was beautiful. Genny paid and thanked the artist.

"That's beautiful," Lucas said, reading the inscription.

Holding hands, Genny appreciated his idea of a short vacation before business.

The two days were refreshing; now it was time to move on to Perugia, the origin of her ancestors.

76

Perugia

House Enrico

Perugia is the ancient capital city of the state of Umbria. The Tiber River runs through the city on the landlocked Apennine Peninsula. Etruscans valued this gateway city as far back as eight centuries BCE. Stone structures with their accompanying city gateways circumvent and adorn the city's two-perimeter ancient walls. The Romans conquered the city and ruled for centuries. Hannibal's surprise attack at the Battle of Lake Trasimene in 217 BCE trapped and drowned 15,000 Roman soldiers in Lake Trasimene, adding to its historic significance.

Perugia was the papal residence during the 13th century; five popes administered from here, and four were elected. Pope Clement V (1305-1314) moved the papacy from Rome in 1309. The elections were presided over at the Palazzo delle Canoniche, which adjoins the Perugia Cathedral. The Cathedral housed the remains of four of the popes, not Clement V, and their tombs, except for Pope Benedict XI, were destroyed during the War of the Eight Saints. His remains are still extant at the Perugia Cathedral, Metropolitana di San Lorenzo, Duomo di Perugia. The geographic coordinates are 43.112685oN 12.389209oE, matching one of the coordinates on the medallion.

Two ancient universities and the world-famous Baci candy factory attract visitors to the city.

***

Genny and Lucas arrived at her grand cousin's residence. Giovanni was Enrico's cousin, and Maria, his wife, lived in the Virgili ancestral family home. Enrico had once lived here before his parents immigrated to America. Enrico and Maria were up in age but looked and moved with a vibrant step.

The house was, as Genny knew, visited when she was a child. Her heightened, wolf-like senses could detect Enrico's scent, unaware whether it was the house or Giovanni. Subtle signs that it was Christmas season adorned their home, not-too-large, traditional beamed ceilings with stucco walls and terracotta floors—a nativity scene reflected in the fireplace's peaceful burn. A small pine tree sat in the corner, undecorated: Mario Lanza's *Guardian Angel* enhanced the Christmas spirit.

Genny deeply inhaled, detecting the savory scents wafting from the kitchen. She felt relaxed and at home.

She introduced Lucas and was hugged by her cousins, who were more like an aunt and uncle.

The home's charm exuded a feeling of well-being, as though time had stood still; the walls emanated tranquil karma and the happiness of generations.

"Splendida ragazza!" Maria pinched Genny's cheek.

In English, Maria said how much Genny resembled her granddaughter.

They had three children, all living in America. They rotated visits yearly and, in the fourth year, vacationed together as a big family. This year, they spent the Christmas holidays alone, at home.

"My dad was upset that I wouldn't be home for Christmas," Genny explained.

"Dr. Cantalupo, la mia famiglia?" Giovanni's face lit up. She smiled.

"You are my family." Hugging Giovanni, scenting Enrico. "We are on sort of a working, research vacation." Pausing "Polenta?" Maria smiled.

"Yes, and some eggs and other surprises," Maria said. "Vieni, mangiamo e parliamo."

They talked while enjoying a lovingly prepared breakfast. Genny asked a thousand questions about Enrico, and Giovanni happily answered them, telling her the family history.

Lucas knew the coordinates matched the Cathedral, but Genny wanted to visit the family plot in the Monumental Cemetery. She told him she felt a connection, something in her dreams.

They were invited to stay for the holiday. Genny and Lucas had picked up gifts for them in Rome. The Virgili were excited and felt a strong attraction and affection toward Genny.

The Cathedral was closed to the public for holiday presentations until the day after Christmas. They would celebrate Christmas Eve Midnight Mass at the Cathedral with her cousins.

After a lengthy breakfast, Maria showed them to their room, which had everything they needed—including a bathroom.

"Enrico stayed in this room when he was a little boy, I was told. He occasionally visited. He was one of my favorites. My heart still aches when we lost your grandmother." With a tear in her eye, hugging Genny, "La Mia casa e la tua casa."

Genny and Lucas settled into their surroundings. Genny was filled with generational vibrations, feeling a peace and Christmas joy that she hadn't experienced before, knowing that Santa Claus may not be real.

77

Secrets of the Tomb

Enrico's Testament

Later in the day, Giovanni, their tour guide**, took them to the
Monumental Cemetery. Along the way, they mainly chatted about
family. Giovanni spoke mostly about his children and
grandchildren. They told him about America, and the conversation
evolved into their work.

"Enrico was so dedicated to his work in archaeology and
ancient civilizations. He would communicate with me and ask me
to collect photos and images of the area. This was ongoing; I
would research records for him. Then, a few years ago, I think it
was a few months before he passed, he came to visit."

"I remember him writing to me that he wanted to see his
ancestral home and family before it was too late," Lucas
interjected.

"I don't recall this," Genny said.

"You were probably wrapped up in school, archaeological
digs, a time in your life when family and friends get lost for a bit,"
Lucas said.

Genny, feeling guilty, knew that was true.

Giovanni continued, "When he arrived, he was different. He was ready to leave this world. He was at peace. I'm not kidding; this has inspired me, Maria. Enrico had found God and believed with all his soul."

Genny and Lucas listened as Giovanni recalled Enrico's last visit.

"Genny, he was on the same course or mission you and Lucas are on. I can feel it. When you asked for a guide, I fudged it because I wanted to see you and tell you this story." He paused a bit and took a sip of water, as they were not that far from the cemetery.

"He asked me to take him to the Perugia Cathedral. The night before, we talked about the Cathedral's history, obsessing over the Knights Templar, Pope Clement V, and King Philip IV of France. He had all of these—I want to say crazy—theories, but I knew him as a child, and everything he ever said or did was logical and well thought out."

"What kind of theories?" Lucas asked as Giovanni pulled into a parking space at the cemetery.

"He asked me to never reveal them, even though I didn't understand them." He looked at Genny. "Only to you can I reveal these theories without breaking my trust. But first, let me finish my story. We went to the Cathedral, and Enrico took me to a restricted, do-not-enter area; I believed this area to be physically unsafe. I asked him what he was doing. I told him that we are old men; this is dangerous. He said he would go alone and told me I was always, 'A little shit pants.' I laughed, knowing this was true, and we snuck down a very short corridor behind the tomb of Pope Benedict XI, leading to a stone stairwell that descended under the Cathedral. It was getting dark, and Enrico had a flashlight. I implored him to return, but he shone his light on the wall, and there were torches. The well-equipped archaeologist lit the torch. We were deep into the old Etruscan underground; we could hear running water. It was probably an estuary of the Tiber River or an ancient aqueduct. We were approaching a chamber; it looked like it contained an altar. It was plain, and there was a tabernacle door in the middle, like the altar in a Catholic Church. Then, I could see an open tomb. Enrico whispered, "Clement V." At that point, we heard footfalls, and a group of police arrested us. They charged us with trespassing. I knew the magistrate, and he knew Enrico dropped the charges. Enrico was never allowed back into the Cathedral. The magistrate warned me that if I got caught one more time, me, my family, and their families could never be allowed into the Cathedral." Giovanni paused, but wanted to finish the story before any questions were asked.

"We went home. I told Maria. She inferred that Enrico was acting irrationally, and she worried about him and his health. He stayed in his room for almost two days. He said he was finishing up on a project. He looked terrible when he finally came out; he wanted to come here, to the cemetery; he had a package or something. I took him, and he asked me to stay in the car while he visited the vault. He returned twenty minutes later without the package. It was a quiet ride home. When we got home, he apologized for his behavior and was back to himself, as happy as ever, as though he had just fulfilled a mission. He took us to a wonderful dinner and said he was leaving in the morning. I took him to the airport; that was the last time I saw him." He took a deep, sad sigh.

"Thank you." Genny hugged Giovanni, "Theories?"

"Your grandfather believed that we, the people of this planet, were visited by people from beyond this world who had great technology; they aided in our growth and altered our DNA.

Our deliberate misunderstanding of their technology made them our God. Enrico believed that the Knights Templar, the Catholic Church, Pope Clement V, and Philip IV of France were all connected to his theory. He also said free will will always make us a unique species. That's all I have. I can't talk anymore." But continued, "You seem to be on a similar quest or following your grandfather. I will not come with you to the tomb." He gave them directions. They left.

Genny and Lucas discussed what they had just heard. Their conclusion had no real answers, but they felt confident they were on a path to somewhere.

The tomb "Virgili" was ancient and time-worn. It was uncertain if any recent interments had taken place. There was a badly worn stela with an inscription and a history, an image of an open carved sarcophagus with human remains, and an angel leaving the body looking back at it.

They entered with flashlights, looking for the journal. At the base of a statue of Saint Michael, Lucas noticed a disturbance in the dirt, as though digging had taken place. Only the eye of a trained archaeologist would have detected the displaced soil. They dug with their hands and found a small box containing Enrico Virgili's journal. They replaced the disturbed earth, checked around, and returned to Giovanni.

Giovanni said nothing to them and drove home.

Genny said she was hungry but couldn't wait to dig into the journal.

"Maria is preparing dinner," Giovanni informed them.

"How were your accommodations last night?"

"The finest. Grazie mille." Lucas politely said.

"I dreamed all night; it was so peaceful." Genny exhaled.

They returned and had an early dinner. It was a long day. They retired to their room and read the journal.

"My dearest Genny, I had hoped and had confidence in you finding and figuring out where my journal lay." That was how the journal began. Tears rolled down Genny's cheeks.

The journal was much more detailed than Giovanni's telling of the story. It was kept over decades and, at times, out of order and all over the place. Enrico documented sites, trying to make his theory believable. He had ideas on space travel, such as the planet being seeded, DNA being altered, and alien colonies living under Antarctica.

He theorized that an advanced civilization left its world because of a cataclysm and traveled tens of thousands of years, finding and seeding the planet and filling it with beings to fit its agenda. Enrico was unclear about its ultimate purpose.

They had trouble determining the connection between the church and the Knights Templar.

What was Enrico looking for under the cathedral? Then they found out why. It was written in Greek. Enrico explained, "that some key, not the kind to unlock a door, but information, could be found under Perugia Cathedral, in the tabernacle at the head of the empty tomb of Pope Clement V. There will be a chalice. Lift the chalice off its base where it sits, and locate a latch, button, or switch that will open a compartment, with evidence of my theories. Take it to Avignon, follow the coordinates you've found, and life's mystery will be answered."

They stopped reading and talked, wondering where he got that information. The journal repeatedly mentions ensoulment and connects it with the Catholic Church and the Knights Templar.

"These are all great theories, but there is no proof. Logic could lead to reasonable explanations." Lucas said.

"That's true, but Enrico seemed rushed towards the end of the diary. He was on to something. Something people do not want anyone to find out." They went to bed and slept on it. Genny had processed all the material, and it became part of her dreamscape. They wondered where the rest of his research and artifacts were hidden or stored.

Genny had memorized the Greek text, and in her dreams, the translation starts according to legend.

78

Christmas

Christmas Eve morning and the day was quiet. They sat around and talked. Genny helped Maria prepare dinner. Maria asked her if she liked this Lucas guy.

"He's my soulmate." With dreamy eyes, she gave her cousin an affectionate hip bump. Genny smiled, and Maria broke into a Christmas Carol: "Oh, Holy Night!" She had an incredible voice. Genny chimed in, and Giovanni and Lucas joined the ensemble. They had cordials, told family stories, and a feast was in the making.

After dinner, they went to Midnight Mass at the Cathedral. Genny and Lucas checked out the place. Giovanni said the stairwell is behind the tomb of Pope Benedict XI, a narrow passageway. Lucas got up and, as subtly as possible, peeked behind the tomb.

They returned home, had drinks, and exchanged a few small gifts. Genny called home, and they were starting dinner. They were very excited to hear from her; they talked for fifteen minutes and looked forward to seeing one another next week.

Lucas called his parents and wished them happy holidays. It was late afternoon in California.

Traditionally, Maria and Giovanni would get calls from their children on Christmas Day. They all trimmed the Christmas tree and drank wine, listening to Christmas carols.

Nothing eventful took place; Genny and Lucas continued privately discussing the journal and were looking forward to continuing their quest.

***

Christmas was quiet; everyone slept in a little later. Maria prepared a fitting breakfast. Genny and Lucas would take them to dinner. The Virgili got their calls, went to dinner, came home, wished each other Merry Christmas, and went to bed.

Genny told Giovanni that they wished that he would stay home tomorrow, and they would be fine. He agreed.

79

The *PRIZE*

Orders from Strassa

Before Stanley boarded his flight to Rome, he called and wished his family a Merry Christmas; the children were delighted and surprised by his unexpected, thoughtful generosity. His ex-wife thanked him and asked where this man had been hiding these last few years. He joked with her, and they laughed; a flash of the past came to mind. Thinking about what could have been.

He boarded his flight and was seated in first class, a very private, secluded seat.

The flight attendants were in the spirit, whether it was their religion or not. They offered him a cocktail, and he declined.

Stanley dropped off to sleep with thoughts of Tina. He liked her and felt a bit sad leaving her alone on Christmas Day in the Bahamas. She understood, he thought.

Midway through the flight, he received a text message from Morgan Strassa. It read. "Possible encounter with the Randolph people. Our operatives report that Cantalupo and Chevrolet are seeking something they can not keep. We have been trying to locate this item for a long time. A recent breakthrough has led us to Perugia. Let them find what they seek and then take it. Do not harm any associates or Cantalupo's family. Use force if need be, but remember, do not kill. You will be picked up at the airport and taken to the US Embassy. You will be given diplomatic immunity and certain powers afforded by the local authorities. An agenda of their possible movement will be provided. They are now under surveillance. Your team has been informed and will be awaiting your arrival. You will drive up to Perugia. Just a note: Randolph and her wife are living it up and reportedly heading to Nice, and it appears, per our operatives, that other members of their group will be heading in that direction. I do not see this as a threat but as an observation. We did fuck them over, LOL, they deserve a break, but we must be on alert; this could develop into something. So Merry Christmas, and return the *PRIZE* ASAP."

Stanley responded, "OK."

The convoy approached the city limits of Perugia, and Stanley commented on what a beautiful region he must return to; he was alerted that the surveillance team had the objectives, entering the Perugia Cathedral and taking a tour.

80

Descent into the Cathedral

Genny and Lucas were waiting for their ride, telling their cousins what a wonderful time they had and that they would be leaving in the morning. Maria jokingly said, "Leftovers tonight!" They all laughed.

The ride arrived. Genny held Lucas's hand; she was sweating.

"You, ok?"

"I'm sorry, but I just got this bad feeling."

Lucas knew that Genny's intuition was to be taken seriously.

"We can call this off. These secrets have been hidden for centuries; another day or two won't matter."

"That's true, but I've got to see this through." Genny was feeling a little better. "Besides, we have to meet with the team in a few days." Lucas gave Genny a reassuring hug.

They were dropped off in front of the Cathedral. Their plan was to take a tour and, at some point, disappear. Entering the Cathedral, a separate tourist entrance, they were surprised when they were asked to check their backpacks and go through a metal detector. They left all their belongings at the door, passports and wallets were checked into a locker, and they were given a key; they were only permitted a camera or a phone and small personal items. They only took their phones and, on Genny's hunch, remembered when she found the disc, the odd circumstances, and a small flashlight.

The tour began, and they slowly found themselves at the back. When they came to the tomb of Pope Benedict XI, they stopped and took photos. Genny disappeared on one side, and Lucas on the other. They met, finding the door and the stone stairwell, and descended deep into the bowels of the ancient structure. With very little light, they proceeded along, aware of sounds like rapidly moving water. Genny's vision was that of a nocturnal predator. With a tracking app, Lucas checked the GPS coordinates and held onto Genny as he gave her directions. After a few turns, they could see a chamber up ahead; there seemed to be some lighting. They entered the ancient chamber, and Genny got a flashback to Belize. The room smelled the same. The altar with the centered tabernacle appeared identical; it had a door, not a slab of stone, and the coordinates had placed them at their destination.

"Security cameras!" Lucas pointed, and they moved more quickly.

They observed the empty tomb of Pope Clement V. and wanted to take photos; their phones had died.

Some light was filtering down from high above. Lucas opened the tabernacle door, and there was the beautiful gold chalice with jewels adorning it. Lucas was moving under a time constraint with the skill of a jewel thief. He lifted the weighty object and heard a click. He raised a piece of material. There was a lever; he turned it, and a compartment in the rear of the tabernacle slid down. He reached in, with Genny shining her light on him, pulling out an elongated, thin oval metal plate. He handed it to Genny. There was nothing else within, no markings or anything.

He returned the tabernacle to the way he found it, minus the metal plate. It only took seconds.

There wasn't a lot of light, but they could see tiny lasered inscriptions on both sides of the plate, looking like star charts and maps. They were anxious to get it out of the building to examine it.

"The legend is true," Genny whispered.

They quickly retraced their steps. In the distance, Genny could hear echoing footsteps.

"Oh, shit, Lucas, let's go!" She grabbed his arm and started heading deeper underground. There were ancient structures and walls under the city of Perugia.

Genny heard a voice, something she wished she would never hear again. The rushing water was getting louder as she pulled Lucas up a small precipice; it was a dead end.

At the bottom stood Stanley with his pack of wolves, aiming their weapons at them.

"So, how did that phrase go in Jesus Christ Superstar? Oh yeah. 'So once again, you are my guest,' of sorts." Stanley laughed.

Genny and Lucas were fearful.

"Genny, no one will get hurt," He tried to assure her.

"Gentlemen, put your weapons away!" He commanded.

"Genny, you have something that the government wants."

Genny realized there was no cigar smoke or stinking booze odors.

Slowly approaching her, he put his hand out.

"Lucas, I love you! Trust me!" She suddenly pushed Lucas into the water and dove in after him. She shoved the tablet into her shirt, and the strong current swept them away.

Calmly, Stanley said, "Find out where this leads to." They left.

***

Genny quickly caught up to Lucas, and they embraced each other so they would flow as a unit down what they believed to be an estuary of the Tiber River.

"Who do you think you are—Indiana Jones?" Lucas said, spitting water.

"Hopefully, this doesn't drain into a waterfall." Spitting water back at him.

They continued with no chance of getting out of the rapidly moving water. The walls were smooth and high, possibly an old aqueduct. As they traveled, seemingly a mile or more, the flow increased as the ceiling closed in on them. Narrower and narrower, the sidewalls and the smooth rock ceiling were closing in. Genny feared for Lucas. Lucas felt the same for Genny.

"It's like a funnel," Lucas spat water.

"Just hang in…" Genny couldn't finish her sentence when they both found themselves being swept inside a narrow tunnel with just a bit of breathable air; for minutes, they held hands, gasping for air, and then they were delivered into a pool of water. The water was sinking to a lower level, but they could float above it.

They could see light above, and an ancient circular wall led to the top. They were in a well. They got their breath and found footing on the sidewall. It was about fifty feet or more to the top of the wall. Their phones were waterproof but drained of power. Genny pulled herself to a small landing, reached down, and pulled Lucas up.

Genny could hear voices above, sounding like chanting or prayers. They shouted for help. A hooded figure bent over the top of the well, and he could not believe what he saw.

"Hang on. I'll get help." He spoke in Italian, and then he left.

Moments later, a rope ladder found its way down the well. Lucas went first while Genny steadied the ladder, and then she followed. Her training was coming in handy.

When they reached the top, they were greeted by Father Antonio, a Benedictine Monk and Prefect at Abbazia di San Pietro in Perugia. He and the three initiates were in prayer when they heard the cry for help and were responsible for pulling them to safety.

81

The Abbey of Saint Peter

Understanding the Artifact

"Welcome to our Abbey. We usually don't receive visitors in this manner." Joking, in Italian, he dismissed the young men.

"Thank you, Father. God works in amazing ways." Genny said.

"Thank you, Father." Lucas agreed.

The priest looked at them and said, "He does." In English.

They introduced themselves. Something had caught the father's eye. Genny saw him looking at her neck and chest. She thought about the metal artifact they had just recovered.

"Yes, Father, is something bothering you?" The dripping, now trembling, Genny asked.

"Your most beautiful cross. We must get you inside. Follow me; we'll get you inside and see how we can help you."

They got inside and were given monks' undergarments and robes. They were very comfortable.

Their clothing was sent to be washed and dried.

"Why did you unquestionably trust us?" Genny asked.

"It's a gut feeling; only God would send someone to us like this." He chuckled but was serious.

"So, let's talk." Father Antonio started. "Before I know anything or you say anything, please tell me about your cross."

Genny was surprised by the request but removed the cross and handed it to Father Antonio. He trembled, almost coming to tears. "Do you know the history of this most holy relic?"

"It was a gift from my grandfather."

"Who may that be?" He felt he was in God's presence.

"Enrico Virgili." He closed his eyes with the response, in disbelief.

"Yes, this makes sense." He closed his eyes.

"Did you know Enrico?" A surprised Genny.

"We met."

He continued with tears in his eyes, "Please let me tell you a story." They nodded. "After Jesus was crucified, Peter took on the leadership of the church, and he went to Rome, where he too was martyred and crucified. This cross was believed to be lost. One story is that one of his followers removed it and returned to Jerusalem. During the crusades, the belief was that the Knights Templar had recovered it and passed it down, generation to generation. Here it is now in Saint Peter's."

"Father, help us, and I gift this to you." He was stunned.

"It belongs here, with you." Genny was sincere. Then she whispered, "Thanks, Pa." No one heard her.

They told him their story without significant details and then asked for absolution. The good-natured man laughed.

"Anyone wearing the cross of Saint Peter does not need absolution. God was watching over you."

It was agreed they could spend the night in a room with separate beds, have their clothes returned, keep the robes, and be provided with two bicycles that would either be returned or paid for. Also, a message, as discreetly as possible, was to be sent to

Giovanni and Maria to say that they were okay and that they would get in touch with them.

That night, they examined the artifact. Lucas had trouble seeing the markings because they were so small, and there were so many on both sides. He recognized some star charts, such as the Orion star system. Genny focused on the plate for an extended period as though she were reading it, turned it over, and did the same. Lucas looked at it again without any new knowledge. Genny repeated her robot-like procedure several times, saying, "We should get some sleep; we must get to Monaco." Genny affectionately held Lucas's hand. Kissing him lovingly and slowly drawing away from him, she sighed as she gazed deep into his beautiful blue infinite eyes, looking like the universe. An intense, loving, telepathic energy touched her. She never felt a greater love. She now knew and was understanding the tablet. Tears of joy rolled down her cheeks.

"You ok, GG?" A concerned Lucas hugged her.

"I just love you so much. We found one another. Please, hold me." She did not reveal her findings. They embraced and soon fell asleep.

The following day, before sunrise, the phones were successfully charged; Genny texted Claire in their secret code, updating her of their situation. Claire would provide them private transport from Florence's Amerigo Vespucci Airport to Nice, where they would be chauffeured to Monte Carlo. Getting to Florence was a 9-hour bike ride; they were looking forward to the challenge. They were going to bike to Monte Carlo if they had to.

They left the monastery with thanks from both sides. Two bikes equipped to handle a monk's robe, which was a standard issue, waited for them. The saddlebags were provided with water and food. Lucas had mapped out a course. They just needed their backpacks.

Father Antonio suggested a monk ride with them as a ruse part of the way. Also, he could retrieve their backpacks safely. He rubbed the cross, humbly hanging around his neck.

The three departed for the short ride to the Cathedral. Keeping a safe distance from the church, Lucas and Genny waited for the monk's return as he retrieved their backpacks.

They pulled into a wooded area when safely beyond the city's wall. The monk gave them their belongings, and they started their trek. Two hours later, the monk returned to go home. They were six hours out from the airport. It was 11:30 a.m. They were making good time; the weather was overcast without any precipitation. Sunset was at 4:44 p.m. They were on schedule, arriving at the airport at 5:20. They left their bicycles in a safe area where they would be returned to the Abbey.

They were expected at the airport, boarding the private jet quickly, and then off to Nice.

Exhausted from biking the nine-hour trek in less than eight hours, they looked into each other's eyes and knew they were forever as one.

82

Birk's Frustration

A Shot of Reality

Stanley and his men retreated through the security entrance they had arrived at. The lead agent approached the tour guide and asked if he knew where the water flowed. He replied that the Cathedral's historian could assist them and then directed them.

Stanley sent his lead agent. A note on the door said she would not be in until 2:00 this afternoon. It was 10:30 a.m.; he called his office to get satellite information. Only a skeleton crew was working today due to the holiday, and they would get the information to him ASAP. All his avenues held holiday detours. It was 11:11 a.m. when the agent reported back to the Director, who was talking to Tina on the phone in his car. He discontinued the call. The lead agent gave the report.

"Our hands are tied for a few moments. Let's grab a bite, plan a strategy, organize our information, and then return. They are either dead, or they can't get far." Birk replied.

They had an early lunch at a local café. He allowed his men to have a holiday drink. They had a round of Sambuca, which smelled so pleasing to the Director.

He waved to the waiter and ordered another round. This time, he ordered one for himself. He downed the fiery shot and tickled a drowsing Smaug. It was a feeling he enjoyed but refrained from another.

At two o'clock, they sat and waited for the historian. A very young student entered. Knowing very little English, she explained that she was an intern and the librarian had the week off.

Exasperated and thinking of Sambuca, Birk asked her if she could help. They would compensate her if she had to work late.

She would not accept a gratuity but said she would gladly do the research, and they could come by 10:00 a.m. tomorrow.

Stanley sighed, "OK." They left.

The information from their office showed an underground stream emptying into the Tiber River further downriver.

The Director dispatched agents to the convergence point to see if they could find anything before dark. Upon investigating and interrogating the area, nothing was obtained. Birk booked hotel rooms and waited till morning.

***

Birk and an interpreter entered the Cathedral earlier than agreed, hoping to catch the intern. On their way into the building, the interpreter bumped into a hastily exiting monk and said, "Mi scusi!" They went to the archives; she arrived at 10:00 am.

Through his interpreter, she told them she had worked until midnight and found some interesting things about the water. She said it was initially an aqueduct constructed by the Etruscans and later modified and improved by the Romans. It has been in disuse for centuries. It runs under the Cathedral and out to the Tiber.

"Yes, we know all that. Is there anything else you can help us with?" Stanley was polite.

The interpreter translated, "There is a string of wells along the path. Possibly still in use, but probably not. They would be very deep." She pulled out a centuries-old map and spread it on the table. It depicted where the wells were located. Stanley took photos and then said, "Grazie." He handed her an envelope that contained a generous gift certificate to a fine restaurant and then wished her, "Buon Anno!"

"Grazie. Buon Anno!" She smiled.

They left at close to eleven a.m. He reviewed the sites with his team, and they were dispatched.

It was close to one in the afternoon when Stanley, dressed in his intimidating black suit attire, arrived at Abbazia di San Pietro and was greeted by Father Antonio. The interpreter asked if they had an ancient Etruscan well on the property. The Father said yes, then an aggressive, accusative questioning bombarded him. Father Antonio gave them *The Sound of Music* and *The Sound of Silence* treatment. They insisted on seeing the well. Father Antonio took them to a grassy wooded area used for praying. There were monks and initiates doing afternoon prayers. Father Antonio showed them the well that was about fifty yards away. It was old, and there seemed to be recent footsteps or disturbed dirt. Stanley looked down the well with his flashlight; the water seemed close to one hundred feet away. He felt confident they could not have come up through this. He thanked them for letting them onto the property.

When they were leaving, the interpreter bumped into a sweaty monk who had just parked his bicycle. Locking eyes with the monk, then said, "Mi scusi." They left. Father Antonio rubbed his cross.

When Stanley returned to his hotel, it was past three. When all the agents reported in, it was close to five. The search was a big negative.

They had dinner together as a large group. Stanley thanked them for their efforts.

"We'll ask the local magistrate if he could arrange to dredge the tunnel for the bodies ASAP. Also, check to see if any bodies have been recovered downstream, " he said to his agents as they ate. Stanley, irritated, had a glass of Scotch Whiskey, hoping that what they found hadn't gotten lost in the water.

At nine O'clock that evening, shortly after dinner, Stanley received a phone call from Morgan Strassa in his room. Morgan Strassa, in his dark, powerful, beyond-the-government, international, and maybe beyond this planet, covert operation, worked 24/7.

"Have you recovered the item?"

"Not yet. They have it in their possession, and when the tunnel is dredged, it will be yours." Stanley confidently answered.

"Don't waste your time. You missed your opportunity!" Stanley was stunned.

"What in the name of Christ is wrong with you? Spending all the time with that woman has made you soft."

"I don't get it?" Stanley asked.

"You don't get it. You let them escape. Do you know where they are now? You fuck-up, disappointment." Stanley was getting irritated.

"Where?" Stanley boldly asked.

"My friend, they are in Monte Carlo." Stanley was speechless.

"I tell you, we are the good guys. I tell you not to kill. I did not tell you to be a weak prick."

"Fuck you!" Stanley stood up to his boss. You tell me this; you tell me that; you tell me nothing! I chase objects and things; I have no idea what they are. You want me to be loyal to you, but you treat me like shit. Well, fuck you, Morgan Strassa!" Stanley, feeling good, now expected retaliation.

"You know, Director, it's about time you returned and strapped on a new set." Morgan Strassa was laughing. "You know, Director, a few Christmas gifts for your kids don't make up for all of the pain you caused them."

"I'm not so certain." He replied.

"Get your crew out to Monte Carlo; it's not a long drive."

The call ended. He called his lead agent to tell him the story and plan for Monte Carlo tonight. They were leaving at dawn, send over a couple of cigars, and get him a "Fucking bottle of whiskey!"

83

Tag

Rendezvous in Monaco

Prishia and Claire arrived in Monaco early on the 26th of December. Prisha felt down, leaving her sister behind, but was optimistic about the future. They relaxed and had brunch sent up to their room. Later that morning, Charlie and Ditmer received a warm and happy greeting. They also had brunch. About an hour later, a little afternoon, Sally arrived, all smiles and hugs. They chatted about their vacations, and Claire informed them that Genny and Lucas would arrive shortly. She had not heard from them.

They agreed to go to the Casino and have some fun. Claire gave them disposable cash and told them to spend it and enjoy themselves.

The casino embodied a festive holiday feeling; they played and gambled throughout the day. Claire had arranged for dinner and entertainment at the main venue. It was enjoyable; Sally blogged away, streaming videos, Ditmer and Charlie were quiet, and Prisha and Claire danced, living it up.

They were seated for dessert when Claire whispered to Prisha. "I have not heard from the kids."

"They're fine, don't worry," Prisha replied. Claire wanted to text, but that was not part of the plan. The day ended, and they returned to their hotel suite.

It was close to eleven in the evening, and Claire said she had a surprise for the group and said, "The plan is to visit another Casino tomorrow unless something changes. I've also arranged for transportation back to Nice, whereby we will fly in a corporate jet to Charles De Gaulle Airport and board a charter for Boston. We will be home to celebrate the New Year." They toasted her.

Continuing to party and tell stories about their adventures, Charlie remained quiet and did not drink, and then Prisha asked if she was okay.

"Thanks, I'm just tired." She spoke.

"Go lie down, honey, it's ok." Charlie did just that.

Midnight, all was quiet. Claire lay in bed, her phone in her hand, Prisha sleeping beside her. She dozed off. It was close to 7:00 AM. The sun was not up when the phone's vibration stiffened her body. It was a text from Genny in their artificial language.

"The prize in hand. Extreme danger! Need help! BIRK IS ON THE TRAIL!"

"What do you need?" Claire responded.

In a series of texts and a few phone calls, Claire had arranged their transportation, trying to guarantee their safety.

"See you tonight. Love Ya." Genny replied, and Claire could feel fear in her message.

"Love you too, GG, don't worry. We'll get you here."

"Avignon!" ☺   Claire thought that's why I love this girl.

Claire didn't awaken Prisha but went and took a shower, wanting to think and get a handle and a head start on the day.

She set up various transportation arrangements for different scenarios while checking Birk's whereabouts through her operatives.

The sun was up a little past eight o'clock. She knew Genny was in motion; they had synced their location devices on their phones.

Prisha awoke to the news. She knew the risks they faced and had an urge to run.

"Pri, I'm going to put this information out before the group, and it's ok for anyone who wants to go home." Prisha agreed, got ready, and packed the few things of hers and Claire's.

When the group assembled, it was well after 9 A.M., and they settled on going for breakfast. They sensed that all was not right.

Claire received a text message from Genny: "Birk still has no idea of our whereabouts." Claire smiled.

She told the group that Genny and Lucas had found something of great importance, but Director Birk was on their trail, and he had confronted them.

Charlie sighed, Sally perked up, and Ditmer asked, "What have they found?"

"Ditmer, I'm not certain, but they are coming here, and then we are off to Avignon as soon as possible. We are in a game of tag and want to stay ahead of Birk. I don't know what we are seeking. I don't know if our safety is at risk. They probably want whatever Genny has. She may not want to give it up."

"So, we will wait for them, get answers, and then decide what is best," Ditmer said.

"If everything goes as planned, they could be here by 8 p.m., God willing." Claire sighed, checked her phone, and smiled.

"We can safely hang out here at the hotel; they have luxurious amenities and a small casino. Let's take advantage of this. Let's meet at 7:00 P.M. They all agreed.

Sally made the most of her day by gambling, relaxing at the spa and pool, and blogging.

Charlie and Ditmer relaxed by the pool and napped in their rooms.

Prisha also went to the spa and pool with worried thoughts.

Claire was the quarterback running the game and checking with her phone every fifteen minutes or less for Genny's location. Planning and a generous donation, with the director of the Palais de Papes in Avignon for permission to tour the facility, unsupervised, a few hours before they opened. The palace director had agreed; he knew Claire and would have consented, even without the donation, but he appreciated it. She had told him it was an architectural archaeology project and needed some information and, more importantly, freedom. He forwarded her plans and schematics of the 160,000 square feet of floor space of the two buildings. He wished her "bon chance" and hoped to see her tomorrow.

It was three o'clock, and she could see Genny's progress. She got a report from her informant that Birk still had no clue and believed them to be drowned. This was good news.

At 5:45 p.m., she got a report from Florence, the party on board, and an eta at 7:10 p.m.

She received another report from the informant that Birk was at dinner, clueless but confident of dredging their remains and finding the article.

At seven o'clock, the group sat around and waited for their friends to arrive.

Claire got a text that the limousine would pick up the party at 7:20 p.m. and get to her by 7:45 p.m.

It was 8 o'clock when the exhausted couple entered the room with a warm greeting. Claire hugged Genny, as if not expecting to see her again, and Prisha did the same. They had changed out of their robes into their clothes on the plane.

84

A Risk Worth Taking

Genny handed the article to Claire. "I'm so proud of you, GG!" Claire was emotional. She took it, put on her glasses, and examined it in her classic pose. Prisha leaned over her shoulder. Ditmer couldn't wait to handle the object.

"Genny, this vibrates, even hums," Claire said.

"I know. The closer we got to you, the more activity we got from it." Genny explained.

"Did you take photos?" Claire asked.

"We didn't have time. Our phones were dead till this morning." Lucas replied.

Claire snapped a picture with her phone, and it failed. They tried again with no luck.

Ditmer examined the object. "Marvelous! Charlie, go get your camera, please?"

She did with the same failed result.

They calmed down, "We have business to take care of." Claire said, "We'll discuss it over dinner." She ordered, and it was sent up.

They sat around the table, and Claire said, "This may be our last meeting. We will be moving shortly and possibly in different directions. As of now, and it will change, we are not under the radar, so let's talk before Lucas gives an account of what's happening." Claire checked her phone.

"I do not know what this tablet is. Yes, I can speculate. We don't have the time to examine it like we did with the others. I'll assume that this is all connected, and there are two facts I'm sure of. Somebody wanted us to find these artifacts, and somebody doesn't want us to have them. We are being guided by coordinates that are marked and appear on mysterious, unknown ancient objects, and as archaeologists, we are being seduced into finding their meaning. We know where to look but don't know what we are looking for." Claire stated.

"We'll know when it presents itself!" Genny confidently stated.

Claire continued, "We are in the same predicament as the last time our lives changed; this time, we know it's coming. Is it worth it?" She held up the object, which almost glowed.

"Before we go any further, I am asking you what you want to do. I want to make this as plain and simple as possible. The object will eventually end up in the hands of the government. Do we want to keep it? Pursue what we will without it?" Claire asked with a concerned look.

"I think that it's some kind of beacon. The vibration wasn't present in Perugia; It developed and strengthened closer to here. I say keep it until we can't. The other thing was that Birk seemed different; he didn't smell. Don't know how long that will last." Genny stated.

Ditmer got up and started talking. "If we had a lab and time, I would be all for this. This may be a dangerous undertaking." Pausing, "Charlie is not feeling well; she's a bit delicate."

"You dirty dog!" Genny got up and hugged the couple. Everyone was excited to hear the good news.

"So, you are both out!" Claire was all business.

"Yes." He replied.

"Congrats!" Claire smiled.

"Sally?"

"Ah, yes, I want to go on this quest." Turning to Genny, saying, "Sorry, I still can see Genny on the floor in your office. I'm full of fear." She got emotional. Genny went over and supported her.

"Genny and I are in; there is no problem if we go alone!" Lucas was emphatic.

"You will not come!" Claire was adamant. Eyeing Prisha in a whisper, "Pri, you don't have to do this."

"I'll go where you go." She spoke.

"That's no fucking answer, Prisha! Your life is on the line; please think this through!"

Prisha was unaccustomed to Claire's hysterical, emotional state.

"No, I want to do this. Yes, I'm scared, but it's risk-reward." She laughed. Claire came over, hugged her, and apologized for her outburst. Prisha knew it was all about protecting your loved ones.

Claire got a text: "They know where you are. Birk was admonished and virtually smoked by Morgan Strassa, sending him off the deep end. He's treating us like shit. He's smoking and drinking like old times. Good luck."

"They know where we are. We are being watched. Birk will be here well before dawn."

"Are we certain of this?" Claire asked a final time.

They all agreed with their decisions. Charlie, Ditmer, and Sally couldn't wait to leave.

"You will be taking all our luggage, Prisha's and mine, with you. Genny and Lucas may have a bag of belongings. We can get by with what we have, and we will head home shortly after our mission."

Claire made a few phone calls as the group congratulated Charlie and Ditmer.

"The jet will fly you to Paris tonight; you can board a FedEx Cargo Plane there and be home in the early afternoon. It all has been arranged. Good luck. The pilot has been informed of who you are; Robert Cantalupo will be your captain." Claire stated as Genny smiled.

Prisha and Claire would dress appropriately and have backpacks filled with possible necessities.

The transport arrived, and the small group left with the luggage. An Audi was also prepared for the three-hour trek to Avignon.

85

The Road to Avignon

Templar Truths

The four sat quietly, passing the object about. They were ready but couldn't get into the museum too early. They were allowed access well before it opened to the public.

"Genny, you will drive. Lucas will be the navigator and storyteller in front. We'll cuddle in the back." Claire joked,

"I want to tell Enrico's story before we go?" Lucas requested.

"On the ride, we can discuss it. Let me show you something." She had plans and blueprints of the palace printed from her phone. Each section of the plan had its coordinates. "Let's match what you have with this map."

"Claire, you're a genius!" Lucas stated.

"Even though you feel that way, you are still not teaching at Harvard without a doctorate in Archaeology." They all laughed.

"It doesn't hurt to suck up a bit, Lucas." Genny teased.

"Oh, that's how it's done." Winking at his love. She stuck out her tongue.

"I'll have that to go." He quipped.

"Now, who is the creep?" She shot back.

"Ok, let's get serious. We are about to die!" Prisha was serious; Claire threw a pillow at her.

They were as loose as they could be.

Lucas checked the coordinates with the plans. "Claire, I'm not looking for a job. You already got me one, but you are a clever gal. Look here; he showed where the coordinates matched. It's a tower, Tour de Trouillas, named after a village in the Pyrenees which the Knights Templar frequented."

"That is interesting." Prisha added, "Possibly an underground tunnel."

"I think so," Claire said, and she handed him another set of plans for the palace's underground.

"I think I see a possible corridor leading deep into the bowels of the structure," Lucas said.

"Of course, that's it because we're going to hell." Genny wasn't being funny.

"OK, we have something to work with. Let's get a few hours of rest and be ready to head out around 3:00 am. We can't get into the palace too early. Let's get everything ready, and we can head out."

"Is there a laundry facility around here?"

"Yes, Genny, the community bathroom has sliders and a washer and dryer."

"Thanks, Pri. We smell like monks. Lucas, take your clothes off; I'll wash them." Turning to Lucas.

"Back to the robes?" He asked.

"No, I'll keep you warm, and we sent them with Sally."

"I know that." He winked.

"Know what?" She asked.

"Both." He kissed her. "We should shower?" She smiled and agreed.

Prisha and Claire were enjoying the adolescent banter and headed for bed.

"See you soon," Claire said.

"K," Genny responded,

It was about 1:30 A.M. Claire got a text. "He's on the way to you. Will be there before sunrise." Claire lay awake thinking of just calling it quits. She didn't know what they were chasing. It seemed it was more of a location than a physical object.

***

Birk's convoy moved like an evil peloton, eating time and distance like a beast with blood in its teeth.

Birk's longtime driver peeked into the rear-view mirror and observed his boss in deep contemplation, sipping whiskey from a flask, chewing, chomping, and drooling on a cigar.

"Welcome back, sir!" Boldly stated. "You have been missed!"

Birk saluted him with the flask and said, "Punch it!" He did.

***

They were on their way.

"We don't know what we are looking for," Claire mumbled, repeating herself. "It seems more like a location rather than an object."

"I agree," Lucas said. According to Enrico's notes, he feels a connection between whatever we seek and the Catholic Church. Enrico believes that it has to do with life. When does ensoulment occur? When does life begin? Enrico's theory was that life begins at conception. Enrico believes the Knights Templar brought back objects and theories that were contrary to the Catholic Church and were persecuted and eradicated as an order."

"This all began in the early 14th Century. The King of France and the Pope accused and persecuted the order, ultimately eliminating them."

"You're right, Prisha." Here are the details from Enrico's journal. "Just bear with me a second."

Genny was at the wheel, enjoying the performance of the luxurious Audi A8s. It was dark, but she had excellent night vision. Lucas explained the directions and got back to his story.

"Philip IV was the King of France from 1285-1314, his death, note the year he died. His kingdom was extremely overleveraged because of excessive spending and the high cost of the crusades. An insurmountable debt was owed to the Knights Templar. Seemingly to renege on his debt, he accused the order of idolatry, sodomy, secrecy, spitting on the crucifix, worshipping Baphomet, and a host of acts that would win his support to disband the order. He convinced the Pope, Clement V, to join him, saying they were getting too powerful." He paused.

"Pope Clement V, Raymond Bertrand de Got, his papacy pontificated from 1305 until he died in 1314, note the year. He was somewhat of an unwilling co-conspirator of Philip IV. Together, they persecuted, sacrificed, and ultimately shut down the order.

"On Friday the 13th, 1307, at dawn, yup, Friday 13th, the Grand Master Jacques de Molay and scores of his Templars were imprisoned by the King. Over time, some confessed to their crimes and then later recanted. November 22, 1307, was the official end of the order. Many of the Templars had remained imprisoned, and Clement V favored forgiveness. However, Philip IV insisted, despite their recantations, that Jacques de Molay, the Grandmaster, and his followers should burn at the stake."

Genny could feel the article close to her body giving off heat, confirming her suspicion that it may be acting as a homing device. Lucas was still telling Enrico's story.

"On the day of the execution, Jacques de Molay insisted that his hands be tied in prayer, facing the Cathedral of Notre Dame; he then said, 'God knows who is wrong and has sinned. Soon, a calamity will occur to those who have condemned us to death,' his life ended." He paused.

"You are a fine storyteller." Claire complimented him.

"Harvard?"

"No!"

He continued, "These are Enrico's notes, which I'll summarize. In 1309, Clement V moved the papacy to Avignon, which was part of the Holy Roman Empire and was subsequently annexed by France in 1791. The papacy's move from Rome is called the Babylonian Captivity (1309-1377).

"Jacques de Molay was executed along with his curse on March 18, 1314. Pope Clement V died on April 20, 1314. It was only a month after the execution. His body, while lying in state, was struck by lightning and burned beyond recognition; he was later buried in Uzeste, France.

"King Philip IV, while on a hunting trip in November of 1314, had a stroke and died on November 29, 1314. Curse complete." He paused.

"Just got a text that Birk's people know where we are headed and are coming for us at a high rate of speed. If worse comes to worst, we'll give up the article, right, Genny?" Claire instructed.

"This thing is acting like a beacon." She handed it to Lucas, who passed it around.

"Yes, Claire," Genny answered. The artifact felt like her medallion, part of her DNA, her soul.

"I must finish these notes; we are getting close. Enrico believed the Templars brought something back from their discoveries under King Solomon's Temple, the Temple Mount. The order's name is The Poor Fellow-Soldiers of Christ and the Temple of Solomon. I'm done." Lucas drank water.

Genny increased the speed. Lucas said less than half an hour to arrive.

"So, what do you think they found, if anything?" Prisha asked.

"They have always been the focus of perhaps retrieving the Ark of the Covenant," Claire added.

"If there is something, it would have to upset the balance of power at the time," Prisha said.

"I agree, Prisha. It's something that will or would have changed the way things are perceived or believed. We are chasing alien artifacts with messages. There is an answer." Lucas said.

86

The Gates Open

They sat quietly as they approached the immense structure. There was some early morning activity, and other international meetings and conventions were constantly held at the palace. Every July, there is a global art exhibition.

Approaching the security guard at his station in the parking area, Claire explained that we were expected and could enter early, according to the Director. The overnight guard was at the end of his shift and was only thinking of a glass of wine and maybe getting lucky with his wife.

"Reverifier!!" Claire irritated. He checked again. This went on for ten frustrating minutes. Claire phoned, awakening the Director. Moments later, the chief security officer came out, and in French expletives, the two argued; finally, seeing a note, the guard apologized a thousand times to everyone. It was his last shift at the Palace. The high-ranking officer, who apologized and invited them to tour at their leisure, escorted them to the main foyer.

***

Director Birk was less than thirty minutes away.

87

Deep within the Soul

Descent and Confrontation

The Palace was not yet open to the public, and the lighting was soft. The hall of Tour de Trouillas had an ancient library odor. Tapestries adorned the area, but could not be appreciated with the dim night lighting. Lucas checked his GPS, and the tablet seemed to agree that they were going in the right direction.

Claire received a text from Sally telling her they were boarded in Paris and departing shortly. Sally texted prayer hands and a heart, which Claire acknowledged with a thumbs-up. Robert wished them happy holidays.

Following the GPS, leading to an off-limits area, they proceeded down a long corridor. It felt like they were sloping downhill when approaching an old wooden door. Believing it was heading outdoors led to an unfinished part of the Palace.

Moving very slowly, uncertain of their direction, they didn't want to waste time by making a mistake. Arriving at a stone stairway, the tablet's response let them know they were heading in the right direction. Descending the worn and unsymmetrical set of stairs, hundreds of feet, a platform every twenty-five steps.

Reaching a small opening, they were confronted with two choices. One passageway was ancient and led in one direction, the other just as ancient but darker, cave-like, seemingly undisturbed, with a steep descent.

Claire received a text that Birk's team had arrived. When faced with a predator, the team felt natural fear.

Lucas checked the GPS, and both paths ended in the same place. Genny checked with the tablet and sensed it wanted to go down the dark, steep cave.

They continued their journey, deep down, hundreds of yards. The walls were filled with scenes depicting stars. Genny recognized them as the Orion system. There were writings that Genny sublimely interpreted. She said nothing as they quietly descended for the next fifteen minutes, when they came upon an opening. The phones and GPS were no longer functioning.

The trail ended in a spacious and natural opening, with large stones scattered about like seats and the remains of what was once an altar. The ground was sandy. It felt spiritual, like a place of worship.

There was another opening in the hall, and exiting from it was a large demonic silhouette with smoke billowing like a dragon's hot, destructive breath, a stench from hell quickly filling the room. It was Birk. He had left his men behind and wanted to handle this himself.

The smell and fear of what he represented were back. The group stopped, not trying to flee, and agreed to hand over the tablet.

With skilled precision, Birk approached the team and tasered Genny and Lucas. They fell to the ground. He zapped them both again. Lucas was out, and Genny was in a stupor. He looked at her and said, "Good, you can watch."

He walked over to Claire and Prisha, who had huddled together, and then physically separated them, asking them to remove their backpacks.

"The tablet?" He barked.

"It's with Genny," Claire said.

He went over and took the tablet.

"I have my prize!" He was excited.

"You must understand I know and am told nothing about this object. Somebody, my people, bosses, gods, want this. I will bring it to them without question. My job is done. The rest is my pleasure." Flashing his drooling demonic grin.

He took off his *Men in Black* suit jacket, tugging at white suspenders. As Lucas groaned, Birk started to sing *Singing in the Rain* and gave Lucas a sharp kick in the stomach. "I always wanted to do that. "Ultraviolence, I think they called it in the movie." Grinning.

Claire implored him to stop; he walked over to her while whistling the tune.

"This group just busts my balls. Why do you have to try to be smarter than everyone? I have some unfortunate information for you. You want to believe this and prove that. You want to find, oh, the fucking truth. Well, I'm going to tell you the truth, but you will refuse to believe it. I will refrain from another movie quote." He roared in laughter. "We, I, Stanley Birk, Director, am the good guy. However, I get pushed, caused by your activities, to act like an animal. I do get satisfaction in it; I don't know why. I'm fucked up!" The group listened in horror to the pacing, confessing madman.

"You know how much I like those old, ultra-violent movies." He drank and blew smoke into Claire's face." Eyeing Prisha.

"You will not get away with this; trust me, help yourself. Take the object!" Claire was stern.

"You rich, confident, fucking bitch! Your trust is fictional, and I don't fucking care!" He started singing the song again and hauled off and slapped Claire so hard she was lifted off her feet, falling to the ground. Now humming and dancing, "Oh! Fuck did that feel good!" He drank and puffed his cigar during his little jig, moseying to Prisha.

Claire had never been touched or hit in her life. The shock was shutting her down as she looked up at Prisha, who was told not to move or there would be much more pain and brutality inflicted.

He walked up to Prisha in his world of stink, "I never wanted to hurt you. I thought you were the most beautiful woman I've ever laid eyes upon. You are brilliant, and I was jealous of that and hated myself for being unable to think as you do. You thought that I hated you. That was just a defense. I admired and fantasized over you." Drooling. "I'm not going to hurt you, but I will hurt them if you don't cooperate. I just want to appreciate you." He gently touched Prisha's cheek as tears rolled down. Then, picking her up, he set her on the ancient altar. He moved his body close to hers. "I'm not going to hurt you, only admire you." Prisha looked at Claire and did not resist. Birk then started caressing her hair. "My god, you are beautiful," and then placed his face close to hers.

Almost as a reflex from his stench, Prisha vomited into his face. He jerked away from her, screaming expletives, and started flailing rights and lefts to her face; she was in a good position to block most of them. She fell to the ground. He stood up, and his eyes started rolling to the back of his head, roaring expletives. Genny watched, knew the meaning of that look, and tried to gather strength.

Birk picked up a boulder and raised it over Prisha, aiming it at her head. The tablet, tucked in his suspenders, started an intense vibration. Birk mumbled, "Thou shalt not kill." The moment just before the boulder's release, Birk was side-kicked in his knee, shattering, splintering bone, and blood spurting into a pattern that would have excited *Dexter*, the avenging serial killer.

Prisha slid away as the boulder landed beside her. As Birk fell to the ground, Genny kicked him in the chest, crushing it. He fell to the ground. As he lay in a pool of blood, Genny said, "Sing to this, you sick prick!" Kicking him in the face, removing his jaw and teeth, and busting his nose.

Prisha rushed to Claire and helped her up.

"I'm ok. You?" Claire said.

"It's been worse," Prisha said, then hugged and found time to laugh.

Genny went over to Lucas, who was recovering from his shock. His stomach and ribs were sore, possibly broken.

88

The Passage and the Portal

They all looked at Claire, unsure of what to do next. They could hear voices approaching from both exits.

"Let's go!" Genny rallied the troupe. "Leave the tablet. I understand and see a possible exit." Genny was led, being pulled by a magnetic attraction.

They helped each other squeeze through a small crack in the wall.

"Now this is Indiana Jones shit." Lucas grimaced, keeping his sense of humor.

They descended. It was dark; old torches were on the wall, and they did have supplies in their backpacks. They lit a torch and, using limited light from their flashlights, observed ancient writings, markings, star charts, and planets on the walls as they went deeper. Thoughts of returning were just another fear that was put aside.

Genny said she smelled something and could see a reflection or some light.

Birk's men found him barely alive and rushed him off for medical care. When he exited the tunnel, the lead agent contacted

Morgan Strassa and sent the photos. The Boss replied," Good work, get it to me; the pursuit is over."

***

It was getting warm, and the group started sweating. They walked towards the light and entered a chamber; they could hear a stone doorway rumble closing behind them. There was a vertical rainbow of colored light. Their bodies started to tingle, and the feeling of euphoria and rapture overtook them; all their pain, injuries, sadness, and memories of them were gone.

Genny got a deja vu, and her body was warm and gently vibrating, a pleasure beyond her ability to describe.

In their psychedelic state, they looked and touched one another in disbelief. They all looked different. Claire wore Aphrodite's face in silk garments. Prisha glowed in the radiance of the look of the Goddess Saraswati. Lucas was a young American Indian boy, and Genny was a young American Indian girl.

The room was scented with their favorite fragrances, which only they could sense. Claire bathed in lavender; Beethoven performed before her. Prisha heard her mother singing in the garden and the smell of the garden's earth after a warm, gentle rain. Lucas listened to an old 78 record that his father often played him when he was a boy; he was savoring and enjoying a Gitane cigarette. Genny was listening to Pavarotti and sipping wine with her Pa. They telepathically communicated.

An image of her mom greeted Claire. They mentally communicated, mutually conveying a loss in each other's absence. Prisha was welcomed by friendly images, which were her childhood pets.

It continued timelessly; they interacted with all beings that held meaning or had passed in their lifetime.

The room glowed in the brilliance of a Warhol painting, with Dalian images, visiting Cezanne in Modern Olympia, scrambled and jumbled in a Picasso, Braque landscape, as though the giants had partied with Timothy Leary and collaborated on a painting.

Time was lost. Each could see the other, but they were not themselves. A presence ushered Prisha and Claire into a room. They began to partially return, closer to their reality, and then found themselves in front of a large, shiny metallic plate with all the qualities of a superior mirror. Prisha looked at Claire, and Claire looked back at her as they investigated the metallic plate. Holding hands, they could see themselves and their other in the mirror. It was like double exposure, an image overlaying an image. The image within was smiling and projecting happiness. They embraced, kissed, and then vanished into the metal.

Moments later, Lucas and Genny entered the room with the metal mirror. Genny was much more cognizant than Lucas, noticing her surroundings. They were in a church. Knights Templar symbols abound; a fully armored Knight with a sword guarded the mirror on one side. The other side was adorned with glyphs and an ancient script that Genny was familiar with. She scanned and retained it.

They looked into the mirror and saw their other, within, happy and smiling. They held hands, and Genny heard "Namaste." She bowed and whispered, "Namaste." They were transported through the soul gateway.

89

Aftermath and Disappearance

Ditmer, Charlie, and Sally returned to Cambridge. As the New Year approached, their fears elevated. They had not heard from Claire and the others for days and were uncertain how to contact the authorities.

Sally thanked Cynthia Robeo for filling in while on vacation and asked her if she could stick around for a few days. After explaining that she hadn't heard from Claire and the group for a few days and was concerned, she agreed to stay on.

Ditmer and Charlie returned home and would not return to work until after the first of the year.

***

In a news blurb, it was reported that Stanley Birk, the Director of the newly created United Aerial Phenomena Task Force (UAPTF), was critically injured while investigating an incident in southern France. This caught Sally's eye with a dire feeling. She contacted the President of the University. The university president told the authorities that the group had not been heard from for days and would like to say they were missing abroad.

***

CNN reported, "Renowned Archaeologist, philanthropist, Academic Director of the School of Archaeology at Harvard University, and the Trustee and sole heir of the massive Randolph Foundation, Dr. Claire Marie Randolph-Mishari, her wife Dr. Prisha Harshita Mishara-Randolph, a professor at Harvard University, Dr. Genny Guiliana Cantalupo, also a professor at Harvard University, and Lucas Johhny Chevrolet, a professor at the University of Massachusetts, in Boston, have not been heard from since December 28th, five days ago. They were on an archaeological tour of Avignon and have not been seen since. Fear of an accident or foul play lingers over the impending search and investigation. Dr. Randolph-Mishari has always been on the cutting edge of archaeology, and recent reports have linked her interest to the dating of Mayan civilization to earlier periods, with possible ancient alien interest. Dr. Chevrolet is well known for his controversial book *Mesoamerica—The Stones of the Gods*, which questioned the dating of the ancient structures of Mexico, Central America, and South America. Dr. Mishari-Randolph recently resigned from a high-profile position as assistant director of the United Aerial Phenomena Task Force (UAPTF). Dr. Cantalupo is a recent doctoral graduate and is a handpicked protégé of Dr. Randolph-Mishari. A side note: reported earlier this week that Director Stanley Birk of the (UAPTF) was critically injured in a department-related investigation that took place in the same geographical location as the missing archaeologists."

***

Local Boston media reported that after ten days, the Archaeological group from Harvard University on an archaeology tour in southern France is still missing and presumed to have met with a sudden, tragic ending.

***

CNN: It's been three weeks since the Archaeological group from Harvard University was last seen. Today, in a miraculous and seemingly incredulous turn of events, Dr. Lucas Johnny Chevrolet and Dr. Genny Giuliana Cantalupo were discovered living at a Hopi Tribe Reservation in northeastern Arizona in Coconino and Navajo Counties. They were teaching Hopi history and their descent from the stars. The chief said, "They just showed up, carried a peaceful aura, and just fit in."

There was no explanation of how they got there or a recollection of their time in France.

They were returned to the Boston Area, where they were met with a Dr. Briscoe, a Captain in the United States Air Force at the Soldiers Home in Chelsea, Massachusetts, for psychological evaluation."

***

CNN: Doctors Randolph-Mishari and Mishari-Randolph were last seen over a month ago until today.   They were spotted in the ancient Mayan City of Uxmal at the Mayan Cosmic University of the Divine Feminine, where they lectured on the divine feminine as the universal sacred power of a woman. They were found and returned to Boston, where they were placed into the care of Dr. Mark Isenberg at the Brigham and Women's Hospital in Boston for evaluation.

They had no explanation or memory of their time in France and did not recall how they ended up in Mexico. They did not resist returning to their Boston home; they packed and left without a question.

***

Sally was so adept at her position that she filled in for Claire in the interim. Cynthia stayed on to help. Ditmer and Charlie returned to work, to a surprised faculty of their marriage and expecting child, sincerely wishing them well while whispering behind their backs. Ditmer was sweating the future and sadly missed his confidante, Claire.

90

Reunion and Reflection

Lucas and Genny were invited to dinner at Claire and **Prisha's**; it would be their first meeting since their adventure.

The room was scented with freshly cut flowers; soft classical music massaged the ears. The hugs felt warmer, more sincere, and more affectionate than ever. The four were mellow and calm. Genny brought a couple of bottles of her Pa's wine that survived the adventures.

They talked with familiarity but felt a strange disconnect. Genny asked, "What were your last memories?"

"I remember being with Claire and my family in India, then in Nice. Oh yeah, the Casino. Then, living in abject poverty as a teacher, I got great pleasure living in Uxmal. How did we get there? I have no recollection?" Prisha explained.

"That is my story, but I feel so calm. Genny, you taught me how to meditate, and now I feel I can reach deep within my soul with great pleasure. It was suggested that we go under hypnosis. I don't know. I couldn't be any happier." Claire held Prisha's hand.

"You remember Birk and his reported injuries?" Genny asked.

"We do," Prisha said, also speaking for Claire. "I remember the artifacts and the mission, but they don't seem to matter. I know this is contradictory to how we used to feel. I feel the mission was a success. I can't explain the time in Uxmal; I remember it all. I look forward to going back to teaching." Claire was quiet. Genny put her hand on Claire's hand. Claire could feel the energy in Genny's body. Genny squeezed her hand, and Claire smiled. They all agreed, not remembering totally what happened, except for Genny.

"Birk got something he deserved," Genny said.

"The last thing I remember is our great adventure, all but the end. I knew we were searching for something; we had a tablet, went to Avignon, and ended up in Arizona. I don't know how. I'll speak for Genny because we have discussed this: our time, like yours, in Arizona, we were poor, happy, and respected. We lived as husband and wife for those few weeks. Excuse the expression; it was heaven on earth, and I thank those involved. I'm happy to get back to teaching and writing." Lucas smiled.

Genny spoke, "Claire, pass on the hypnosis. Time will bring back those lost moments. Don't allow anyone inside your mind. Your dreams will guide you and Prisha; eventually, you will recall and grow strong together. I am confident." Genny spoke with maturity, a shaman.

Claire knew that Genny was special. How much, she had no idea, but trusted her.

"I am finding my way back through my dreams." She was not being forthright, even with Lucas. "I'm happy; Lucas is part of me. I said this before, but I'm certain he and I were and are always." Her friends toasted her romantic statement, but she was speaking the truth.

91

Moving Forward

The semester moved on, and things gradually returned as close to normal as possible.

Charlie and Ditmer ran their world-class lab with such efficiency that it was written up in Tier 1 academic journals. Waiting, getting excited for the arrival of their new family member, they never spoke about the disc, medallion, or tablet. They destroyed and deleted everything involved with them. They remained close friends with their associates.

***

Sally continued to blog and write. She was becoming well-known in her circle. She dated Cynthia and Dan, the UPS courier. The three were good friends; sometimes, they would go down to Harvard Square to party.

***

Prisha continued to teach at the university, with great fulfillment, in her degree area and archaeological history. She and Claire were inseparable. Claire backed off from running the Family Trust and appointed a trusted Co-Trustee. She also taught and lectured for a few days. Prisha and Claire would spend at least one evening a month with Lucas and Genny.

***

Stanley Birk took many months to rehab, receiving advanced technological treatment, but not at Genny's level. He would recover and spend additional time in rehab for his addiction and demons. He accepted a transfer to run the security at Area 51 in Nevada, and Tina went with him.

Lucas and Genny lived in Enrico's home in East Boston and felt his spiritual presence. Lucas couldn't be happier with his work; he was highly respected at his university, and associates in his field would attend his lectures. He had become an exciting raconteur, called the Mark Twain of the archaeological world. He never realized that he was searching for something he had already found.

He and Genny were writing a sci-fi novel interpretation of Genny's tablet translations, but not all of them. The book has already been accepted for publication. It was about a distant, futuristic race of beings whose dying solar system forced them to explore the universe for a new home, terraforming Earth, recreating their world, starting a new life on Earth, and coming as gods along with their artificial intelligence. Marriage was part of their future.

***

Genny continued to see Dr. Briscoe at least once a month. Her physical and intellectual growth was increasing daily. She continued to dream, relate, and interact with the spirits at Avignon. She had retained everything; she didn't share it because she didn't want the bad memories to surface for her loved friends. She knew they would dream and remember as one remembers a dream.

Genny had mentally retained all the material on the disc, medallion, tablet, and soul gateway. She believed they contained information and facts that were harmful and dangerous to public knowledge. She understood Morgan Strassa, but not the violence; coupled with fear, it was a tool to control animals and men. There was a need for secrecy. It was real, and she had all the proof inside her head.

The relatives of the Virgili family in Perugia permitted her to restore the family vault. Claire would help with the expenses. Her plan, which she revealed to no one, was to add a new stela at its entrance and construct a tomb for Enrico, with an inscription of the tablet inscribed on the face of the tomb and within the tomb, placed within a sealed chamber his journal and a journal that she has written in his honor, translating the messages that he believed.

Epilogue

The semester ended…Prisha invited her family to visit her. Genny and Lucas planned to return to Arizona for a few weeks, talk with the people they met, and try to retrace all that happened there. Lucas then had a lecture series planned for late July and early August; at that time, Genny was returning to Perugia.

All the alien writings and communications went from Genny's inner thoughts to paper. She could recreate and transcribe the disc, medallion, and tablet precisely as she saw them, forwarding the symbols and writings to a stonecutter in Perugia to prepare Enrico's tomb and its lid. The cutter would make a miniature cist that could be hermetically sealed; he was informed that it would contain a small amount of Enrico's remains. The truth is that it would have his journal and Genny's journal, the account of the past year's events, along with her translations of the alien writings. A lock of Enrico and Genny's hair would be placed within the journal. The lapidary was to clean the vault entrance and repair and expand the stela to include the names and dates of all deceased entombed. He was also contracted to rehab the vault, inside and out. Genny wanted the vault to have meaning and become a showcase in the cemetery, capturing the interest of tourists and interred family visitors. The cost was exorbitant; the project was presented to Claire, who graciously provided the funding.

On her arrival, her cousins lovingly greeted Genny. She would stay with them during her visit. Shortly after the incident, Genny communicated with them, thanking them for their wonderful Christmas. Now, she wanted to hug them and thank them personally. Giovanni had overseen the vault project and would not accept compensation; he was honored that a tomb was set in place for him and Maria.

Genny carried a rectangular urn containing the documents. Giovanni also believed Enrico's ashes or personal effects were in the container, and he was partially correct.

The tomb's rehabbed site was stunning. The exterior was sandblasted and then treated with alabaster, conveying a visual message saying, "We were important. Remember us." The inside was just as beautiful.

They approached Enrico's tomb, and beside it was Giovanni's; they both felt a sense of sadness.

The tomb lid was leaning against the wall. Genny approached and inspected the tomb cover with the intensity of reviewing legal documents. During the renovations, new construction, and additions to the vault, Genny was in continuous contact with the lapidary and his associates. She insisted it had to be perfect, exactly as she described it. It was a difficult task, but easy-going Genny was firm on the contract; they would have to replace it if it was not to specifications.

She stared and read every symbol. The lapidary, breathing heavily, waited for a response,

"Magnifico! Grazie." A teary-eyed hug ensued. The stonecutter was relieved.

She handed him the urn, and he placed it within the cist and then sealed it. He put the lid, with the help of his workers, onto the tomb. They sealed the tomb. A Catholic priest admiring the vault entered, and it was explained to him the meaning of the ceremony; he offered a prayer, a befitting end to a spiritual journey, and all was laid to rest.

***

Genny peacefully dreamed as she crossed the Atlantic Ocean, heading towards home. Armed with new hardware and tweaked software, vibrating at a higher frequency, life-saving gifts from Dr. Lewis and Area 51, she accepted who she had become. Her feelings and emotions were no different than they were in the past, and life only changed if she chose to do so.

In meetings with Dr. Briscoe, they discussed that her near-death or death experience at the hands of Stanley Birk might have altered her perception of life. The question is, "Did she cross over to the next life?" They couldn't be sure, but her nights were filled with dreams of her past lives and guiding spirits, who claimed they knew and had met her.

Why me? Why this quest, she wondered? They want to be remembered. Pa was so close and maybe did understand, she thought.

Vivid, surrealistic silent films continuously played as she dreamed of an exploding solar system as a city-size starship escaped, crossing the universe for years, centuries, and possibly millennia, heading toward Earth. Horrific hallucinogenic images of billions of beings dying. Their DNA strands were saved, combined into a single strand, guarded by the survivors, and self-adapted AI during their journey.

Genny dreamed of climbing onto a rotating double helix, hearing these billions of voices in a choral symphony, Ode to Joy, awaiting rebirth. She rode atop the vibrating strand as it merged into her genome. According to the tablet, the alien host, man, receives a soul-bearing companion at conception, leaves at death with a life of experiences, and awaits another rebirth.

The recurring dream of time reversing, her life being rewound, like in *The Curious Case of Benjamin Button*; at conception, meeting her spiritual hitchhiker who smiles and jumps aboard, hiding, and then growing forward, at the hands of fate, searching for its soulmate. She lovingly whispers, "Lucas."

Genny dreamed of Avignon; the intense pleasure it brought convinced her that it might be heaven. She was happy for those who believed and might experience its joy and beauty, filled with hope, and rewarded their faith.

She awoke, wondering and, at times, questioning the tablet's translations and sharing almost everything with Lucas and her friends, but she kept these challenging, deep, personal thoughts buried in her soul. Her belief, if true, was theirs to discover, as well as the unforeseen bliss and joy that may be waiting. She laughed and struggled like she knew the end of a good book or movie and didn't want to ruin or misunderstand it, getting it all wrong. Anxiously looking forward to her next meeting with Dr. Briscoe, she pulled up her sleeve, admired her tattoo, and felt satisfied. Opening her laptop, the blank screen briefly reflected her doubled-exposed image. She had an overwhelming longing and a strong feeling of the absence of Lucas, missing his presence, scent, and essence; she needed to hug him, her family, and her friends.

ACKNOWLEDGMENTS

Thank you, Diane Severin and Denis Filipitti (H&W). Diane, without your "volunteer reviewing" and skillfulness, I would not have been able to move forward with this project. I hadn't seen you in nearly fifty years, and having you both over was a pleasure. You are always welcome.

Michael Archdeacon, your contributions and our exchange of ideas have been instrumental in shaping this project. Your progressive outlook on life, even when it seems alien, has always been a source of inspiration. Thank you for your valuable input and suggestions.

Michael Wildrick, my nephew, thank you, thank you, thank you, thank you, thank you for the beautiful gifts. An Apple today keeps the writer engaged, lol.

My friend Dave Tick is always encouraging and helpful. I want to thank him for the past, present, and future.

Maureen Cecca Sacco, Moe, my sister, graciously and eagerly read a draft. I really appreciated it and apologize for not getting back to discuss how it was done, but I will at some point. Also, Josh Sacco, my nephew, requested a copy. He's out there playing bass with his band, Bonus Cat. Good luck, Josh!"

My daughter Amanda, who has always supported my work, is managing a lot with a new baby, a three-year-old, a full-time high-pressure job, and supporting her husband Matt through the police academy. Yikes! Love Ya!

My parents, John and Carmela, have long since passed away. I want to thank them and apologize for lessons learned too late. I wish they were here so I could hug them, tell them I miss them, and express my love for them.

My Spin Bike over 16,000 miles of friendship and thought. Thanks.

Giuliana Adele Cremone and Robert Hayes Cremone are my grandchildren and the true loves of my life. When they read this, I will probably be gone. Pa loves you.

Geno! Oh, Geno!

Book characters trek

Through plot's darkroom imagery

Ending...Beginning.